LESS THAN PERFECT

Janet Franks Little

ANESSA BOOKS

ISBN: 978-1-7322225-4-0

Cover designer: Victoria Landis,
http://www.victorialandis.com/book-cover-design.html

Formatting by Anessa Books, http://anessabooks.com

Published by Anessa Books
Virginia, USA

TABLE OF CONTENTS

DEDICATION

This book is dedicated to greyhounds that once raced or are still used to entertain gamblers, and to Kook and Klepto (pictured). Check out Klepto's antenna leg scene in Chapter 2 and Kook's manicure scene in Chapter 26.

ACKNOWLEDGMENTS

I'd like to thank fellow author, Karen Moser, who writes as K.D. Alden and Liza Kendall. She allowed me to meet her two greyhound rescues, Kook and Klepto, and educated me about the breed. I learned that the only place a greyhound should race is into human arms for a loving embrace.

Less Than Perfect

CHAPTER 1

"WHY DO WE have to share?" a high-pitched voice whines.

"Because we're not getting one for each of you," a rough, low-pitched voice answers.

"I want my own, if she gets one," a second childish voice chimes in.

I pause with my hand on the doorknob. This in-house visit was set by the rescue organization for this morning. I was only given their last name and that they had two children. The doorbell rings again, and, copying my usual runway preparation, I lengthen my spine, take a deep breath, and swing the door open with a well-practiced smile. "Hello."

A man and two little girls face me on my Florida home's open porch. The children tilt their heads back until they make eye contact with me, looking like open-mouthed Pez dispensers. They are adorable duplicates with wild red hair around their pixie faces. It tumbles over their narrow shoulders and down their tiny backs. Freckles dot porcelain cheeks below pale blue eyes.

I assume the man with them is their father. He has an athletic and muscular build, piercing jade-green eyes, and brown sugar stubble covering the lower half of his face. Even though he's bald, most women would find him attractive. He would be on eye level with my six-foot height if I weren't standing on the doorsill in sandals with one-inch heels.

"You must be Mr. Stabler."

"That's right. You can call me Justin." He disengages his hand from one child and extends it.

When I grasp it, heat seeps through his palm to mine. My stomach melts, and warmth spreads lower down my body. I hold on longer than necessary to determine why this is happening to me. Justin gives a slight tug, and I release him. "And I'm Annie Warden."

"These are my daughters, Eden and Savanna," he says, nodding left then right.

I smile down at the children. "It's nice to meet all of you."

Eden announces, "We're seven years old and in first grade."

"That's good to know." I turn toward Justin. "Did you have any trouble finding my place?"

I live in Parkland, a former ranching and farming area in the northwest corner of Broward County that didn't become a city until 1963. It is home to excellent schools, parks, and quiet neighborhoods, most of them gated communities. However, where I live is unrestricted and unregulated, except for city ordinances.

"The directions I was given were good," Justin answers. "We live only ten minutes away in Coral Springs."

"Please, come in." I open the door wider.

Justin and the girls enter the foyer. He scans the rooms he can see from here but says nothing. The interior of my four-bedroom, one-story house, built in the early 1980s, looks like a fledgling or drunken architect designed it. Nothing makes sense. The living room requires a step-down, the kitchen is centered across from the front door and hidden by a wall that doesn't quite reach the vaulted pecky cypress ceiling, and the primary bath is large enough to include a queen-sized bed. But the property was undervalued when I bought it after my divorce. I wanted the fenced-in, acre-large backyard that I could fill with dogs, horses, goats, or any creatures of my choosing.

The children's eyes skid to the five greyhounds behind a series of freestanding pet gates in the living room. Eden points at them. "Look, Daddy, there they are. Aren't they beautiful? I learned all about them in my library book."

Savanna stiffens and steps closer to her father, watching the quintet of canines with wary eyes.

Eden bounces in place. "I love them all! I can't decide which one I want."

I bite my tongue. This isn't a greyhound buffet where anyone can pick a dog and take one home. The rescue organization I foster dogs for has strict adoption policies to match the best possible owner with a large breed, former racer.

Before I can speak, Justin puts his hand on his daughter's head. "Remember what we talked about in the car? We're here to see the dogs and learn about them. We're not going to get one today."

With his handshake still warming my palm and the gentle reminder to his child, this stranger has awakened something dormant in me. My skin buzzes with a weird sensation. I gesture to the dining room table and chairs. "Why don't we sit down and talk first?"

"But I want to see the dogs," Eden wails.

I move two large cushions from a nearby rattan armchair to the white-tiled floor in front of the pet gates. "Why don't you sit here? You can watch the dogs and let them get used to you."

Eden grabs her sister's hand. "Come on."

Savanna shakes her head, causing her springy hair to bounce around her face, and moves slightly behind her father rather than toward the greyhounds. The dogs raise their noses to catch the new human scents in the air.

Eden puts her fists on her hips. "See, Daddy, this is why the dog should be mine, not hers."

Justin places a hand on Savanna's shoulder. "She'll join you when she's ready."

Eden plops down on one of the cushions while we move to the dining room table. Justin sits across from me, and his daughter climbs onto his lap. Savanna puts her elbows on the glass tabletop and stares at me, no longer displaying the same fear she had with the dogs.

She reminds me of someone assessing my strengths and weaknesses. For what, I don't know, but that same hard look reminds me of go-see appointments. A photographer may take test photos, a designer might ask me to try on outfits, or a casting director could require me to walk the runway.

Under Savanna's scrutiny, I inject foster-mom confidence into my voice. "Tell me about your experience with dogs in general or greyhounds in particular."

Justin leans sideways to look around his daughter. "Well, I grew up with several dogs. We were supposed to feed and walk them, but my parents did that."

"Have you ever had responsibility for a dog as an adult?"

"My wife had a Yorkie when we married, but she died."

Savanna's heart-shaped face crumples and her blue eyes fill with tears. "I miss her, Daddy."

"I know, honey. We all do." Justin hugs his daughter and shrugs with an apologetic look in my direction.

Silent alarm bells sound in my head. A greyhound is very different than a Yorkshire terrier. If their little dog died recently, why does this family think a greyhound would be a suitable replacement, especially when Savanna is still grieving? Is she used to a much smaller pet, and that's the reason she's reluctant to get close to my dogs?

I murmur, "I'm sorry for your family's loss."

Eden comes over to the table. "Why is Savanna crying?"

"I was telling Annie about Mommy's dog."

"That's why we should get one. Then we won't be sad anymore. That's a good idea, isn't it, Annie?"

Impressed with her sound reasoning, I nod. "It's hard on everyone when a family loses a vital member. The loss leaves a big hole in your heart. What was her name?"

Justin pauses before answering. "Lucy."

I must ask this question. "Why are you interested in greyhounds?"

"Eden saw a news program about Florida tracks shutting down and the dogs needing homes. She's been insisting our dog be a former racer."

The little girl nods vigorously. "I know they need a special collar and can run as fast as a car."

Unlike her grieving sister, Eden appears ready to move on to a new pet. Why are the two children responding so differently to the loss of the Yorkie? If their mother had the dog before she married, it may have been a senior when the girls were born and not interested in playing with them. Or Eden may be a dog lover, and Savanna is not. I need to know why a red flag popped up about this family.

"Eden, why aren't you sad that Lucy died?" Instead of responding, her head whips toward her father like children do when unsure how to answer an adult's question. Looking at Justin, I add, "I'm only asking to be sure you're adopting a dog for the right reasons."

Three faces stare back at me: a hostile-looking father, a teary-eyed child, and a frowning perplexed one. Finally, Justin speaks in a slow, measured tone. "What are you trying to say?"

I clear my throat. "I want to know why you want to replace your Yorkshire terrier, Lucy, with a much larger and more active greyhound."

"Lucy was my wife, not the dog."

CHAPTER 2

THERE HAVE BEEN a few horrifically embarrassing times in my life. Five years ago, at a fashion show in the Bahamas, the too-large bikini bottom I wore slipped on a turn at the end of a runway and exposed my naked butt to the audience.

Once, in the ladies' room of a London club, a woman in the next stall sounded distressed. I asked, "Are you okay?" When no one answered, I crouched on the floor and craned my neck under the divider.

A man was fucking a woman from behind. He met my shocked gaze and said, "Like what you see, luv? Wait your turn, and I'll do you next."

"Annie?" Justin stares at me with his grass-green eyes.

My cheeks explode with heat. "The Yorkie wasn't named Lucy."

"No. The dog died before the girls were born. My wife, *Lucy,* was killed in a traffic accident four years ago."

"I'm so sorry I misunderstood."

He flashes a weak smile. "It's okay. When you asked for a name, I thought you meant my wife. The dog was called Bubbles."

An awkward silence stretches between us. Finally, I let out a breath and stand. "Is everybody ready to meet the greyhounds now?"

"Yes! Yes!" Eden gives small claps of her hands.

Justin doesn't answer but lifts her daughter off his lap and stands.

15

"Savanna, are you ready?" I ask.

She nods and takes her father's hand. We move to the step-down living room, where three greyhounds stretch out on an L-shaped sectional, and two occupy oversized dog beds.

I stop by the gate that opens into the room. "The white ones on the floor belong to me. On the sofa are the dogs in need of homes."

"What are *your* dogs' names?" Eden asks.

"The one with the black around her eye is Juno. The other one is Bella. They were both former racers and had the same father but different mothers. I didn't know that until after I adopted them and looked at their pedigrees."

A frown wrinkles Eden's forehead. "What are pet-a-greens?"

"*Pedigrees* are charts that give the background of purebred dogs. Like family trees, they tell who their parents, grandparents, and great-grandparents were."

Justin studies the canines in the room. "Did you grow up with dogs?"

"My father and his brother operated a kennel for over ten years. They bred and trained greyhounds to race rather than to show." I don't tell him that I had nothing to do with the business or greyhounds until I was an adult.

He cocks his head. "Not all of them are racers?"

"The American Kennel Club dogs are bred for their health and to improve the breed, but most greyhounds are bred to race. Those are the ones registered by the National Greyhound Association."

"Eden wants to give a retired racer a home, but maybe we should consider adopting a puppy instead. What do you think?"

Justin's intense stare is so potent it almost feels like he's touching me. "Um, well, to be honest, buying a puppy is expensive. Greyhounds are sometimes unsuitable for racing, but the females are often kept for breeding. If a dog doesn't want to run or is not a good racer, there's usually a long waiting list to buy one."

"Is there any other way to get a puppy?"

"If a kennel has too many dogs to train, they'll have an auction. The puppies may show promise as racers, but it's a matter of space and time. Even these dogs can sell for thousands of dollars. But I wouldn't want to raise a greyhound puppy even if I got one for free."

Savanna touches my hand. "Why not?"

I crouch to the child's level. "Any puppy is a lot of work, and greyhounds are *huge* with lots of energy. Like Eden said, they can run as fast as a car, and they love to chew."

Justin raises one palm. "I think we can rule out getting a puppy. I take it most adoptions are adult dogs."

"Yes." I look up at him. He is handsome even from this perspective. "They're trained and ready to live a life of leisure in a family home. Rescue groups ensure the dogs are neutered or spayed, vaccinated, medically cleared, and tested for small animals."

"What do you mean they're tested for *small animals*?" Justin frowns and takes a tiny step backward, pulling Savanna away from the gate.

"People have nothing to worry about. Like all hounds, the breed is prey-driven. Racers train to pursue small animals. Sometimes, they can't live with little dogs, cats, rabbits, or guinea pigs. We test them, but there's no guarantee they won't attack one in an adopter's home." As much as I hate giving a prospective adopter this warning, I'm obligated by the rescue organization.

As I crouch by her side, Savanna taps my shoulder. "Do they like little kids?"

"They *love* people and other greyhounds. From the time they're puppies, that's who they're with all day." I rise to my full height. "Would you like to go into the room and meet them face-to-face now?"

Both girls nod with vigor.

"Okay, you need to stay calm. Sit down on that section of the sofa and wait. Juno and Bella will probably be the first to greet you. Then we'll see if the others are interested. It's like meeting a new person. Sometimes you want to be their friend, and sometimes you don't. The same thing happens when you meet a new dog."

The girls follow me inside and sit where instructed. Juno and Bella rise from their dog beds and approach. This happens almost every time a prospective adopter comes to my house. It's as if they know they're off the adoption block and can be friendly and curious without being judged.

Each of my greyhounds stands in front of one child. Eden and Savanna run their hands over the dogs' heads, down their necks, and lower to rub their chests. After several minutes, one of the rescue dogs, a large black male, pushes his way between Juno and Bella, forcing Eden to pet Bella with one hand and the foster dog with her other one.

"This guy is named Felix. He's three years old and competed in ninety-three races. He's mild-mannered in the house but very energetic in the yard. He tested okay with small dogs but didn't like cats. I've only had him for two weeks, so I'm still learning about his behaviors."

A second foster joins Felix. My dogs drift back to their beds without the girls' undivided attention. Eden reaches out and strokes the newcomer's back. "This one looks like Bella. Are they sisters?"

"No. This is Fancy." The greyhound has black around both eyes and her ears. She is covered with ticking, which are flecks of black on her white coat. "Fancy is fine with small dogs and cats. She's less than two years old and only raced four times."

"Why only four?" Justin stands on the other side of the gate with a wide stance and his arms crossed, the picture of a coach conferring with a pitcher on the mound.

"Probably because she came in last each time. Despite her training, she was not a good racer."

The third dog never moves from her place on the sofa. Sometimes, she lifts her head and opens an eye to peer at the kids but then flops back onto the cushion and ignores them. Her coloring is similar to Fancy's but with dark brown brindle markings instead of black.

Justin points with his chin. "What's the story on that one?"

"Lady is almost five and competed in nearly two hundred races. She's okay with small dogs, but her cat testing is still pending."

Eden studies Lady. "Is she tired because she raced so much?"

"It could be that, or it's because she's an older dog. Now that she doesn't have to race and train, she has become very lazy. That's what I call her—Lazy Lady."

The girls stumble over the tongue-twister nickname and laugh. Savanna casts a worried glance at Lady. "Can I go over there and say hi to her?"

"Sure. First, say her name and talk to her so she knows how close you are."

"Be careful," her father warns.

Savanna slowly approaches the end of the sofa where Lady lies. The little girl sits on her heels and speaks in a soft voice. "Hi, Lady. My name is Savanna." The greyhound opens her eyes and lifts her head. "Can I pet you? I think you're pretty."

The dog tracks the girl's slow hand as it reaches toward her. When Savanna rubs her little fingers between Lady's ears, the dog closes her eyes and drops her head. Savanna rises and strokes the back of the greyhound's neck. Lady rolls to her side, exposing her mottled chest and abdomen.

I smile. "She loves having her belly rubbed."

Savanna runs both hands from the dog's breastbone, over her ribs, down the soft stomach, and back again, a kiddie pianist sweeping the length of a keyboard. Lady emits a soft groan, flips on her back, and lies with her front legs extended like twin antennae. Savanna stands and hunches over the greyhound, never slowing her long strokes.

Fifteen minutes later, we all gather at the front door. The two girls chatter about the virtues of all three fosters. Eden's favorite is Fancy because she's the youngest and doesn't want to race. Savanna likes Lady the best because she was a winner and now deserves a well-earned rest. Felix is big and shiny, like the horse on the cover of the *Black Beauty* book their Grandma read to them.

Justin opens the door. "We'll talk more at home about the dogs."

"I recommend studying about greyhounds online. Check posts by people who own them. That helps you know all the pluses and minuses of the breed."

"Girls, thank Annie for letting us see the dogs today."

"Thank you." The words are spoken in unison.

Eden flings her arms around my hips from one side, and Savanna does the same on the other. I place one hand on each little girl's back, holding them close. Unexpected maternal feelings course through me.

"Can we come again? Please, Daddy?" Surprisingly, this comes from Savanna, not the more gregarious Eden.

Justin smiles at his daughters. "Sure, if it's okay with Annie."

"Give me a call, and we'll set a date."

"It's time for us to go." Justin puts his hand on Savanna's back.

His palm covers my hand where it rests between the little girl's shoulder blades and remains for a heartbeat before moving away. In those two seconds, a hot tingle spreads up my arm, and my heart lurches. Justin pulls a thoughtful face as though he's just as surprised as I am.

I walk the family out and wave goodbye, wondering how disappointed the girls will be if different dogs are here on their next visit or if I'll ever see them again.

CHAPTER 3

"HOW IS WORK going?" I open the carton containing the chocolate cake covered with ganache and layered with salted caramel that I bought at a French bakery. My usual contribution to this monthly event is either wine, beer, or a decadent dessert,

"Oh, a new year is crazy, regardless of the school." Francesca, or Frankie, as the family calls her, is the new principal at a middle school in Palm Beach County. She reaches for several plates from the cupboard. "Will you grab the platter up there, Annie?"

I stand behind my much shorter cousin and remove the sizeable oval dish from an upper shelf. One Sunday a month, Frankie has a family dinner, which includes her husband, Dale, their two kids, both sets of grandparents, and me if I'm in town. Frankie's four-bedroom, three-bath Boynton Beach house sits in a newer subdivision where the builder used six different architectural plans. People have individualized their exteriors with varying colors of paint, which still need to be approved by the homeowners association. The result is the same limited palette of pastels and neutrals.

Frankie pulls a large aluminum pan from the oven, lifts a corner of the foil cover, and waits for the steam to escape. She brushes her wild, dark hair off her forehead. "I've got to tell you one funny thing that happened this week. After dismissal, I saw this new teacher just out of college standing by his classroom door. He rested his head on a locker and said, 'How in the world did you get yourself into this?' All first-year teachers have a tough time, so I patted his back and asked him if he was okay. He turned around and said, 'I will be as soon as I get this kid out of his locker.'"

I bark a laugh, and Frankie joins me.

My niece, Natalie, a little girl with dark hair like her mother's, enters the kitchen dragging a reluctant toddler by the hand. "Mommy, Jonas stinks."

Frankie unties her apron. "Annie, will you take the ribs from the pan and put them on the platter?"

"Sure." When I peel back the remaining foil, the smoky tang of the meat mixes with the sweet aroma of Kansas-style barbecue sauce.

Frankie picks up her son. "Let's get you cleaned up, smelly boy."

Natalie climbs onto a barstool. "Guess what, Annie?"

"What?"

"Grandma says she'll text me when I learn to read." Natalie started preschool two weeks earlier. She insisted they teach her to read because she learned how to play and eat snacks in daycare.

"That's a nice thing to look forward to. I know you'll be a great reader."

"What do old people talk about when they text?"

"I don't know. You'll have to ask one."

She frowns. "I just did. Hi, Grandma!"

"Hello, sweetheart, and hi, Annie." My aunt, Linda, enters the kitchen, followed by her husband, Milo.

She is average height with shoulder-length, well-cut light brown hair. My mother, who I only know from photographs, and her sister, Linda, looked very similar when they were younger, except Mom was half a head taller.

"Grandma," Natalie says, "What are you going to text me when I can read?"

"I don't know, honey." Linda puts a large salad bowl covered in plastic wrap on the kitchen counter. "Probably funny pictures of dogs and recipes."

"Don't send any diet ones. Mommy has those already."

"What recipe do you want me to send you?"

"One for Pop-Tarts."

Linda pauses. "Um, I don't think I have that one."

Her short, mustachioed Italian husband approaches Natalie and kisses the little girl's head. "How's my girl?"

"I'm good." Natalie's brow wrinkles. "Are you glad I'm not a boy, Grandpa?"

"I sure am. Are *you* glad you're not a boy?"

Natalie shakes her head like a shampoo model on a TV commercial, brushing her hair away from her cheeks. "Yeah, I *love* being pretty and smart."

Aunt Linda hugs me. "How are you doing, sweetheart? Are you home for a while?"

I embrace my aunt in return. "I'm fine. I have a photo shoot next month in Madrid. Until then, I'm finishing up book cover designs for some publishers and authors." With my modeling career slowing, I use my graphic design skills to do fashion layouts for online sellers and other tasks such as book covers.

"Overseas flights. Ugh! I don't miss all the flying and traveling we did when you were younger. Of course, I was younger too, but I never could adjust to the different time zones as easily as you did."

Linda refused to allow me to travel alone as a seventeen-year-old model. For three years, my aunt and I journeyed the world. At first, the bookings, especially the international ones, were exciting and glamorous until the reality of the situation hit. Long hours, a stressful work environment, and maintenance of my appearance no matter how I felt. But I'm a seasoned traveler now and still enjoy foreign shoots. My body adapts to different time zones as easily as a reset watch.

Linda steps back and eyes me. "And who are you wearing today?"

The dress is acid yellow with short sleeves and a mid-thigh hemline. I covered the elastic waistband with a black Chanel belt. On my feet are white socks and Converse sneakers. I spread out the skirt and twirl. "This is by A Loves A, and I picked it up at Dillard's."

Frankie enters the kitchen with little Jonas on her hip. "Hi, Dad."

"How's my little man?" Milo lifts the toddler and kisses his plump cheek.

Linda hugs her daughter. "Hi, honey. Annie's got the ribs handled, and I brought my Caesar salad. Is there anything else I can do?"

"No. Everything is set up on the patio. Dale will be home from golfing any minute, and his parents should be here soon."

A door opens, and a voice with a Desi Arnaz accent calls out, "Lucy, I'm home!"

Hearing the name again reminds me of the embarrassing incident with Justin Stabler yesterday.

Frankie's husband walks past the kitchen, and Natalie climbs off the barstool. "Daddy!"

At the same time, little Jonas squirms in his grandfather's arms. "Dada!"

Both kids run to their brown bear of a father, who is sweaty and red-faced from his outing in the South Florida heat. Dale must have rushed home without freshening up in the locker room. No doubt Frankie gave him strict instructions to not stop for a beer in the clubhouse. He lifts his son while Natalie inches up his leg like a squirrel scampering up a tree. With both children on his hips, he neighs and trots off, the human equivalent of a horse. The kids squeal in delight.

Dale's parents arrive a few minutes later, bearing a baked bean casserole. I often wonder if Dale will one day look like his dad. Roger and his son top my height by several inches. The older Forbes has a belly that protrudes as if he carries a large watermelon under his shirt. Both father and son have broad faces, but Roger's has melted into his neck with a series of double chins.

Dale's mother, Dawn, has long, grey hair that must have been a glorious blond at one time. She has no discernable waistline, a motherly bust, and an affinity for oversized earrings and nail art.

"Annie." Dawn kisses my cheek. "It's so nice to see you again. It's been a while."

"I missed last month's dinner because I was away for work."

She shakes her head. "It's amazing you're still modeling. You're what? Thirty-two?"

"Thirty."

"Well, you don't look it, and you're still so tall and thin."

I raise my eyebrows. "There's not much I can do to change my height."

"No, of course not." Dawn tilts her head back to eye the top of my head. "Why do you still keep your hair so short? Have you ever considered letting it grow out? It makes you look like one of those boys in a band from South Korea."

Aunt Linda and I cast meaningful glances at each other. "I like it this way. The style works for me."

Soon, everyone is seated at an oval glass and aluminum table on the rectangular patio with an amorphous-shaped pool in the center. The backyard slopes gently down to a lake. Frankie loves her property, but, like many parents of small children, she is hyperaware of how lakes and pools can be hazardous. Although both her kids were enrolled in swim classes at a young age, childproof fencing surrounds the pool, and a strict rule is that the screen door to the backyard must always remain locked.

After finishing our rib dinner, followed by my bakery-bought chocolate cake, Dale, Roger, and the children drift into the house. The women continue to sit at the table with the residue of the meal and two partially empty bottles of wine.

Aunt Linda twists in her chair to face me. "How many greyhounds are you fostering now?"

"Three. But a widower and his twin daughters came to look at them yesterday."

"How old are the girls?" asks Frankie.

"Seven. They're in first grade."

"And how old is the father?" Her smile becomes a sly grin. "Just a rough estimate will do."

The memory of Justin's hand touching mine causes my attention to waver for a few seconds.

"Look, Mom." Frankie points at my face. "She has dreamy eyes."

Linda ignores her. "Are they going to adopt one of your foster dogs?" She loves the breed but doesn't own one herself. Instead, she's my dog sitter whenever I go out of town.

"I don't know. Eden and Savanna really want a greyhound, but Justin isn't too sure."

Frankie drawls, "Is *Justin* hot?"

"He is if you like…" I almost say bald men, but the hairless head of Dawn's husband pops into my mind.

"If you like what?" Frankie's eyes narrow at my hesitation.

I halt again before saying men who aren't taller than me. Linda's husband, Milo, is the same height as his five-foot-six wife. "If you like men still grieving for a dead wife."

Dawn pours herself more wine. "My advice is to forget about getting involved with a widower. It's impossible to compete against a ghost."

"That's okay. I'm not into dating anyone right now."

She waggles a manicured finger with three colors of polish on it. "But you shouldn't give up on it entirely. After all, finding a man after you turn thirty isn't easy."

I snort. "Trust me. I know. Finding a nice, normal guy today is like trying to find the least damaged bananas on a clearance shelf."

The other three women at the table laugh, but I don't.

CHAPTER 4

DESPITE SAYING THAT I wasn't interested in dating, a little starburst thrill pops inside my chest when Justin Stabler calls again. "Hi, Annie. It's Justin. We came to see you last weekend."

"Yes. I remember. Have you and your daughters reached a decision?"

"We've been doing a lot of research online that says greyhounds are great with children. The owners write that their dogs are mellow, intelligent, and clean."

"That's right. I didn't want you to only take my word for it."

"I saw there's a Meet and Greet this weekend with several greyhound groups. Are you going?"

Three South Florida rescue groups are combining for an adoption event at a park on the county's western edge. "Yes. I'll be there."

"The girls want to know if you still have the same dogs."

"I do, but a family is adopting Felix, the black male."

"Eden and Savanna decided they want one of the females. It seems I'm out of luck getting another guy in this house."

A voice in the background says, "Daddy, did you ask her about Fancy and Lady?"

"She still has them." Squeals and handclaps follow his response.

When the noise dies down, I say, "If you attend the Meet and Greet, there'll be at least a dozen other dogs there. The girls might make a connection with another one."

"I don't know. They're pretty sure it will be either Fancy or Lady. Anyway, I'll look for you on Saturday."

After the call ends, a cozy feeling courses through me. Why did Justin say *I'll* look for you and not *we'll* look for you? I force myself to recall my rules for engagement with men. The first and most important one is to pretend indifference until the other person's return attraction is confirmed. At my age, it's pathetic for a woman to develop a crush on a man who does not reciprocate her feelings.

The following Saturday is an overcast day. A rainstorm thunders early in the morning, and grayish billows hang heavy in the sky. Glimmers of sunshine peek through the leaden blanket, promising a bright day, only to disappear again as if the sun is playing tug of war with the clouds.

Thankfully, where the Meet and Greet is being held isn't muddy, despite the earlier shower. When I arrive at the park, several people sit in lawn chairs with their dogs on the grass or blankets. Others mill under a covered pavilion. I retrieve Fancy and Lady from their crates in the back of my SUV.

A tanned woman frantically waves at me when I enter the picnic area. Debbie Hale-Brown is a board member of the rescue group I belong to. When I reach her, she squints up into my face. "I'm so glad you brought your fosters, but I thought you had three ready for adoption."

"I left Felix at home with my dogs since he'll be going to his new owners tomorrow."

"What a coincidence. The only one I have right now is being placed tomorrow, too." Debbie executes a twirl and opens her arms wide, mimicking Maria von Trapp on a mountaintop. "I'm here by myself today. Maybe we'll meet some unattached men who are not only interested in greyhounds—if you know what I mean."

Debbie Hale-Brown's marriage ended two years earlier, and since then, she's been on the hunt to find a man and re-hyphenate her name. With a stocky cheerleader's body, the younger woman is attractive and well-groomed with long blond hair extensions. Today, she's dressed in a pink shirt, a white denim skirt, and enough makeup to excite a Mary Kay rep.

As we walk to the pavilion, Fancy and Lady greet each new dog with excited whips of their skinny tails, straining to close the distance for better sniffs. Thirty minutes later, they lie on the cool concrete floor of the pavilion.

I am seated on a picnic table bench, talking with a couple considering the adoption of a second greyhound, when a little girl's voice cries out, "We're here, Annie!"

An older woman walks toward me with Eden and Savanna. Justin is nowhere to be seen. A twinge twists in my chest. The prospective adopters thank me and move off with their dog. Fancy stands, her tail whipping back and forth. Does she remember the twins? Eden and Savanna talk to the older woman and point to my two dogs. I stand and smooth down the legs of my red Brunello Cucinelli walking shorts.

When they draw near, the older woman has a wide-eyed look that starts at my longer-than-average legs and continues up to my face. "Hello, I'm Cecilia Sonnenberg," she says. "Eden and Savanna's grandmother."

She is a petite woman with the faded hair of middle age. Her strawberry blond locks were probably as dark as her granddaughters' hair at one time. Tiny particles of vanilla-colored face powder sprinkle the drawstring lines around her mouth. Cecilia has a nondescript pageboy hairstyle and the sagging face of the perpetually dissatisfied. Her figure appears formless in elastic-waist pants and a button-down blouse worn loose.

"It's nice to meet you. I'm Annie Warden." I push disappointment with Justin's absence aside to greet the girls. "You two will have such fun today meeting more greyhounds."

They move their heads in tandem to view the other dogs around the shelter. Eden runs her hand along Fancy's back. "We still like yours best."

"But you need to meet the others just to be sure." I give each girl a sandwich bag with several dog goodies inside. "Ask the foster mom or dad if you can give them a treat. If they say yes, put one in your palm under the dog's nose. And ask if you can pet them before touching them."

Cecilia looks around the pavilion. "Is there anything else we should do?"

I pull a paper out of a canvas shopping bag. "Here's a list of possible questions."

She scans it with a fixed expression. "We're supposed to get answers to all twenty-two of these?"

"No, but if you're interested in a dog, you should learn as much as possible. The idea is to get the best match."

Cecilia emits a grumbly sigh. "Seems like a lot of work to get a dog. I told Justin to go to the pound and pick one out, but the girls are set on adopting a greyhound."

"Grandma!" Eden rolls her eyes. "Come on. I want to meet the other dogs."

"Hold on. We'll get to it." Cecilia's gaze drops to my naked ring finger. "Eden and Savanna were very impressed with you and all the dogs in your house."

I plaster on the prim smile I save for people who think a thirty-year-old single woman with no children and an excess of large dogs constitutes a mental defect.

"Grandma, let's go." This time, it's quiet Savanna who voices her pique.

I sit on the bench to be closer to the children. "Check out the other greyhounds. Remember what you learned about meeting a strange dog. I'll be here when you're done."

They exit the pavilion and approach a trio of dogs lying on a blanket under a tree. I lose sight of them when two more prospective adopters stop and ask about Fancy and Lady. When they move on, Debbie plops down beside me and bumps my shoulder."I saw you talking with those red-headed twins. It looked like you knew them."

"They came to my house last weekend to see the dogs."

"Are they the Stablers? I emailed a guy named Justin the directions to your house." She scans the area until she lights on Eden, Savanna, and their grandmother in a far corner under a popup tent. "Is that their mother? I know women have babies later in life, but I wouldn't want to pay for my kid's high school graduation with a social security check."

"She's their grandmother."

"Is she raising them?"

Before I can figure out a polite way to tell Debbie it is none of her business, a deep-timbered voice says, "Hi, Annie, sorry I'm late."

CHAPTER 5

IF DEBBIE WERE a dog, her ears would have perked at Justin's voice, and maybe they do under her hair extensions. She scampers off the picnic bench and hustles over to him. "Hello. I'm *so* glad you came today."

Over her shoulder, he looks my way with a who-hell-is-this expression. "Uh, it's nice to be here."

I roll my eyes, causing Justin to grin.

"I'm Debbie Hale-Brown. Are you interested in adopting a greyhound, Mister. . .?" She purrs in a soft, husky voice, a little more passionate than is appropriate.

"Stabler. Justin Stabler."

"*Justin Stabler!*" Debbie squeals. "I was the one who answered your email and set up the appointment to see the foster dogs."

"Um, thank you."

"You're very welcome.

I have a revelation watching Justin and Debbie interact. They appear so *right* together. He's taller than her by half a foot or more, and her long hair contrasts with his shaved head. Despite the thrill I experienced when I met him, did I read too much into the incident? Not all guys want to be with a small-breasted, too-thin woman who is taller than them, and has a pixie cut only slightly longer than most men's hair.

Justin looks at me and says, "Are Cecilia and the girls here?"

Debbie takes hold of his hand and pulls. "Come with me. They're over this way."

Justin glances back like he's an innocent man being lead off to prison.

For the next hour, I speak with more possible adoptees, including a newly married gay couple interested in Lady. When the two-hour event ends, the Stablers are nowhere to be seen. Maybe they found another greyhound they preferred and are reluctant to give me the bad news. Or maybe Justin wants Debbie to coordinate the adoption from this point. I sling my canvas tote with paperwork, water, bowls, and dog treats over my shoulder and wave farewell to the other foster parents. My phone rings after loading Fancy and Lady into crates and turning the ignition key.

"Hello?"

"Hi. It's Justin. The girls and I would like to know if we can meet you somewhere to talk?"

Uh-oh. Why can't he tell me whatever it is over the phone? "I guess so."

"We're in the parking lot across the road and saw you get into your car. Can you suggest a place we can all go with your greyhounds?"

"There's a dog park not too far from here. Do you want to follow me?"

Justin relays the information, and a chorus of excited yeses follows. "We're in a black BMW."

"Is your mother-in-law with you?"

"No, she left soon after I arrived. It's just me and the girls."

On the way to Barkham Park, I rehearse my speech when he tells me they found another dog they like better than mine. Or I will do my best to graciously accept his desire to work with Debbie instead of me.

I pull into a parking space, and Justin backs into the one beside me. Our driver-side windows power down. He points to the fenced-in area. "Are we allowed to go in there?"

"Yes. I have a pass."

The wet and dreary morning has transformed into a sunny afternoon with white clouds scuttling across a brisk blue sky. I get Fancy and Lady from the back of my car, and we enter the first double-gated area for large dogs. A black lab and mixed breed dog with some husky in him come forward, sniffing through the chain link fence. I check for signs of aggression or dominance. The six other dogs in the enclosure ignore us.

Before opening the second gate, I turn to the girls, "Have you ever been to a dog park before?"

They shake their heads.

"Okay, walk in and keep moving forward. Don't touch the dogs. Don't talk to them, and don't make eye contact. We're going to walk over to that empty bench under the tree. Ready?"

I stride forward like I'm on a high-fashion runway. Several dogs rush in front of me. I bump the ribs of a pushy German Shepherd with my knee when he doesn't move away fast enough. The others fall into step until it appears I have six leashed dogs instead of two. I hope Justin and his daughters mimic my entrance.

On the bench, the girls clamber onto the seat beside me. Justin sits at the opposite end. Eden and Savanna stare wide-eyed at the dogs crowding around us. They pull their arms close to their chests.

"Ignore the dogs," I tell them. "Look and talk to me or your dad."

Justin watches the nosy canines out of the corner of his eye. "Why do that?"

"We're claiming our space. Our body language tells them we have as much right to be here as they do."

The four strange dogs saunter off after sniffing Juno, Bella, and the human legs. The greyhounds' slender bodies quiver with excitement. They sense a place where they can run loose. "Why don't you girls pet Fancy and Lady? They're too excited for me to let them off-leash right now."

"Why can't they be loose like the other dogs?" Eden reaches forward to stroke Fancy's back. Her sister does the same with Lady.

"Because they could hurt themselves or another dog. I want them to run, not race."

The girls stroke the greyhounds and distract them with warnings. "This is a park. You need to play nice."

"If you go too fast, you can hurt yourself."

"You don't want to make the other dogs feel bad because they can't run as fast as you."

After a few minutes, I unclip the leashes. Juno and Bella take a few tentative steps on their stick-thin legs, shake from head to tail, and then trot off to the fence line, sniffing the ground.

Savanna kneels on the bench. "Why aren't they running?"

"They will as soon as they've figured out the area. Keep your eye on them. You'll soon see something beautiful."

The former racers do a slow circuit around the three-acre area. Then, without warning, they accelerate, running neck and neck with each other, mouths open and paws barely skimming the grass. Eden and Savanna jump off the bench and clap their hands. After two circles and several figure eights around the park, Fancy and Lady return to us smiling, panting, and collapse on the grass in the shade of a live oak tree. The twins sit next to them, petting their heaving sides and telling them how beautiful they are.

Justin watches his daughters with one arm extended across the bench back. I copy his position. Our fingertips lay inches from each other. "Thank you for taking time out of your day to bring us here. We tried to get back to you, but Debbie insisted on introducing us to more people and dogs. After a while, Eden complained she was thirsty, and Savanna needed to use the restroom, so I told Debbie we had to leave. She made me fill out an application. In fact, she wrote down everything as we walked to our car."

Oh, no! Debbie will never allow me to complete the adoption now, even if the Stablers choose Fancy or Lady. I could see the fire in her eyes when she spotted Justin. Although she's committed to finding homes for greyhounds, her priority is finding a husband. Justin is the perfect prospect to fulfill both causes. He's single and willing to rescue a dog. She will likely insist on doing the home check at his residence. And, if the adoption is approved, Debbie will be the one to place Fancy or Lady with the Stablers.

Justin frowns. "If she took my application, does that mean you won't be the one in charge, even if we pick one of your dogs?"

Keeping my voice as neutral as possible, I say, "I'm sure that's what she plans."

CHAPTER 6

CLOUDS MOVE OVERHEAD, and the sun suddenly shines on Justin's face, making his eyes glow in the split second before he blinks. "What if I insist we want to work with you? After all, you know the dogs better than she does. Besides, the girls seem to be as taken with you as they are with your dogs. And so am I."

My breath hitches in my throat. "I feel the same about you and your daughters."

His fingertips inch forward and touch mine. "We're on the same page then."

"Daddy!" Eden drapes herself over her father's shoulder. "Can we walk around the park?"

"Don't go out of the gate."

I turn toward her. "Walking in here is fine, but don't run. Some of the dogs might chase you."

Eden glances at the two greyhounds stretched out on the grass. "Can Fancy and Lady come with us?"

"Call them and see if they'll follow."

Eden moves to the winding sidewalk that snakes around the area and slaps her knees. "Come, Fancy. Come, Lady."

The younger greyhound rises and ambles over to the little girl. Lady lifts her head, and then drops it onto the grass again.

"Are you coming, Savanna?" her sister asks, hugging Fancy's neck.

With a sigh, the other twin leaves Lady's side, and they set off on the pathway like a trio of girlfriends.

Justin chuckles. "I guess we know which dog they're adopting."

"Or which dog is adopting them. I won't ask you to fill out another application, but how about answering some questions for me?"

"Sure, as long as I get to ask you some."

I'm pinned in place by the determined masculine intensity. "Okay, but I go first. What's your occupation?"

"I'm a civil engineer for Broward County and have been doing it since I graduated from college. What do you do when you aren't caring for greyhounds?"

I rarely share information about my career as a model with new people. Over the years, there have been many backlashes about my thinness, height, edited photos, unhealthy eating habits, and unrealistic expectations for young women. I no longer maintain a social media presence for that part of my income because of comments posted by trolls.

"I'm a graphic designer doing mostly print ads and other work for publishers. What does a civil engineer do?"

"I oversee government building projects."

"Do you do the designs?"

"No. I hate being stuck in an office all day. I'm mostly on-site with the contractors."

That explains his golden-brown skin. His jaw and cheeks have strong angles, and his pale green eyes are reminiscent of sunbaked grass. If he wasn't so male with his face stubble and bald head, he could be pretty instead of handsome.

"Do you and the girls live in a house or apartment?"

"I own my own home, and it has a fenced-in backyard. Several people at the park asked me that today."

The sun has moved, and we no longer sit in the shade. Beads of sweat dot my forehead. On the other hand, Justin is in his element. His powerful forearms extend from the stretched T-shirt sleeves, and his skin glistens. I squint up at the sky. "Can we move to a different seat?"

"Not much of a sun worshipper, are you?"

"If I could tan like you, I would be."

We settle on another bench in partial shade under a leafy tree. Our other alternative is under the pavilion, where several people occupy picnic tables. But there is no privacy for us to talk. Lady follows us to the new seat and squeezes herself under it. The twins continue strolling around the park, petting some dogs or chatting with their owners. Fancy romps in the open grassy area, playing the canine version of tag with another dog.

I turn to Justin again. "Does your mother-in-law live with you and the girls?"

"No, but her house is two doors away. Lucy insisted on moving close to her after the twins were born." His voice has a clipped quality to it, and I wonder why.

"With your work schedule and the girls in school, how many hours a day will a dog be alone in the house?"

"Cecilia will come over at noon to let it out, or she'll keep it with her. We haven't decided that yet."

"Is her backyard fenced in too?"

"Yes. You'll see that when you do the home check. If there's anything that we need to change, let me know." There is a heavy pause before he says, "Would you—"

"Annie!" Eden and Savanna run toward us and point to the open field. "Fancy pooped, and a lady says we need to clean it up."

I stand. "Let me show you what to do. Where is it?"

The girls look at each other and give dramatic shrugs.

"Well, which lady told you?"

They point to a large woman with a buzz cut shorter than my hairstyle, wearing Levi's and an X-men T-shirt. The poop monitor looks like a corrections officer or a hockey coach. She's deep in conversation with another equally intimidating but younger woman.

We approach, and I catch their attention with a hand wave. "Excuse me. Where did the greyhound make a mess?"

The older woman scowls. "You're supposed to keep an eye on your dog."

There is no dog anywhere near these two women. "Which one is yours?"

The woman scans the park and points to the far end. "He's the Rottweiler over there. Why?"

"I was wondering which eye you were keeping on him."

The woman snarls, "You know what, bitch? Find your dog's mess yourself."

"Thank you. I will."

We walk away, and Eden hisses, "She called you a bad name."

"I know, but I choose to ignore it." I head to a metal stand holding a roll of plastic bags and pull one off. "Let's see if we can find some poop to pick up."

Savanna's brow wrinkles. "What if it's not Fancy's?"

"It doesn't matter. At least we cleaned up some dog's mess."

Eden raises her hand. "Can we do it too?"

"Sure. We'll all be poop pickers."

The girls race to the stand, grab two more bags, and join me. We walk a grid until we find three different piles. I show them how to insert a hand inside the bag and pick up the feces. Savanna closes her eyes with a look of disgust and misses several pieces. After I knot the bags shut, the girls carry them to a nearby trash bin with their arms extended away from their noses.

"Will we have to do that when we get our dog?" Eden asks.

"Yes. Whenever you take your dog for a walk or to a park, you shouldn't leave a mess where someone might step in it or need to clean it up. Also, you don't want your backyard to be dirty either."

"Daddy will have to buy us bags," says Savanna.

"You can also get a pooper-scooper. It's like a double shovel."

That sends the girls into paroxysms of giggles. Eden rushes to her father. "Daddy! We need a pooper-scooper."

"What have you been teaching my daughters?" Justin gives a sidelong look at the two women on the far bench.

"How to clean up after a dog."

"Good. Maybe they'll learn to keep their room clean too."

I check the time on my Apple watch. "I'm sorry, but I need to head home and let my other dogs out."

I withdraw a whistle from my pocket and blow. There is no sound, but Lady crawls out under the bench, and Fancy charges across the park with two more dogs. I feed my two greyhounds and the other dogs liver treats from a sandwich bag in my purse. Like Lady and Fancy, these canines must also be whistle-trained.

I attach leashes to the dogs' Martingale collars and ask the twins, "Do you want to walk *the girls* to the car?"

Eden and Savanna nod. I instruct them to hold the leash in a relaxed but firm grip and how to keep the dogs at their side and not pull ahead. After loading the greyhounds in their crates, I start the engine to cool off the interior. At the same time, Justin checks that his children are buckled into the backseat. We meet between our two vehicles.

He flashes a huge smile. "I can't thank you enough, Annie. This was a great day. I know Eden and Savanna will talk about the dogs and everything they learned for quite a while."

"Good. I'm glad you had fun at the Meet and Greet."

He balls his hands deep into the front pockets of his cargo pants. "There is one more thing I'm curious about."

"The whistle?"

"What?"

"Are you wondering about the whistle I used to call the dogs?"

He raises a single eyebrow. "No, I want to know if you'll have dinner with me tomorrow night."

I blurt out, "I'd love to."

His grin scrunches his eyes halfway closed. "Do you have a restaurant preference?"

"Some place casual is fine."

"Have you ever been to Packy's?"

"I've never even heard of it."

He describes an Irish sports pub in Lighthouse Point where Buffalo Bills fans congregate to watch football games. In addition to the restaurant and bar, Packy's has pool tables, dartboards, and sponsored tournaments for both games. "Their food is good, but the only night of the week they don't have any specials is Sunday. The Bills aren't playing, so we won't have to deal with noisy fans. The one perk tomorrow is there's no charge to play pool all day."

"Sounds like fun. Let's go there."

"You mean that?"

I nod. "Yes."

"Then I'll pick you up at seven."

CHAPTER 7

THE NEXT EVENING, I'm deep in my closet. Justin is due in thirty minutes, and I can't decide what clothing suits an Irish sports bar date. It has been over a year since I've had a date. After my divorce, I experimented with internet dating.

When I told Frankie about it, her response was, "Are you nuts? That's one surefire way to end up as the lead story on a true crime podcast."

Although, I never met a man who I feared or made me uncomfortable, I did go out with three distinct types before I closed my accounts. There was the eager-to-impress guy who planned an out-of-the-box date. Or the one who expected me to arrange the activity, pay my half, and then pursue him afterward. And, of course, there was the *one-and-done* who said he had a great time and would call, but I never heard from him again.

One of my first internet dates was with a beefy investment banker who insisted I would love playing paintball. I ended up bruised all over for two weeks. When he called again with an offer to skydive, I told him I wasn't interested in pursuing a pain-filled or death-defying relationship.

Another epic fail took me to a show at the planetarium. The guy fell asleep and had a wet dream. It was too late to wake him when I realized what was happening. In the middle of a film about Halley's Comet shooting through the night sky, he shot through his underwear and khaki pants. I was sympathetic to his predicament and offered him my L.L. Bean sweater to hold in front of his zipper on the way to the parking lot. He said he'd have it cleaned, but I never saw him or my sweater again.

After that, I decided I was not desperate enough to risk my life, disfigurement, or the loss of apparel until tonight.

I finally don my favorite Guess jeans with a red, white, and blue striped Land's Ends T-shirt and Ulla Johnson barely-there flat sandals. I spend fifteen minutes applying and then removing makeup. Stepping back, I appraise my face in the mirror. Even though pounds of cosmetics have been used on my face, eyes, and lips over the years, I have never been confident doing it myself.

The doorbell rings as I tuck my credit card, cell phone, and driver's license into a Coach wristlet and thread the attached leather loop through my belt. When I open the door, Justin leans against the jamb. His stance is casual, but his expression says he is happy to see me. His dark jeans hug his muscular legs, his white dress shirt sleeves are rolled up his thick forearms, and he's wearing ankle boots in grey suede. I close the door behind me, lock it, and pocket the key.

Justin stares as if seeing me for the first time. "You look different."

"Good different or bad different?"

"Just different. More polished, but still beautiful."

Beautiful? No one has ever used that word to describe me. I have been called statuesque and editorial, but not beautiful. One photographer said, "Annie, darling, you are either the most confidently awkward model I have ever worked with or the most awkwardly confident one. I can't decide which it is."

I smile at Justin. "Thank you. You look wonderful, too."

When he starts the car engine, the sound system comes to life with Taylor Swift's song, *You Belong with Me,* blasting from the speakers. Justin quickly switches it off. "Sorry about that."

I frown at him with a note of faked regret in my voice. "I don't know if I can go out with a man who listens to Taylor Swift. My first boyfriend loved her. He kept loaning me his CDs, convinced her music would grow on me, but it never did."

Justin laughs. "I agree. I'm not crazy about it either."

"Yet her music is playing in your car."

"I have a playlist for the girls that doesn't drive me insane. It's better than the *Frozen* soundtrack playing over and over. They listened to it when I dropped them off at my sister's house for a sleepover."

That little nugget of information means he doesn't have to return home to relieve a babysitter. "What other songs have you downloaded?"

"You want to hear them?"

"Sure." The music will pass the time until we get to the restaurant.

Justin taps the screen, turns on the sound system, and skips past the current song. Next is *Happy* by Pharrell Williams. He looks at me with raised eyebrows. I wrinkle my nose. He uses a button on his steering wheel to play the next one in the queue. *Roar* by Katy Perry begins. I nod my approval. The only sound in the car is the music until we reach Packy's.

The parking lot is half full of cars. The pub is housed in a typical one-story square building covered with beige Hardy board siding and a flat roof with a green-shingled overhang. The dimly lit interior exudes the pub atmosphere: a circular bar surrounded by stools, dozens of televisions with their sound muted, tables and chairs, an empty dance floor in front of a raised small stage, two pool tables, and not-too-loud music playing from speakers. A large group of people sit around the bar, but only four tables in the restaurant are occupied. The yeasty smell of beer overlays the greasy aroma of fried food.

A woman bartender says, "Take a seat wherever you want."

I look around the room. "I wasn't expecting a stage and dance floor."

"On Friday and Saturday nights, live bands play. We'll have to come sometime."

Our first date has barely begun, and he is already offering a second one. A definitive response will depend on whether I have a good time tonight.

At a table, Justin pulls out the chair next to the wainscoted wall. I take a seat, and he sits across from me. A young woman wearing a green Packy's T-shirt arrives with napkins and menus at our table. She has metal piercings through her lip, nostril, and eyebrow. Her head is half-shaven, with the other side sporting chin-length blue hair. "What can I get you to drink?"

"I'll have a Budweiser," I order.

Justin widens his eyes. "Make it two."

After the waitress leaves, I cock my head at him. "You looked surprised when I asked for a beer."

"I assumed you would want a cocktail or wine."

"Why?"

"Because you're too elegant for pub beer."

That's the second adjective from him that has never been used to describe me. "I'm not beautiful nor elegant. I'm a too tall, too thin, thirty-year-old woman with too many dogs who—"

"Is beautiful and elegant."

"Justin, you might need a seeing-eye dog, not a greyhound."

He throws back his head and barks a hearty laugh. The waitress returns with two frosty beer bottles and places them on the napkins. We open our menus and discuss options, settling on sixteen Jack Daniels glazed wings and a basket of homemade potato chips with honey mustard dipping sauce.

He closes the menu. "Do you want to split the Ultimate Brownie Sundae for dessert? We should order it now because they sometimes run out."

Split the dessert? I planned on ordering one just for me. "Sure, we can share."

After the server leaves with our orders, he stares at her retreating form. "I don't get it. Why do people who can grow hair shave their heads? Or half their heads?" He must see my somewhat shaken expression when he looks my way again. He blinks and sputters, "No, Annie. I wasn't referring to your hair. It looks good on you. Besides, it's not shaved, just short."

I force a smile and take a long swig of my beer.

Perhaps to distract me from his comment, he says, "Tell me more about yourself."

"What do you want to know?"

"Who was your first boyfriend?"

I'm surprised by his question. "I was a bit of a late bloomer. I hit six feet tall by the time I was fifteen. Many teenage guys don't want a girl taller than them, let alone one with no curves."

"How old were you when you had your first boyfriend?"

"Eighteen."

"Did you meet him in high school or college?"

"I didn't go."

His eyebrows arch. "You didn't?"

"I only was in high school through my junior year, and I didn't go to college."

"Do you mind me asking why?"

I hesitate to give him the truth, but this man thinks I'm beautiful and elegant, so why not? "When I was seventeen, I started modeling full-time. I finished high school online but never attended college. To answer your original question: My first boyfriend and I were with the same agency and met when we did a photo shoot together."

"I wondered if you had ever done any modeling."

"I still do, but my work as a graphic designer is my full-time job. My turn now. Who was *your* first girlfriend?" After I voice the question, my heart skips a beat. What if his dead wife, Lucy, was his first and only love?

"Her name was Kelsey. She was fourteen and a cheerleader. I went to every football game to see her in that short skirt, doing those spastic arm movements and shouting out the *give-me* letters."

I laugh. "You are such a dude."

"How many boyfriends did you have after the male model?"

"One."

His forehead furrows with a slight, confused frown. "Why only one?"

"Because I ended up marrying him."

CHAPTER 8

JUSTIN'S EYES TRAVEL over my face, "Are you divorced?"

"Four years now. We dated for three and were married for two. Unfortunately, it was at the height of our careers, so we spent as much time apart as together."

"What did he do?"

"Thierry was a professional basketball player for the LNB Pro A, the French equivalent of the NBA."

A picture forms in my mind of my six-foot, ten-inch husband in his gray suit on our wedding day at the *Mairie* or town hall. Even though the local mayor, who was the officiant, assured us of anonymity, word spread that Thierry Benoit, one of the stars of Limoges CSP Elite, was getting married. By the end of the ceremony, a wall of townspeople gathered outside. As the *police municipale* escorted us from the building, flowers were torn from my bridal bouquet, and women hurled threats at me for taking one of France's most eligible bachelors off the market.

That should have been my first clue that the marriage was doomed. To this day, I have only told Frankie and Aunt Linda the real reason behind my divorce. Still, I'm sure many people, including Thierry's fans, did the math and figured out why the marriage ended.

Justin's brow creases. "Your husband's name was *Chitty*?"

"Close enough. Although it's a popular name for boys in France, it's difficult for English speakers to say."

"Here are your wings and chips." The server arrives with a tray perched on her shoulder.

After she transfers the food to the table, Justin motions for me to go first. I bite into a wing and half-close my eyes, savoring the sweet, spicy tang of the Jack Daniels glaze. I chew, moan, and swallow.

Justin smirks. "Do you need some time alone with that wing?"

"Would you be insulted if I said yes?"

"Not if you let me watch."

His *trying-to-be-cute* response makes my heart pound a little faster. "Now you know my guilty pleasure—bar food."

As we eat, I talk about my diet and exercise regimen (dog walking, swimming, and eating whatever I want on the weekends), owning and fostering greyhounds, and my travels. Justin shares that he competes in Iron Man competitions every other year, the difficulties of being a single father of two girls (everything pink, girly, and bedazzled), and some county-wide building projects he's overseen. Two more beers have been consumed when our Ultimate Brownie Sundae is placed on the table, and our tongues are loose.

Justin digs his spoon into the dessert. "Was the time you and your husband spent apart the reason for the divorce?"

I chew and swallow a mouthful of the sinfully rich and decadent goodness. "I learned a hard lesson marrying Thierry, one I should have known before saying I do. A marriage doesn't save a failing relationship any more than a pregnancy saves a failing marriage."

Justin's head snaps up. "Why would you say that? I mean, about a pregnancy."

I point to myself with the spoon. "Because that's what *I* was. An attempt by my mother to save her marriage."

"Your parents divorced after you were born?"

"They might have if my mother hadn't died giving birth to me."

"Annie, I'm so sorry." His gaze fixes over my left shoulder toward the stage and dance floor with a somewhat anguished look.

Is he thinking about his motherless daughters?

Then, he focuses on the chicken wing he holds. "Were you raised by your father?"

"No. From the start, I lived with my mother's sister and husband. Her daughter is less than a year older than me, and we grew up together. My dad remarried when I was twelve. After that, I only saw him when he and his new wife came to Florida during the winter. That's the relationship we still have."

Justin looks at me for the first time since he learned about my mother. "He doesn't sound like he was cut out for parenthood."

"Not everyone is, but I was lucky to have my Aunt Linda, Uncle Milo, and my cousins, Francesca and her brother, Tony. They're my family." I push my empty bottle of beer to the end of the table. "Can I ask about your wife?"

"What do you want to know?"

"Anything you're willing to tell me."

"Lucy was on the turnpike when another car lost control and hit her. The girls had just turned three the day before. Of course, they have almost no memories of their mother except for photos, videos, and what Cecilia and I tell them. Their grandmother showed them pictures of Lucy when she was in high school. There were a lot of them with Bubbles, her Yorkie. That's what started the girls wanting a dog, any dog. Then Eden saw the news report about greyhounds. And you know the rest."

The server arrives and gathers our empties. "Is there something else I can get you guys?"

Justin shakes his head. "You can bring the check. We'll play some pool, so I'll run a tab for drinks we order."

I excuse myself to go to the ladies' room. While washing my hands, I stare into the mirror, unable to see how Justin thinks I'm beautiful and elegant. Greyhounds are beautiful and elegant. Does he think I look like a greyhound because of my thinness and long legs? That's what they said about my father and his brother when they ran Warden Kennels. Both tall and lean men were often compared to the dogs they bred and trained.

Upon my return, Justin stands. "Are you ready to play pool?"

"I didn't tell you before, but I've never played. You'll have to be patient with me."

Both tables are in use. We take seats nearby, and he gives me instructions about the game. I have difficulty keeping a straight face when he says, "Some players like a long shaft while others like a shorter one. What's important is to get one with a nicely shaped tip."

He points to one of the tables. "See, that's a nice, tight rack right there. You want to make sure all your balls are touching."

I cough to cover my snort of laughter. Eventually, a couple leaves, and Justin pulls two cue sticks from the wall rack. I gather the balls from the pockets and roll them across the table to him. He positions them inside a plastic triangle, and then instructs me to hold the cue in two ways. He does this by standing beside me and not in a sexually suggestive position behind me. His fingers on my arm and hand send tingles up and down my spine. After several practice shots, I have more stability using what he calls the *closed bridge,* where my long forefinger curls over the shaft.

"Remember to stroke the ball. Don't poke it. Play through the cue ball, driving it forward with your follow-through."

He suggests a game of Eight Ball, takes the opening shot, and careens several balls into two different pockets. He's either an excellent instructor, or I know how to position my body after years of being photographed because I do well for a novice player. Justin wins each of two games either by sinking the eight ball or because I send the white cue ball into a pocket. We relinquish the table to other people who are waiting.

Justin narrows his eyes at me. "Are you sure you've never played pool before?"

Using my index finger, I paint an X over my heart. "Swear to God and cross my heart."

"You could become a good player with more instruction and practice." He turns toward the line of nine dartboards along one wall. "What about darts? Ever played?"

I shake my head. Two men throw at a board at the far end, and we choose one in the middle.

Justin hands me three darts. "The board is numbered one to twenty, but the numbers don't go in order."

After explaining the points for landing in a red or green space or the bullseye, he demonstrates where to stand and how to hold the dart. "Let's play until one of us gets a hundred points or more."

After my third win, Justin fists his hands on his hips. "Have I just been hustled?"

"I swear I've never played darts before." I don't mention being on a junior archery team for several years. I'm not athletic, but I have good eye-hand coordination.

When we leave Packy's, he slings an arm around my waist and pulls me close. "Annie Warden, despite being beautiful and elegant, you're not a bad pub date."

"Wow, what a ringing endorsement."

At his car, a soft smile creases his mouth. It seems he wants to say something but is reluctant. Justin's body looms toward me, close but not touching. His body heats the surface of my skin, and then he reaches out a hand. Dozens of tiny wings beat in my chest. His mouth draws closer. I close my eyes partway when he grabs the car door handle, pulls it, and steps back to widen the opening.

Lust, disappointment, and embarrassment swamp me. God only knows what shows on my face from that emotional stewpot. I duck and fold my long body into the front passenger seat, not daring to look at him.

CHAPTER 9

THE DRIVE BACK to my house is quiet. Justin doesn't offer to play music, and I don't ask. We pass shuttered businesses and stores with dark plate glass windows. Streetlights illuminate the odd person here and there, walking briskly along the sidewalk or hurrying through a crosswalk at a red-lighted intersection. For the most part, few other vehicles are on the road, neighborhoods are silent, and most people are asleep preparing for their Monday workday.

In my driveway, I turn to face Justin when he parks. "I had a good time tonight."

The motion detector light above the garage door snaps on and highlights the planes of his face. "I did, too."

Is asking him if he'd take me back to Packy's to hear live music on Friday or Saturday too presumptuous? He said I was *not a bad* pub date, but maybe he was just being polite. Out of the blue, I imagine getting naked with him as slow, soft music plays. Where the hell did that come from? I enjoyed the past several hours, but he still isn't my type. I like men taller than me, lanky like me, and with thick heads of hair. I like smooth-talking, cock-swinging bad boys who, in the end, don't treat me well, even though I hope for more but never demand it. I like guys who other women look at and wonder what they see in the gawky woman at their side.

Justin shuts off the engine and exits. I track his movement around the hood of the car. When I swing my jean-clad legs out and stand, he is inches away from me with the metal and glass door between us. Without thinking, I lean forward and kiss him. He puts his hand on my neck and kisses me hard as if we're not expecting to see each other for a long time. His mouth opens over mine, and his tongue sweeps inside. He tastes of beer and something I have not discerned in a while. A man hot with intoxicating desire for me. I revel in the sense of him in my mouth.

When the kiss ends, we both smile. Justin pulls me to his side and shuts the door. At the front entrance, he wraps an arm around my waist, and his mouth again seeks mine. His warm, sexy scent fills my nose. I breathe the maleness of him deep into my lungs. Everything else around me recedes as he makes love to my mouth. My palms slide to his bulky shoulders as his slick tongue teases and coaxes. We return each other's passion and possession in equal measure. My toes curl as I run my fingertips over the smooth scalp at the back of his head. I am needy and greedy for more.

He groans into my mouth, a sound of lust and yearning that flames a feminine fire deep inside. I step back into the shadows, and he follows. The coolness of the concrete on my back does little to diminish my body heat. He grinds his erection against me. I wrap one long leg around his waist as he presses me tight against the wall. I raise my other leg and link my ankles behind him. His mouth moves to the side of my throat, sending shivers up and down my spine.

"You're killing me, Annie." His words warm places inside me that have been cool for a long time. He thrusts against me, and his voice drops into a deeper, hotter place. "You're so beautiful. I want to eat you up. One juicy bite at a time."

His words create warm flutters in the pit of my stomach where liquid heat pools. My nipples pucker painfully tight. I squeeze my legs around him, wanting him so much that my inhibitions and reasoning burn away.

"Inside." I'm unsure if I mean we should go inside the house or if he should be inside me right where we are.

He walks backward to the front door as if I weigh nothing. "Key?"

I uncouple my ankles, and my legs slide down the backs of his thighs. I release one hand from his neck, dig into my wristlet, and hand him the key. The only light inside is from the galley kitchen. He closes the door behind us, and our mouths fuse. Within seconds, his hands are everywhere.

His mouth is on my neck when he mutters, "We need to stop."

"No, we don't."

I unbutton the top two buttons on his shirt, and he pulls it over his head. At the same time, I tug mine off. He unfastens my bra and covers my small breasts with his palms. I push my jeans down my legs.

"Dammit!" My skinny-legged pants won't come off without removing my sandals.

"What's wrong?"

"My shoes."

He kisses the space between my breasts, drops to one knee, and licks a slalom path down my inner thigh. He unties the leather strap bows at the front of my ankles and slips the sandals off. He grasps the bottom hems of my jeans and holds them down as I free my feet.

All thoughts of not going through with this evaporate when Justin tilts his face up. My body tightens under the scalding heat of his gaze. It is as seductive as a physical caress. He rises, and my gaze dips from the hollow of his throat to his defined chest muscles. I follow a trail down his tight abs under golden brown skin, past his navel, to the waistband of his jeans.

Justin removes his boots and socks and pushes his pants and underwear down his powerful thighs. There isn't an ounce of fat or an inch of loose skin anywhere on his body. More intense heat pools between my thighs when I see his impressive erection. His muscles bunch when I touch his flat belly and then brush the hard length of him. My thumb slides up and down the thick pulsing cord beneath the skin. He groans.

I take his hand and lead him to the living room sofa. "Sit."

I strip off my thong and straddle his lap. A shiver works through my body and pulses in my abdomen when the thick head of his erection brushes me. Hot and ready for him, I direct his mouth to my breast.

"Wait!" He pushes against my thighs. "In my pocket. Condom."

At first, I think there's no need for that, but then it hits me. There's another good reason for using protection. "I'll get it."

I climb off and pad over to his jeans. When I bend and rifle through the pockets, he groans. Packet in hand, I rip open the plastic pouch and remove the latex ring. Dropping to my knees, I position the lubed condom over the head of his penis and roll it down the shaft.

Once again, I kneel astride him and lower myself, inch by solid inch, until fully seated. I'm so ready my body quivers with intense pleasure. For a few moments, I'm satisfied with him buried deep within me and unmoving.

He draws my face forward. With a consenting moan, I kiss him, surrender to his desire, and then ride him slow and steady. His palms skim my ribcage with every arch of my back. As I move faster and harder, my rising and falling hips bring us closer to ecstasy. In tandem, Justin drives himself into me, matching his upward thrust with my downward one.

Caressing and stroking.

In and out.

I never want this whirling vortex of hot pleasure to end.

"Come on, Annie. I've got you."

After a few more deep thrusts, I tumble into a fierce, torrid climax, long and hard. The world falls away until all that remains is the pounding in my chest and head. My inner muscles clench in out-of-control spasms, holding him tight. An explosion of curses collides with his primal and possessive pleasure. Lightheaded, I slump forward, my arms boneless at my sides, palms face up on the cushions. Justin wraps me in a tight embrace. Our heaving chests coordinate with each other's breaths. Inhale. Exhale. Inhale. Exhale.

Time stands still and rushes by at the same time. Like a swimmer rising to the surface after an arduous dive, I reorient myself, lift my head, and open my eyes. Justin stares at me with the same starry-eyed enthusiasm I'm sure reflects on my face.

He murmurs, "Okay?"

"I'm great. You're good at that."

"You're the one full of surprises." Justin traces the line of my eyebrow with his fingertip. "I never expected you to be that passionate."

"What do you mean? Why wouldn't I be?"

"Because you're so beautiful and elegant." I shake my head, but Justin stills the movement with his hands on my ears. "I'll keep saying it until you believe me."

"It'll take a while."

"I don't have a problem with that."

A soft yip sounds from the other side of the house.

"Uh-oh, someone needs out of their crate." I crawl off him.

"I forgot about your dogs." He stands, removes the condom, and looks around. "Is there a bathroom I can use?"

I point to a doorway next to the living room. "Through there. But before you go, do you want to spend the rest of the night here?"

"Can't. I need to get home."

My self-assurance evaporates. His kids are at his sister's house until morning. "Sure. Okay."

"Hey." His arm whips around my waist. "What's wrong?"

"Nothing."

He checks his watch. "I need to leave for work in five hours. Soon, I'll want to spend the whole night, but that will take some planning."

Another louder and more forceful yip comes from the back of the house. Justin walks to the guest bathroom. The ambient kitchen light highlights the muscle movements in his broad back and tight butt until he disappears into the dark hallway.

In my bedroom, four large dog crates line the wall. I open the French doors to the patio and then unlatch the wire gates. One by one, each dog streaks outside in a fast-moving line. I stand in the shadows of the covered lanai and watch them as they do their business, sniff the ground, and engage in short sprints with each other, flashing in and out of the motion detector's light beams.

A lock clicks, and Justin steps out of the door to the kitchen. He's dressed. To my surprise, I place an arm across my breasts. I've been naked or nearly naked in so many backstage dressing areas or designer workrooms that I am usually not self-conscious about my nudity.

He kisses my shoulder and girdles my waist with his hands. "My God, you're tiny. My fingertips almost touch front and back."

Tiny? Another word no one's ever used to describe me.

"You look like a goddess standing here in the moonlight."

In my early twenties, I did a photoshoot where several of us had been painted white and dressed to resemble marble statues. In a sense, I was a Greek goddess—but it was only a photographic illusion.

Justin's warm breath coasts over my shoulder. "Leaving you is the hardest thing I've had to do in a long time. Stay just as you are. I want that picture in my brain until I see you again. Good night, Annie."

I remain silent and still until the front door closes, and all the dogs gather around me in the darkness.

CHAPTER 10

JUSTIN AND I text over the next two days, but it's mostly about my foster greyhound, Fancy, and his adoption application. He doesn't ask me out again, nor do we talk about our last date. I hope it's because every interaction occurs when his daughters are nearby. I get questions like Eden wanting to know what Fancy's favorite toy is or Savanna worrying that Lady will feel bad if they don't adopt her.

Then my phone rings. I stare at the screen with a resigned sense of dread. I had hoped I wouldn't receive this call but knew I would.

"Hi, Annie, it's Debbie Hale-Brown. I'm letting you know I've contacted the references on Justin's adoption application. Everything appears to be in order. Since they're first-time owners of any breed, they'll need some extra support when they get their dog. I'll contact him to schedule a home check, and if everything looks good, I'll stop by your place to pick up Fancy."

I inhale a deep breath. "That's not how it's going to work, Debbie."

"What do you mean?"

"The Stablers contacted me first. I conducted the initial interview. They came to *my* house to see *my* foster dogs. I urged them to attend the Meet and Greet. I should have been the one to take their application and confirm the information."

Besides, I'm the one who Justin asked out. I'm the one who had sex with him. And I'm the one who plans to do it again.

"Oh, Annie, it doesn't matter who does what. I don't have any foster dogs with me right now, and you still have another one to be adopted. I can take over."

"I appreciate you contacting the references, but as far as conducting the home check and settling the dog, I've had Fancy living with me, and I know her best." I struggle to keep irritation and anger out of my voice.

"You can tell me whatever they need to know. I'll be the point of contact with them from now on."

I hesitate. I can use this as a test to determine if Justin truly wants me to be the adoption liaison and whether he wants to continue a romantic relationship with me. "You know what? Call him. If he agrees to have you take over, I'll understand. But if he says he wants to work with me, you'll need to step aside."

"I can assure you that won't happen."

"Why not?"

"When I met him, there was an instant bond between us. Justin said he'd be thrilled to hear from me as soon as I confirmed his references. I have no doubt that this adoption will lead to a closer relationship between me and his family."

"You're telling me this *attraction* happened while you talked to him for less than an hour in the park?"

"Romeo and Juliet fell in love at a party."

I can't believe she's comparing her and Justin to a three-day teenage relationship that caused six deaths. "Just call him, Debbie, and tell me what he says."

"Fine. I will." The words sound like they are uttered through clenched teeth. "But you'll see. He'll want me to handle everything."

That evening, my phone rings, and Debbie's name appears on the screen. "Annie, it's me again. I spoke with Justin, and we agreed you should handle the home check."

I resist the urge to say I told you so, but in my head the childish taunt of nah-nah-nah-nah-nah resounds.

Debbie sounds flippant, but her voice is a bit shrill. "It seems the girls are set on having you help them with Fancy since you live close to their house. I'll scan the application and email it to you tomorrow. Don't forget to mail me back all the signed paperwork and his payment once he takes possession. And, Annie, there's one more thing."

"Yes."

"This isn't over yet."

Fifteen minutes pass before my phone rings again. This time, it's Justin. "Did you get a call from Debbie this evening?"

The low rumble of his voice causes an anticipatory thrum to settle low in my body. "I just got off the phone with her a little while ago."

"Talk about a woman who won't take no for an answer. She's worse than two-year-old twins."

I laugh. "I tried my best to convince her I should remain in charge of the adoption, but she just wouldn't have it."

"I believe you. When I insisted that we wanted to continue the process with you, she acted as if I was jilting her at the altar and running off with the maid of honor."

I pause as a thought occurs to me. "Did you tell her about us going out Sunday night?"

"No. Did you?"

"I'm not crazy enough to throw gasoline onto that fire."

He chuckles. "Instead, you left me to deal with the she-wolf."

"Sorry about that, but she said there was an *instant bond* between you at the Meet and Greet."

"Yeah, if you mean she attached herself to me like Velcro."

"Well, don't worry. I'll handle everything from now on. The next thing we need to do is schedule a home check."

"Will this weekend work? The girls are anxious to get Fancy here."

"What about you? Are you excited to add a new member to your family?"

"If it means Eden and Savanna will stop bugging me, then I'm more than ready."

We confirm the home check for Saturday morning, followed by me bringing Fancy in the afternoon if everything and everyone is ready for her. I ask about the preparations they've made for the adoption.

Justin lists the purchases of a large crate, a dog bed for the family room and another for the kids' bedroom, toys, food, and water bowls. "The girls demanded I buy Fancy a new pink collar and leash. We found the Martingale one you recommended online, but they were disappointed it doesn't come with rhinestones."

"I can bring a glue gun, and the girls and I can bedazzle the one you bought. After all, Fancy should live up to her name."

His laugh is a deep, rich sound that tickles my spine. "No. Don't encourage them. I'm already surrounded by so much girly stuff, it's a wonder I don't sprout tits."

"Maybe if I spend time at your place, I can get some too."

His voice lowers into a husky, rough-and-tumble octave. "Yours are more than fine just the way they are. They fit you and me perfectly, and I can't wait to try them on for size again." My heart flips around my chest when he murmurs, "Annie?"

"Yeah?"

"I'm hard just thinking about it."

A child's voice in the background says, "What are you thinking hard about, Daddy?"

The squeak of a swivel chair sounds. "Eden! What are you doing out of bed?"

"I got thirsty. Are you talking to Annie?"

"Yes, I—"

The little girl shouts, "Hi, Annie. When are you bringing Fancy to us?"

Justin speaks into the phone again. "I've got to go. We'll see you on Saturday."

Before the call disconnects, Eden squeals, "She's coming on Saturday?"

Yes, I'm coming on Saturday and maybe more than once.

CHAPTER 11

I ARRIVE AT Justin's house at ten on Saturday morning. The drive takes less than fifteen minutes. His neighborhood comprises three and four-bedroom brick-faced or stucco-walled houses on one-quarter to one-third acre lots. Unlike my semi-rural, anything-goes neighborhood, this suburban development is the kind of place where lawns are neatly mowed and edged, as well as given regular treatments of weed and feed. The main road is lined with sidewalks, so the girls can exercise a dog without walking in the street. At the main entrance to the neighborhood is a small park with playground equipment and a walking path. The Stabler house is tucked into one of the smaller cul-de-sacs.

The blue-painted front door is flung open before I reach it. "You're here!"

Eden and Savanna barrel out and wrap their arms around my hips. I stagger slightly under the twin onslaught.

"Girls!" Justin scolds. "Remember what we talked about."

Eden releases me and faces her father. "But we don't have Fancy yet."

He meets my gaze. "We've been practicing leashing an imaginary dog and not opening the door until it's secured."

"Look what Daddy made." Savanna pulls me inside. "See."

A large eyebolt is anchored into the wall with an attached carabiner. From the metal clip, a dog leash is attached.

Justin shrugs. "I was afraid the dog might pull loose from a kid's grasp, so I fastened the bolt to a stud."

I nod in approval. "This is an excellent idea."

"We've been pretending to put the leash on first, then answering the door." He frowns at his daughters. "Until today."

"We forgot," the girls say in unison.

"All you have to do is forget one time, and Fancy's gone."

Their father's warning sobers them, and they cast fearful glances at each other. Eden turns a pleading gaze at me. "We won't forget when she's here. We promise."

Savanna's eyes glisten with tears. "We would *die* if anything bad happened to her."

"Don't worry. That's one of the things we'll work on together." I point to the floor. "If you put a throw rug here, it'll help her know where to wait until the signal is given to come forward."

"I'm sure we have one around here," Justin says.

"No, Daddy," Eden whines. "We need to get Fancy a rug just for her."

"A pink one," Savanna chimes in.

Justin examines his defined chest muscles under the snug, gray T-shirt, checking for sprouting tits.

I laugh. "I don't think you have anything to worry about yet."

Eden grabs my hand. "Come see the toys that we bought for Fancy."

The living room on my right seems to double as a playroom. Games, dolls, and small plastic characters litter the beige carpet, furniture cushions, and the tops of wood end tables. An eight-by-ten photograph in an ornate gold frame holds my attention for several seconds. It shows a young woman in a typically unnatural senior photo pose. She has long red hair that streams down her shoulders and back. A sprinkle of freckles across her nose is a reminder that, although she is on the brink of adulthood, her childhood is not that distant. Bright blue eyes complement her oval face.

"Annie?" says one of the girls. "See Fancy's new toys."

"Hold on a minute." I sweep my hand toward the scattering of playthings around the room. "Are these *your* toys?"

The twins nod with puzzled expressions.

"Would you be upset if they get ruined?" Eden and Savanna frown at each other with a silent twin communication of *why-is-she-asking-us-this*. "If you leave your toys lying around, Fancy might chew on them."

Eden picks up a stuffed green frog from a nearby basket. "But we bought some just for her. Like this one."

"That's nice, but remember, she was a racer who never had anything to play with. I don't have kid toys at my house, so how is she supposed to know the difference? She sees you playing with something and will think she can, too. And she plays by chewing and ripping things apart. Also, she could swallow some of the smaller pieces, making her very sick."

In a tentative voice, Savanna asks, "Sick enough to die?"

"Yes. It happens all the time."

Both girls look stricken and suck in their rosy, freckled cheeks. They gather the toys in their arms and head toward the back of the house.

I raise my hand in a stop gesture, but Justin lowers my arm. "Let them finish. If this is all it takes to get them to pick up their crap, I can't wait until Fancy is here." The two little girls reappear and scoop up more. Justin calls after them, "I hope you're putting those away and not dumping them in your room where Fancy can still get them."

Eden and Savanna flash wary glances over their shoulders before disappearing from our view.

He moves us out of their sightline and draws me against him. "That'll keep them occupied for a few minutes. I missed you."

The tip of his tongue touches the corner of my mouth. I slide my hand up his muscled, bare arm. Parting my lips, I invite him inside. His tongue completes a light sweep. It's a new sensation kissing a man who is my height. No backward head tipping. No gaps between our bodies. We touch from chest to knee, every inch close and tight.

He slides one hand under the edge of my striped Saint James top. The small of my back tingles when his thumb brushes under the waistband of my short denim skirt. My hands skim over his shoulders. The kiss becomes hot and greedy. Our bodies rub against each other as his hand skates up my back and under my bra. My tongue tangles with his, drawing him deeper.

Without warning, his mouth breaks away. "Annie. Annie. You drive me crazy."

His words warm me. He traces the curve of my ear with his lips and kisses my jaw. I can't get enough of his mouth. From every angle, I silently beg for every kiss in his arsenal. The open-mouthed, small pecks that are like tiny raindrops. The demanding ones that fill my mouth. I lose myself in the moment and forget where I am when two things happen simultaneously.

From the back of the house, high-pitched voices blend into one. "We're done!"

In the foyer, a single doorbell chimes, followed by the snick of a key in the lock.

Justin and I spring apart. He falls onto a nearby armchair, his bottom teetering on the edge of the cushion. I spin around and come face-to-face with Lucy's photograph. Her eyes no longer appear guileless. She seems to stare at me—the woman who moments ago kissed her husband as if he came with reward points. I shift my eyes away and study the ceiling, checking for cracks.

"Hello. Anybody home?"

"Grandma!"

Justin's mother-in-law, Cecilia, steps inside and shuts the front door. She bends forward with open arms. Eden and Savanna rush toward her but veer away at the last moment.

"Look who's here." Eden rushes to me.

Savanna stands in the middle, looking between me and her grandmother. "Annie says we can't leave our toys out because Fancy will chew on them."

"It might make her sick and she could die," Eden adds. "Is the room safe now, Annie?"

Justin stands up with a flicker of aggravation on his face. "Cecilia, you didn't call to say you were going over."

Instead of looking apologetic, the older woman lifts her chin. "The girls told me the *greyhound lady* would be here this morning, so I stopped by to learn about caring for the dog. After all, you asked me to tend to it when you're not home during the day."

"*I said*, if we passed the inspection and Fancy was here, I would call. Annie hasn't been able to get any farther than where she stands now. The home check has barely begun."

"Are you asking me to leave?"

The atmosphere between Justin and Cecilia is a sparking wall of tension. An awkward silence stretches for several seconds before he clears his throat. "Well, you're here now."

In a bright, rushed voice, I tell the children, "The room looks much better, but have you checked under and behind the furniture for any little thing left behind? You may not see it, but a dog will find it. Since Fancy isn't a puppy, she won't chew things like electrical cords, shoes, or books, but it's still a good idea to keep small things put away until she gets used to living here. She's been trained to know what's off limits at my house, but you'll have to teach her not to touch things that don't belong to her in your house. Let's make sure all the rooms are dog-safe."

The twins and I do a cursory search of the living room and then proceed into the dining room, kitchen, and family room. We put remote controls in drawers, books on shelves, toys in their bedroom, clothes in laundry baskets, and shoes in closets. In each room, my eyes are drawn to photographs on walls, tables, and shelves. Most are of the twins at various stages from infancy to the present day.

One enlarged print in a silver frame engraved with Mr. and Mrs. lettering hangs on the dining room wall. It shows Justin and Lucy with broad smiles at a wedding chapel in Las Vegas. Justin has light brown hair, and, to my surprise, it's curly, although the bare expanse of his forehead shows he is well on his way to early male pattern baldness. He wears a suit and tie while Lucy, who is a younger version of her mother, has on a lacy, white shift. I wonder how Cecilia felt about her only child being married in a place where laundered money outweighs clean hotel sheets.

Justin and Cecilia move into the living room as the children and I work. Despite whispering, their strained voices seep out of the room, if not the actual hissed words.

In the girls' bedroom, they put away a variety of items while I sit on one of the twin beds. Lucy has a presence here also. On a nightstand is a photo of teenage Lucy cross-legged in the grass, her hands on her knees like a kid in a school photo. Above each single bed is a collage of the twins with their mother.

I point to the one hanging over the white headboard with Eden's name painted in fancy pink script. "Is that you and your mom in all those pictures?"

She looks up from inserting crayons in a flip-top box that I remember from my childhood. "Yeah. That's me and mommy."

"Who made the collage for you?" I ask even though I know the answer.

"Grandma. Every year, she changes them so we don't forget."

I imagine Justin cannot forget Lucy every night when he tucks his daughters into bed either.

Savanna asks, "Do all dogs chew up things?"

"Sometimes they don't chew them. They only steal them. I have a friend who has a greyhound named Klepto. Do you know what a kleptomaniac is?"

Her nose scrunches. "No."

"It's someone who knows stealing is wrong but can't stop doing it. Her dog, Klepto, always steals flip-flops and hides them in the dog bed. She doesn't take sneakers, sandals, or any other type of shoe. Only flip-flops.

That's how she got her name. My friend knows where to look every time her shoes go missing."

Eden giggles. "Don't tell Daddy, but he puts things in his closet when he wants to hide things from us."

"How's it going in here?"

Our three heads turn in guilty *we-weren't-talking-about-you* swivels. Justin stands in the doorway, more relaxed than when I shepherded the girls out of the living room and left him alone with his mother-in-law.

Savanna cranes her neck to peer behind her father. "Where's Grandma?"

"She went home. I'll call her if we pass inspection and Annie brings Fancy back here."

Eden crawls across the carpet toward me with her child-sized hands pressed together like a penitent. "Are we passing?"

"So far, so good. The last thing I need to see is the backyard. You finish up in here while I go outside with your dad. Okay?"

Justin and I move to the covered patio and walk to the far side of the house, where a chain link fence separates his property from the neighbor.

We stand in the shade of a tall Ficus hedge, and he takes my hand in his. "Annie, I'm falling in love with you."

CHAPTER 12

SWARMS OF BUTTERFLIES take flight in my stomach. Oh, my God! He's falling in love with me already? What do I say to him? My feelings aren't there yet, although I'm very attracted to Justin.

I keep silent, and he tugs me against him. "I can't believe the world's most perfect woman can get my twin terrors to clean up their mess without complaint."

I release my breath, grateful that I waited to respond. "Justin, I'm not perfect. Far from it."

"Damn close. After you told me you were...I mean, you *are* a model; I Googled you. You've had quite a career."

I lift one shoulder in a tiny, self-deprecating shrug. "I started when I was seventeen, so I've been doing it for a while."

"Don't most models stop in their twenties? Your online page says you're thirty and still working. I can understand why." He runs his hand up my arm. "Your skin is tight, and I already know your tits are amazing. You have the waistline of a teenager and a thigh gap I could watch TV through. Kids and dogs love you. How could you be any more perfect?"

"No one is perfect." I wiggle free of his embrace. "Let's walk the rest of the fence line. The girls should be finished soon."

"Did I say something wrong?"

"No, it's just that first impressions can be wrong or not show the whole person."

He tilts his head to one side. "You're right, of course. We have a lot to learn about each other. I want you to know that from what I've seen and found out so far, I think you're perfect." I open my mouth, and Justin raises his hand. "I know, I know. You don't like the word. I promise I won't use it again, but I'm attracted to you. Not just how beautiful you look on the outside, but how beautiful you are on the inside."

I force myself to smile at him. "I'm very attracted to you too."

He rubs a hand over his bare scalp. "I figured I had a shot since you like short hair, or in my case, no hair."

"You're lucky you have such a beautiful head."

And he did. Some bald men have bullet-shaped skulls like Uncle Fester. Frankie's father-in-law, Roger, has a bowling ball attached to his neck. As Justin Googled me, I clicked on bald and beautiful men online. I was surprised by how many good-looking and sexy bald men there are: Dwayne "The Rock" Johnson, LL Cool J, Vin Diesel, Taye Diggs, Bruce Willis, Pitbull, and Jason Stratham. I laughed when a picture of Stratham and his girlfriend, Rosie Huntington-Whiteley, appeared on the screen. Justin Stabler looks similar to the English actor, and I did a Victoria's Secret runway show with Rosie years ago. Even though she stands a few inches taller than her boyfriend, this power couple looks great together. Maybe Justin and I are not so mismatched after all.

"You know," he says, "they've done studies and found bald men are perceived as more dominant, masculine, and confident than men with hair. The only negative is we're thought to be four years older than we are."

"I agree with the study. I mean, not about age, although I don't know how old you are."

"I'm thirty-three."

"I guessed right." In truth, I estimated he was seven or eight years older than me. Maybe the study was on point about baldness and age perception.

We stroll along the fence line and reach the gate next to the side wall of the two-car garage. Justin faces me with a snarky grin. "Do you know why dating a bald man is a good idea?"

"Please enlighten me."

"We're super sexy."

I place my hands on his shoulders. "I agree."

"Baldness is a classy look that goes well with jeans or tuxedos." He pulls me against him.

"I can see that."

"But the most important reason is how we became bald."

I frown. "How is genetics a reason for dating?"

Justin cups my breast. "DNA triggers the hair loss, but U-turns under the sheets complete it."

My palm caresses the back of his head, and hot dampness moistens my panties.

"Why are you rubbing Daddy's head?"

Our arms drop, and Justin looks over my shoulder at the girls behind me. He says with no hint of being caught unawares, "I bumped my head, and Annie checked that it wasn't bleeding."

I turn to face our interrupters. "Don't worry. He's okay."

Eden shakes her head. "That happens a lot when he's shaving."

"Hey, you try cutting the hair on the back of your head," Justin growls.

"We do want to cut our hair!"

"Like Annie's," Savanna adds.

"But you won't let us."

Justin doesn't look at me. "You know why you can't."

The girls sigh in unison. "You. Promised. Mommy."

Does he prefer long hair on a woman? Many men do.

At last, he gives me, or maybe my hair, a quick sidelong glance. "Does the fence and gate meet with your approval?"

My eyes dart to the lift latch. "It's a good idea to put a simple padlock on here so no one will inadvertently leave it open. It happens, especially if you have a lawn or pool service. I use one set with my house number to help workers remember the combination. Since it's outside, be sure and get one that's waterproof."

"Daddy, can we get a pink lock?"

"No." He squints at the sky. "Let's go inside. It's time for lunch."

We troop into the house. Justin enters the kitchen and asks, "Grilled cheese sandwiches, okay?"

"With potato chips?" Eden bounces up and down.

He opens the refrigerator door. "With carrot sticks."

"No, Daddy. We're still hungry after we eat carrots."

"Can we have Oreos?" asks Savanna in a soft and uncertain voice.

In his hands are cheese, butter, and baby carrots. He bumps the door closed with his hip. "Plates have to be cleaned before cookies."

I tuck my purse under my arm. "What time do you want me to return with Fancy?"

All three Stablers gape at me, and then Justin puts the items he holds on the counter. "Aren't you having lunch with us?"

The girls attach themselves to me like suckerfish. "Please stay."

"But there are things for me to do at home before I can bring Fancy here." The girls' arms drop away from my waist. "Anyway, what time is good for you this afternoon?"

"We've got nothing else planned."

"How about two o'clock then? I'll let myself out and see you in a little while." I cross the beige tile floor to the front door and pull it open.

Debbie Hale-Brown faces me with her fist raised. I stumble backward, catching myself with a death grip on the doorknob.

CHAPTER 13

"**ANNIE!**" **DEBBIE LOWERS** her arm. "I was just about to knock. How did the home check go? Did the Stablers pass with flying colors?"

"Why are you here?"

"Who is it?" Justin emerges from the kitchen, wiping his hands on a dishtowel.

I turn around at the sound of his voice.

Eden leans one shoulder against the kitchen wall. "It's that other dog lady. The one who won't stop talking."

Debbie breezes past me. "Hi, Justin, you're such a wonderful father that I felt confident you'd have everything prepared to bring one of our rescues into your beautiful home. I thought I'd save Annie the trouble, so I brought the adoption paperwork for you to sign and to get your check." She smiles into Eden's frowny face like she's forced to admire someone's ugly baby.

I close the front door. I guess I'm staying after all.

Debbie is dressed again in pink and white. This time, her short, chunky legs are encased in white skinny jeans, and she is wearing a silky, rose-colored tank top. She positions herself to present a view of her freckled cleavage for Justin when she bends forward to address his daughter. Widening her heavily lined blue eyes like an overeager children's entertainer, Debbie asks, "Do you remember me from the Meet and Greet? Are you Eden or Savanna?"

"I'm Eden. Annie knows who we are."

Debbie straightens with her disingenuous little smile, still firmly in place. "Well, she's had more opportunities to get to know you. I hope I will, too."

While she speaks to Eden, Justin catches my attention with panic in his eyes. He mouths, *Help.* I place my purse on a chair and extract a pen.

"Debbie, I was headed to my car to get the paperwork. Is yours in here?" I pluck a manila folder from under her arm, open it on the kitchen counter, and flip through a couple of pages. "Okay, Justin, here's the adoption contract. This states that Fancy is current on all her vaccines, has been spayed, and is free of intestinal parasites and heartworms. As the adopter, you promise to take care of her with food, water, and indoor shelter. You will keep her healthy and provide a safe collar with rabies and I.D. tags. If the adoption doesn't work out, you can return the dog to the rescue organization within seven days and receive a full refund. After that, you forfeit the adoption fee. You can't give or sell her to someone else. If you do, it's a breach of contract, and the group can take legal action in which you'll have to bear all costs and attorney's fees."

My skin prickles with the eyeball daggers Debbie is likely throwing my way. She probably has a wax doll that looks like me, ready to be impaled with straight pins. "Number fourteen addresses liability and damages from dog behavior. On my copy, I listed that Fancy has not displayed aggression toward smaller dogs or cats, but you need to take care if she spots a rabbit or squirrel outside. I wouldn't recommend having pets like hamsters or guinea pigs." I talk and write these items on this copy of the contract. "Of course, we discussed the possibility of her chewing things in the house until she is trained to leave them alone. This may or may not occur, and she might develop other behaviors later."

"Annie, you didn't tell him about number eight." Debbie's long, pink fingernail taps like a tiny woodpecker on the paper. "It says you must allow a representative from our rescue group to visit the premises and make sure the terms of the agreement are being kept."

Justin's forehead furrows. "For how long?"

"As long as the dog is alive or in your possession."

"Come on, Debbie," I drawl. "When have we ever done that?"

"I don't recall, but he has to be made aware of the provision before he signs."

Justin swipes a hand over his stubbly jaw. "Can I designate the representative?"

"We want Annie!" Eden adds.

Debbie looks at me with an unblinking stare. "There's no guarantee she'll be associated with our group for that long."

Her chilling words cause me to freeze, but Justin pulls the pen from my stiff fingers. "I'll put her name down as my preference, and if she's unavailable, the group can assign a replacement of my choice."

Debbie instructs Justin to initial each page, sign, and date the last one, with me witnessing his signature. While we wait for him to locate his checkbook in his office, Debbie taps the toe of her kitten-heeled shoe on the tile.

Eden opens a deep drawer and pulls out a loaf of bread. She motions to me and Savanna. "Let's help Daddy get lunch ready."

The three of us butter one side of eight slices for cheese sandwiches and work to convince Debbie I'm as comfortable in their kitchen as they are.

Savanna says, "Don't forget we like our sandwiches cut down the middle and not in triangles."

"Can I get out the potato chips?" Eden licks her lips.

"Nice try," I laugh. "Remember, it's carrot sticks for you."

Justin returns with a completed check, hands it to Debbie, and escorts her to the door. There's some low conversation between them before he returns to the kitchen.

After the sound of her car engine fades away, Justin says, "I'm happy to see you're staying for our adoption party lunch. After all, it wouldn't be the same without you."

CHAPTER 14

AFTER LUNCH, I return home to prepare my usual gift basket for new adopters, containing dog shampoo, training treats, a gift certificate to Chewy.com, a collapsible water bowl, waste bags, a leash dispenser, a bone-shaped cookie cutter, and an environmentally friendly mishap spray. When Fancy and I return to Justin's neighborhood, Cecilia is watering hanging baskets of leggy pink begonias at a house two doors from his. I open the hatchback and get Fancy from the crate in my SUV.

"Can I help?" Justin's mother-in-law is at the end of the driveway. She comes forward and pats the dog's head. "I take it this is Fancy. The girls haven't stopped talking about her."

"Yes. They chose this greyhound, and she seems to have chosen them."

"How old is she?"

"Her birthday is in November, and she'll be two."

Cecilia runs her hand down Fancy's back. "She's younger than most former racers, isn't she?"

"Yes. The girls will have her as a pet for a long time."

"Justin has never picked out a dog before, and I know you're anxious to place this one into a home. You can tell me if there's something wrong with her. I won't say anything. It's just that the girls would be heartbroken to lose their pet to a health or behavioral issue soon after getting her. I can prepare them for that if I know ahead of time."

I tighten my lips. What type of person is critical and considerate at the same time?

"Well?" Cecilia arches one pale, almost nonexistent eyebrow in reproof. "Is she defective?"

"No. She's perfect. Fancy doesn't like to race, which makes her a wonderful pet, especially for a family of first-time dog owners. She's less likely to run competitively or chase small animals."

"I thought greyhounds are bred to run."

"They are, but racing isn't a genetic given. Not all hounds like to hunt, and not all water dogs like to swim." And not all grandmothers are sweet, lovable women.

The twins spill out of the house. They slow down and become quiet, heeding my earlier instructions not to excite or spook the dog. Eden ignores her grandmother and approaches Fancy with her hand outstretched. The greyhound cranes her head forward for a sniff, and then her whipcord tail wags, slapping my thigh. Savanna quickly hugs her grandmother around the waist before extending her hand to the dog.

Justin's gaze focuses on Cecilia, and his face goes blank. "What are you doing here?"

"I was out front watering plants when Annie arrived. I thought she might need some help."

"Does she?"

"She hasn't said so yet."

"Maybe you haven't given her the chance to ask."

"Why don't we do it now?"

"Why bother?" There is a honed edge to his voice. "The kids and I are here. We can help her if she needs it."

This conversational exchange contains the same overt hostility as the one earlier. Dread sinks like a weight in my stomach. I can't leave Fancy in a house ripe with conflict. Dogs are sensitive to human emotions, and a new home is already stressful without the added burden of tension from the humans.

"I can help too," Cecilia snaps.

"Just this morning, you agreed to wait until I called you, yet here we are." He flings his arms wide. "Like always, you just go and do whatever you want."

Cecilia's face tightens. "What is wrong with you? I'm just here to be of assistance with this dog you're getting for my granddaughters."

"That's the problem. You act like the doting grandmother, but you really want to be in charge of everything. It was the same with Lucy. You handpicked her clothes and college major, but your biggest failure was not stopping her from marrying me. I refuse to let you do the same thing with my daughters."

I glance down at the children. They are a study of discomfort. Savanna sniffs back tears and frowns like a sad little clown. Eden stares at her hand stroking Fancy's back, ignoring everyone else.

"Stop this." I don't shout but inject firmness in my voice. "I'm sorry, but I don't think this adoption will work out. I'm canceling it right now."

The twins gasp. Tears fill their eyes and trickle down their freckled cheeks. "No. No."

Justin's head jerks my way. "What's wrong?"

My chest explodes. I'm about to break the twins' hearts and ruin a budding relationship with the first man who has attracted me in years. Still, Fancy's well-being is my top priority. "Girls, why don't you go in the house? I need to speak to your father and grandmother."

"But—"

"Go inside," Justin commands in a gentle voice.

"But—"

"Now."

The children run up the driveway, sobbing. Fancy strains against the leash to follow them, but I gesture for her to sit and wait.

After the front door slams shut, I face the so-called adults. "I can't put Fancy in a home filled with conflict. I don't know what is going on between you two, but dogs are susceptible to stress. Being placed in a new environment with new owners is hard on them, let alone one where people are fighting. In good conscience, I can't leave her here. She might act out, and I wouldn't blame her if she did. The best thing I can do for Fancy is to cancel the adoption."

Cecelia levels a glare one might see on the mug shot of a serial killer. "You can't do this to Eden and Savanna."

"Up." Following my command, the greyhound jumps into the car with a confused expression. Hopefully, my apologetic face and kissing her nose let this sweet girl know she did nothing wrong. "Yes, I can. I will do whatever is in the dog's best interest. Unfortunately, I can't do anything for the girls who have to live with your bickering. Maybe they're used to it or just as stressed as Fancy would be if she lived in this house. Either way, I won't put this dog in a home that isn't ideal for her."

Cecilia thrusts her chin forward. "I'll call that other woman from the park, Debbie, what's-her-name. I'll get her to give the dog to the girls."

Justin puts a hand in front of her. "Threatening Annie won't get us anywhere. She's right. We've put her in an awkward position, and the only people getting hurt are Eden and Savanna."

Cecilia says nothing but crosses her arms so tight over her chest that her knuckles turn white.

Justin turns toward me. "I'm sorry you've gone to all this trouble. We will try to resolve our differences so that Fancy will have a good home with the girls. I'll call you later."

Justin walks up the asphalt driveway with his mother-in-law following him. Fancy stays with me. Piercing wails sound from inside the house. Two distraught, white faces press the front window with wide eyes and open mouths. I climb into my car with a pervasive feeling of sadness choking me.

CHAPTER 15

I JUMP EVERY time my phone rings the rest of the day, but Justin doesn't call. However, early Sunday morning, it does ring, waking me from a sound sleep. "Hello," I mumble.

"Annemarie, it's your father."

No light filters into my bedroom through the vertical blinds. "What time is it?"

"Hang on."

"Dad? Hello? Are you there?"

"I'm back. I had to get my glasses. It's 5:10. Why did you want to know the time?"

Something isn't right. The cadence of his voice is slower than usual. "I wanted to know if you knew how early you called me."

"I just told you. It's 5:10."

Every conversation with my father is the same push-pull of words without listening, thought, or feeling. "Okay, then, let me rephrase my question. Why are you calling at this ungodly hour? Couldn't it wait?"

What a stupid question. This is Dennis Warden, whose wants and needs are always more important than mine.

"I'm calling to tell you Barbara passed away."

For the last eighteen years, my father has been married to Barbara Seaver Graham Putnam de Longhi Warden, the heir to a pharmaceutical fortune. He is the wealthy socialite's fourth, and now final, spouse. Being Barbara's husband has been his most successful and long-running job. Thirty years ago, when his brother died of cancer, followed two days later by my mother's death from an aneurysm during my birth, Dennis became the sole owner and operator of Warden Kennels and the only parent of a newborn daughter. He claimed the business demands were why he couldn't raise me himself. Ten years later, he lost the kennels through failed ventures, bad investments, and outright mismanagement. I should be glad my father was also not taking care of me. Who knows what kind of far-from-normal childhood I would have had?

At that time, someone suggested he become a *walker*. In Palm Beach County, walkers and gigolos are prevalent among mega-rich women. Unlike a gigolo, who is often a young man and sexually active with his benefactor, a walker escorts socialites to *The Season's* charity balls, galas, and club parties in exchange for free meals and entertainment.

My father is tall and lean, with a full head of ashen hair and a toothpaste model's smile. He can easily be mistaken for an actor in a TV commercial about erectile dysfunction. Another advantage is that Dennis wears a tuxedo like he was born in one. With excellent recall skills that he utilized for greyhound racing records and pedigrees, he quickly learned the lineage, source of wealth, previous spouses, and sexual proclivities of all the most influential people in Palm Beach's jet set. He made both married women and diamond-rattling divorcées jealous of whomever he escorted.

Soon, he was the darling of society hostesses and attracted Barbara's attention. She claimed she wasn't looking for a fourth husband but was quoted in a society column as saying: "All my girlfriends wanted Denny to escort them, and I got tired of waiting my turn."

I was twelve when I met my stepmother a month after the wedding and honeymoon. Barbara was a pleasant woman with big blue eyes and whitish-blond hair. The only change she made in my life was the expensive birthday and Christmas gifts mailed to me every year. When my father and Barbara occupied their Palm Beach Towers condo during *The Season*, they invited me to dinner at the Everglades Club or Trevini Ristorante, their favorite eatery. They spent the rest of the time between her homes in New York, Maine, and Italy. I was never invited on any of those trips or to stay at any of those residences.

The grind of an ice dispenser and the clink of cubes into a glass sound in the background. "My wife's funeral was yesterday."

"Her funeral was on Saturday?"

He pauses. "What day is it?"

"It's Sunday."

"We buried her on Friday."

"What happened to her?"

"She went to a clinic for a minor procedure but never woke up. The autopsy determined she had a heart attack."

Barbara was at least a decade older than my father and minimized their age difference with frequent visits to her dermatologist and plastic surgeon.

"I'm sorry to hear that."

"I'm calling because I need a place to stay for a while."

"But you live in four different houses all over the place."

"Not anymore. Barbara left everything to her boys. I'll get an annual stipend for the rest of my life, but that's it."

I never met any members of my stepmother's family. In our infrequent phone conversations, Dennis often complained about his stepsons. They were less than twenty years younger than him and living off their mother's generosity. He also griped about the *spoiled brats* they fathered. I once asked Dennis if Barbara insisted on a prenuptial agreement before their marriage. He reluctantly and bitterly said there was one. It was understandable. After all, she had been married three times before, had two sons, several grandchildren, and significant assets.

"Annemarie, are you listening? I have a week to get everything out of the New York apartment. I'm going to ship my belongings to you. I'll let you know when I get to Florida. See you soon."

Wait a minute. I did not say Dennis could live with me. I redial the number, but the phone sends me to voice mail. "Dad, we need to talk more about you staying with me. Call me back as soon as you get this."

Our father-daughter relationship has always been an emotional tug of war. The more I begged to be loved at most or considered at least, the more he pushed me away. For so long, I felt like a seasonal piece of clothing tucked away in the back of a closet and pulled out when the weather demanded. When modeling commanded all my time, I was no longer obsessed with my father's indifference and neglect. A busy career filled the void, and being a fashion model replaced my designation as Dennis Warden's unwanted daughter.

But the sad part is that thirty years later I am still a daughter with daddy issues.

CHAPTER 16

UNABLE TO FALL back to sleep, I let the dogs out and put kibble in their bowls for an early breakfast. I work to revise several book cover designs for a publisher and send them off for review. Then I dial my cousin's number. "Hey, Frankie, are you available for a girlfriend afternoon?"

"As long as it includes two kids, or, at least, one while the other's napping."

"What's Dale up to?"

"He'd better not be *up* to or *up* on anything. He's at his parents' helping his dad pressure wash the house."

"The roof, too?" I have a horrible vision of Dale and Roger sliding down a slippery slope of wet tiles like two grizzly bears.

"No. I told him I would kill him if the fall didn't. He swears his parents already had the roof cleaned by a company with workers who weigh less than one of Roger's legs. They're supposed to be cleaning the walls, walkways, and patio. Dawn wants to change the color of the house. Again."

"I'm surprised you didn't go along to supervise."

"Are you kidding? Have you seen my father-in-law without a shirt? That's a sight you can't un-see."

Spending time with Frankie has always been my feel-better-again tonic. After the unfortunate events of yesterday and my early morning phone call,

I crave her much-needed advice. I drive to her Boynton Beach house with the makings for strawberry margaritas, Bob Armstrong Dip, and restaurant-style tortilla chips.

Frankie frowns at the food in my insulated Yeti cooler. "Why would you bring this? You know I'm trying to lose a few pounds? Do you also get kicks throwing doughnuts into Weight Watcher meetings?" She opens the bag of chips and eats one. "Oh, well, it's Sunday. I'll go back on my diet tomorrow."

"Where are the kids?"

"I called my mom. She and Dad got them, so you and I can have a real girlfriend afternoon."

After mixing the drinks and assembling the dip, we set up lounge chairs by the pool. I strip off my shorts and T-shirt, exposing a modest one-piece swimsuit in lime green. Bikinis don't flatter my figure. The models for the Sports Illustrated swimsuit edition are more athletic and better endowed than me, and, of course, now they're much younger. I slather sunscreen all over my body, plop a floppy hat on my head, and stretch out on the lounger. On the other hand, Frankie wears a bikini with a bandeau top, not caring about her not-so-skinny thighs and pooched stomach.

She sprays her darker-toned skin with SPF-35, binds her curly black hair on her head with a scrunchy, and lies on her stomach. "Not that I'm complaining, but tell me why we needed this girlfriend afternoon."

"Remember me telling you about the guy with twin daughters who came to look at my foster dogs."

Frankie scoots her forearms back and raises her upper body. "Please tell me you got naked with him."

"Why do I bother leading into a story with you?"

"Well, did you?"

"Yes, we had sex."

"Do you have a dick pic?"

"Oh, my God! You're a middle school principal."

"What? I'm not at work right now. I'm spending the afternoon with my best friend. So, do you?"

"No! Just let me talk, okay?"

I relate the Meet and Greet and visit to the dog park. Frankie asks a couple of questions, but she is uncharacteristically quiet during the recounting of Justin asking me out. I finish and wait. "Frankie?"

Nothing.

"Are you awake?"

"What?"

"Did you fall asleep?"

She rolls onto her back, lifts her sunglasses, and rubs her eyes like a toddler. "Sorry. It's been a rough week. What were you saying?"

"I don't want to repeat the whole thing."

"I heard everything up to the dog park."

I retell about Justin wanting me, not Debbie, to handle the adoption. "Because she had the completed application, I asked him questions about himself."

"What did you find out?"

I relay the basic information about Justin and tell her about our date at the sports bar.

Frankie reaches into the Yeti cooler and refills her margarita glass. "Are you at the part where you slapped his happy sack like a bad girl, and he sucked all those cobwebs from your vag."

I recoil. "Francesca!"

"Hey, I've been married for eight years and have two kids. I spend five days a week with hormonally challenged middle schoolers. I deserve some vicarious pleasure through your sex life. But, let's face it, up to now it's been about as exciting as an Italian widow's. Do not deny me a cheap thrill."

After reporting what happened on the sofa, I'm forced to add excruciating details to Frankie's probing questions, such as, "Describe his penis. Do you think it's bigger or smaller than Dale's?"

"Having never seen your husband's junk that is not a judgement call I'm prepared to make."

"All I need is an estimate."

When my sexual encounter has been thoroughly dissected, I say, "The problem is, as good as the sex was, it might end up being a one and done."

"Why? What happened?"

We drink more tequila and eat more as I describe the unknown feud between Justin and Cecilia, Debbie's intrusion into the home check, and my cancellation of Fancy's adoption.

Frankie offers insightful opinions on the Stabler-Sonnenberg toxic relationship and humorous views on the chutzpah of a man-hungry woman. She is supportive of my decision to take Fancy back home with me. "Have you heard from Justin since you left yesterday?"

"Nope."

"It doesn't sound like he's mad at you. He recognized you had to do what was right for the dog."

"But you didn't hear Eden and Savanna crying. The hardest thing ever was getting in my car and driving away. Maybe Justin doesn't hate me, but the girls probably do."

Frankie narrows her eyes. "Be honest. Which would upset you more? Never seeing Justin again or never seeing his daughters?"

"You know what? I need to swim a few laps." I jump up from the lounger, throwing my hat and sunglasses on the empty cushion. Rushing to the pool coping, I prepare to dive into the deep end.

Frankie shouts, "You can't run away. I'll just ask you again when you come up for air."

I take a deep breath, plunge headfirst under the water, and swim along the bottom. The cool relief of a silent chlorinated world delays me facing

Frankie's probing question. A similar one has batted around my subconscious since yesterday.

CHAPTER 17

I SWIM LAPS like a shark is after me, smelling blood in the water. When my lungs and muscles scream for relief, I grab the edge of the pool and gasp for breath.

Frankie bobs over with her margarita glass held above the water's surface. "Do you have an answer for me yet? If the question is too hard, watch my lips move. Who will you miss more? Justin or the twins?"

"I…don't…know."

"You said he's not the typical kind of guy you're attracted to. Maybe his kids are what makes you want to be with him."

"I hope not. That would mean I'm a…a what?"

Frankie sips her drink. "It's not like you're a creepy pedophile trolling for single parents of young children. But I get the whole *Hot Dad* allure. From the way you described him, he doesn't have a dadbod."

"What's that?"

"It's somewhere between a beer gut and a six-pack. You know, rounded but not fat. Like Dale. You said Justin does Ironman competitions and works out, so his physique probably turned you on, despite his lack of hair and height. In addition, he's responsible, caring, and protective of his daughters, something Dennis never was. I'm sure you would find *that* appealing."

Bringing up my father's name reminds me I also want her opinion on his phone call this morning.

Frankie continues, "Let's face it, fatherly commitment and love is heartwarming to any woman. A nurturing dad hunk is hot and kind of...*forbidden*. I mean, you're not supposed to want to jump and hump one. I guess what I'm trying to say is, it's understandable you're attracted to him *because* he has kids. There's nothing wrong with that."

Frankie's words are a cooling balm. Suddenly, I'm weightless in the water. My heavy burden sinks to the bottom of the pool, and the slightest ripple could float me away. I wrap my arms around her neck and kiss her cheek. "I love you."

"Hot damn!" We jerk apart. Dale steps from the house wearing baggy, gray jersey shorts and a rumpled T-shirt with sweat stains. "Hot lesbian sex right here in our swimming pool. Can I watch?" Then he spies the bowl of dip and chips and detours away from us. "What have we here?"

Frankie sucks air through her teeth. "Welcome to my world. And you wonder why I want details about a single woman's sex life."

We change out of their swimsuits in the house while Dale polishes off the rest of the margaritas and food. In the kitchen, Frankie opens the refrigerator and peers inside. I load our glassware into the dishwasher. "There's something else I want to tell you. It was some news I received at five this morning."

"It can't be anything good at that time of day."

"Dennis called." I close the dishwasher.

"What did your deadbeat dad want?"

"To move in with me."

With a strangling noise, Frankie spins around. "Shut the front door! You're lying. Why?"

"Barbara unexpectedly passed away."

"Oh, my God! Did she leave the bastard high and dry? Wait a minute. Wasn't there a pre-nup?"

"He said he gets an annual stipend, but all the property and her estate go to her children. He has a week to vacate the New York apartment."

"Why does he have to move in with you?"

I shrug. "I didn't get a chance to discuss the details with him. He said he would be shipping some of his belongings for me to store."

A vein pops out on Frankie's forehead. "You need to tell that son of bitch to rent a storage unit and dump his crap there. Do *not* let him or his stuff into your house. Or better yet, tell him to find another rich wife he can make miserable until she dies, but do *not* let him anywhere near you."

"Why don't you tell me how you really feel?"

"Mommy!" Natalie runs into the house. "Is today Sunday?"

"If yesterday was Saturday, what day do you think today is?"

"Forget it. You don't know either." Natalie pats my leg. "Annie, is today Sunday?"

Obviously, she has had enough teachable moments. "Yes, it is."

"I gotta tell Grandpa." She runs from the room.

I follow her outside and greet my aunt and uncle. Dale emerges from the house with my empty cooler and loads it into my vehicle.

Linda hugs me. "We promised Natalie we'd order pizza for supper. Why don't you stay?"

"I'd love to but I need to let the dogs out. They've been alone all afternoon."

"Well, I'm glad we got to see you."

While driving back to Parkland, I review Frankie's comments about Dennis and, more importantly, Justin. Suppose I allow my father to get close to me again. Will he eventually find another cruel way to write me out of his life as soon as I outlive my usefulness? He never saw fit to house me, so I'm not obligated to do the same with him. As for Justin, there's nothing wrong with finding a man with kids attractive. I'll give him a couple more days to contact me before reaching out to salvage our relationship and Fancy's adoption.

Shortly after I enter the house, my phone rings, and Justin's name appears on the screen. "Annie, how are you?"

"I'm fine. How are you and the girls?"

"We're doing better. Are you busy right now?"

"No."

"I just called my sister, and she's willing to take the girls. I was hoping we could have dinner and talk."

"Sure. Where?"

"You choose."

I don't want to discuss sensitive topics in a restaurant. "Why don't we eat here where it's quiet and we won't be interrupted?"

A tangible sigh of relief emanates over the phone. "That's a good idea. I'll pick up some takeout. What would you like?"

"Surprise me."

CHAPTER 18

I SLIP INTO a tropical print romper with a halter neck and apply mascara and lipstick. Before Justin shows up, I decide to leave another message for Dennis. If necessary, I'll flood his voicemail until I hear from him. In the past, he only returned my calls when he was good and ready. This time, he answers after two rings.

"Annemarie, what do you want?"

"We need to talk about you staying with me."

"Why? Are you having second thoughts?"

"You could say that."

"I just did. Were you not listening?"

"Yes, I was listening, and I've decided you can't live with me."

"Why not? It will only be temporary."

"We've never lived together before."

"But I'm your father."

Raw emotion burns in my veins. "In name only. Uncle Milo is my real father. He was there for me day in and day out. He attended my school events. He made sure I did my homework. He taught me how to drive. He sat with me during chemo treatments when Aunt Linda couldn't. Where were you?"

There's a beat of silence before Dennis responds. "You know, I was never cut out to be that kind of parent. Fatherhood was forced on me when your mother got herself pregnant."

"Weren't you there too? Or did she impregnate herself with your stolen sperm and a turkey baster?"

"There's no need to be coarse. Linda and Milo were better suited to raising you, and they were well compensated for their efforts."

My father never contributed to my care except for putting me on his health plan. Instead, the proceeds from my mother's life insurance policy were signed over to my aunt and uncle, but I'm sure I cost them more than the settlement.

I fight to keep my voice firm with a thread of resolve. "I know I was a mistake because you've told me that for thirty years. Well, you've also been a mistake and a poor excuse for a father. No longer will I let you be the one calling the shots in our relationship. This time I'm the one walking away. I don't want you to live in my house."

I hate the cutesy sayings plastered all over Pinterest about the importance of family above all else. My aunt, uncle, and cousins are the ones that matter to me. My father's selfishness, rather than parental love, has always been the groundwork for our relationship. If he had disappeared after I was born, I doubt my pain and disappointment would be any less. Now, it's even more painful after seeing how well Justin stepped into the role of a single father.

In a slightly impatient and put-upon tone, Dennis says, "We'll talk again when you've calmed down. I'm going to be visiting some friends before I reach Florida. I'll call in a few weeks."

"My mind is made up."

"Are you done now?"

"No." I grip my phone. "There's one more thing. Don't bother sending your belongings. Whatever you ship to me will remain outside or be put in the trash. Good-bye, *Dennis*."

As soon as I disconnect the call, tears flood my eyes, and the doorbell rings. Scooting off the bed, I run to the front door and say, "Just a minute." In the kitchen, I rinse my face with cold water, then dry my cheeks with paper towels, removing any makeup I applied.

Gentle knocks tap on the front door, and Justin's voice filters through. "Annie? Are you okay?"

"Coming."

As soon as Justin sees me, his smile dies. "What's wrong?"

"Nothing." I wave a dismissive hand. "I just had another unfortunate phone call with my absentee father." I glance down at the bulging bag of food he's carrying. "Oh, my God, how did you know I love that place?"

The white plastic is printed with *Rock N Roll Ribs*, a local joint started by two musicians, one being Nicko McBain, the drummer for Iron Maiden.

"The girls and I love their food too."

"Please tell me you brought baby backs." Justin and I engage in a grin-off over the delight of barbecue.

"See for yourself."

I follow him to the kitchen, where he places the bag on the counter and removes two flip-top Styrofoam containers. "I wasn't sure which sides you liked so I ordered a variety."

I bring plates, silverware, and napkins to the dining room table. "What do you want to drink? Beer, wine, soda, water?"

Justin sets the containers in the center of the table. "Beer."

"There's nothing better with ribs."

We eat and talk, avoiding the most awkward topic until our appetites are sated. Justin cleans his hands with a wet wipe. "I want to apologize again for what happened yesterday. It's kind of embarrassing to have an outsider call us on the carpet for what Cecilia and I have been doing to the girls."

The word *outsider* pings in my chest like a loose piece of gravel hitting me.

Justin scoots his chair back, crosses one foot over his knee, and rests the beer bottle on the heel of his sneaker. "I told you before that Lucy wanted to move close to her mom when she was pregnant. I was against it. Cecilia has always been a force, especially when it came to managing her daughter. I admit she was helpful when the twins were infants, but she always needs to be the one in charge. She'll ask what you want, then she'll do whatever the hell she pleases.

"When this whole greyhound adoption came up, Cecilia thought getting a dog would be good for the girls. After we met with you, Eden and Savanna became even more excited. That's when Cecilia went cold on the idea. The more we talked about greyhounds, the more she brought up issues like the breed is too big for the girls to handle, and they don't live as long as small dogs. It was like she spent hours trawling the internet looking for every excuse for why we shouldn't get one of your dogs. Then I realized the problem wasn't the greyhounds. It's you."

CHAPTER 19

A STAB OF pain shoots through me like heat lightning. I straighten my spine and press a palm to my chest.

Justin's eyes widen with a vivid green flash. "No. No. There's nothing wrong with you. Shit! That didn't come out right. The problem is Cecilia. You're that word I'm not allowed to say."

I exhale and relax against the chair's back.

He plunks his beer bottle on the table. "Every time the girls talk about you in front of their grandmother, she gets this sour expression. I should say she gets an even more sour expression than usual. She doesn't like you."

"But I've done nothing to her."

"What you've done is make my daughters fall in love with you. Cecilia is jealous of the girls. She's afraid they'll love you more than her." A mingling of irritation and anger plays across his face. "I didn't realize until you came along how possessive she'd become of them. She was the same way when I was dating Lucy. We ended up eloping to Vegas after finding out she was pregnant because her mother refused to pay for...or attend our wedding."

A mental image of a young couple under a *Cupid's Wedding Chapel* sign flips into my mind. "Can I ask you a question?"

"Sure."

"How did you feel when you learned Lucy was expecting?"

"To be honest, I wasn't happy. I had just finished getting my degree and was a year into my job with the county. I had student loans and not a lot of money." Justin scratches the side of his neck. "At the time, I thought she was going to break up with me. Things hadn't been good between us for a while."

"But you married her anyway."

"She was pregnant with my child, I mean, children. I had a responsibility to those babies. I hoped we could make our marriage work for their sakes, and everything was going well until she died."

"Have you and your mother-in-law been able to resolve your differences?"

"For now, we've agreed not to argue in front of the kids. There are a lot of things Cecilia and I disagree on, but she loves Eden and Savanna and doesn't want to see them hurt. You were right. We were stressing them out. They told us in very clear terms how our arguing made them feel."

I bite my lip then say, "Do they hate me for canceling the adoption?"

"Are you kidding? It's just the opposite. You've become their superhero because of your concern for the dog. It's me and Cecilia that are in the doghouse, so to speak."

"You know, I want the girls to have Fancy. They need her, and she needs them. Since I brought her home, she's been moping around the house. If she's not outside, she just lays in her crate. It's like she's just as disappointed as the girls."

"I know you can't put a dog on hold, but is there something you can do until we can prove she'll have a good home with us?" Justin appears to hold his breath, like a defendant awaiting a verdict.

"You have a trial period of a week to finalize the adoption. We could try again next weekend. Otherwise, I'll need to call Debbie and tell her Fancy is available to be adopted by someone else."

"I guess we have a week to prove ourselves."

We're silent for an awkward length of time until I blurt out, "Do you want another beer?"

"One more."

"Let's sit on the patio. The dogs need to go outside."

The greyhounds race around the yard, except for Fancy. She sniffs Justin's legs and stares into his face as if asking him where Eden and Savanna are.

He rubs her neck, and her eyes moisten like she's on the brink of tears. "That's it. I'll do anything to make this adoption work. I can't stand making another little girl sad."

I give this sweet man an indulgent smile. I guess Frankie is right. Women love warm-hearted fathers.

Fancy joins my dogs in the yard, and Justin turns in his chair to face me. "Do you mind me asking why your father made you cry? I remember you said that you didn't see him much while growing up."

I give Justin the highlights of my father's marriage to a wealthy socialite. "He called early this morning to tell me she died and has given most of her estate to her kids. He has a week to move out and wants to live with me."

Will Justin's reaction be like Frankie's? Or will he give me a platitude about family being family no matter what happened in the past?

"Let me get this straight. The guy who never took care of you wants you to take care of him. I'm sure his wife left him enough to get his own place, but, if he's been sponging from her for the last eighteen years, he probably expects to do the same with you. Why should he spend any of his inheritance if you'll pay his living expenses?"

Justin is so right about Dennis. I know Barbara left him better off than he let on, but he always preferred using OPM—Other People's Money.

"He reminded me again that he never wanted to be a father." Despite my best efforts, a hint of emotion colors my voice. "I'm sorry. It's hard when your only biological parent is a shitty human being."

Justin stands and holds out his arms. "Come here."

I rise to my feet, wrap my arms around his neck, and rest my cheek against his ear. His muscled arms pull me into a fierce hug, which molds me against him. I feel protected and special.

He put his lips close to her ear. "Annie?"

"Hmm?"

"If you're a mistake, you're the greatest one your father ever made."

When we kiss, he tastes like yeasty beer and the sweet tang of barbecue sauce. Each press of his lips and sweep of his tongue weakens me further. I anchor myself to him, kissing him back harder. He groans, grasps my bottom, and squeezes. His hips roll against me, pressing his hardness into the notch of my thighs. Electric thrills sizzle through me. Goosebumps ripple over my skin as he kisses my jaw, nips my earlobe, and sucks on my neck. I grip him tighter, aching for the safety of his embrace, his mouth, and the taste of his skin. I want him with a fierceness that makes me willing to be taken anywhere, even on the patio.

"Annie." He murmurs against my lips. "We can't."

"Yes, we can." I cover the hard bulge behind his zipper with my hand.

"I have to pick up the girls."

"I thought they were at your sister's house for the night."

"Not for the night. Just until eight o'clock which is…" He squints at his watch over my shoulder. "In twenty minutes."

"But you want to do this. I can tell."

"Yeah." He glances down. "That guy blows my cover all the time."

"How about a quickie?"

"I want all night to make love to you again."

"Promise?" I rub against his hardness.

"I promise the next time we're alone together, we'll both be naked, and I'm going to lick every inch of you just to know how you taste." His gaze slides to my mouth, down my throat, and to my breasts. He lightly bites the heel of my palm, then places his lips at the corner of my mouth. "I'm going to start to nibble right here." His fingers slip under the edges of my halter top and brush the sides of my breasts. "And here." My breath catches as he runs his hands down and raises the short hemline of the jumper. He slides one hand under the elastic leg opening of my panties. "And here."

"Oh, God."

"But not tonight." He kisses my forehead. "I'll call you tomorrow."

A few minutes later, he is gone, leaving me with an aching need for him and him alone.

CHAPTER 20

THE FOLLOWING SATURDAY morning, four people waited outside Justin's house when I turned onto his street. Standing between their father and grandmother, the twins prance like show horses.

I exit my car, and Justin smiles that soul-warming smile of his. "Thank you for giving this another go with us."

Eden tucks her hand in mine. "We want Fancy to live in a quiet house with no fighting."

Her grandmother says nothing.

"Are you in agreement with this, Cecilia?"

"I will do whatever is in the best interest of my granddaughters."

"Good. We'll first walk Fancy around the new neighborhood, the yard, and, finally, take her in the house." When I open the hatchback, the greyhound leaps from my car like a kid high on sugar. She dances around, licking the twins' faces. "Girls, listen. I'm going to tug on her leash. At the same time, you tell her to sit."

Eden and Savanna point their index fingers at the greyhound when I jerk the leash sideways. In commanding, but high-pitched voices, they say, "Sit!"

Fancy plops her bottom on the driveway, quivering in place. The girls pet her for several minutes and tell her how good and pretty she is.

Cecilia squints up into the sunny sky. "I'll wait inside the house."

The rest of us walk down the street. When the greyhound displays no overt anxiety or excitement, I hand the leash to the girls. Fancy walks between them, relaxed and confident.

Justin shakes his head. "They look like they've been doing this for years."

"I told you they're meant to be together."

He clasps my hand in his. "Maybe there are more of us meant to be together." He tucks our joined hands behind my waist and kisses my temple.

Eden asks over her shoulder, "Are you watching how good we're doing?"

"We're watching," Justin answers. "Keep it up."

I instruct them how to approach people with or without dogs, and the signs when Fancy needs to relieve herself. Back at the house, we walk the dog around the front and backyards to identify her boundaries. Inside, Fancy is reintroduced to Cecilia, who pets her head without much enthusiasm. The greyhound stands still with a disinterested expression, like a sullen teenager forced to submit to the attentions of an elderly and embarrassing relative. After a few seconds, she spins away with a dismissive flick of her tail and rejoins the children, wearing an open-mouthed smile as if saying, "Duty done. Let's go play."

Fancy steps into her new crate, and after a few sniffs, she lies down as if trying it on for size. She slurps water, eats kibble from the bowl on an elevated stand, and noses through a basket of dog toys. To my surprise, she mouths a stuffed rabbit and follows the girls into their bedroom instead of choosing a familiar chew toy.

When neither the dog nor the children return, I turn to Justin, "It looks like Fancy has settled in. Call me if you have any questions or problems."

"You've done a great job preparing us." He slings an arm over my shoulder. "Would you like to stay for lunch?"

Cecilia's gaze narrows on his familiar gesture. I resist shrugging him off. "Thanks, but I should leave you to spend time with her on your own."

"Why don't you two go out for lunch, or later for dinner, and I'll stay here?" Cecilia says. "The girls said you went on a date one night, and I assume it was with Annie. I'm not blind. I can see you two are attracted to each other. I'm just saying that if you want to spend some time alone together, I'm willing to take care of the kids and dog."

"Uh, that's very nice of you to offer." Justin seems flummoxed.

"Well, what are you waiting for? Ask her out."

"Would you like to go out for lunch or dinner?"

"Dinner sounds good."

Cecilia levels her gaze at me. "When would be a good time for him to pick you up?"

"Seven?"

She turns to Justin. "Will that work for you?"

"Sounds good to me."

I say my goodbyes to the girls and Fancy. The greyhound ignores me and lies on the floor while Eden and Savanna parade dolls up and down her back.

Justin steps outside with me. "I don't know what's going on with Cecilia, but I'll take advantage of it. Where would you like to go tonight?"

So far, he's paid for a date at Packy's, fed me a grilled cheese sandwich lunch, and bought my favorite barbecue takeout. In most dating relationships, a couple spends an inordinate amount of time figuring out where and what to eat. "Why don't you come to my house, and I'll cook dinner?"

Meeting his endless verdant eyes, it appears we're thinking the same thing. "I'd very much like to eat at your place."

We kiss against the closed door. The one deep kiss is like an unspoken promise of the insane sex we will have later tonight.

He touches his forehead to mine. "What can I bring?"

"Yourself and a pocket full of condoms."

CHAPTER 21

MOST EVENINGS, I cook my dinner by reheating entrees prepared by others and purchased for exorbitant prices at deli counters or from freezers. Linda insisted Frankie and I learn to cook. The problem was my aunt is as useful and skilled in the kitchen as a leaf blower. Everything she prepares is packaged, frozen, or canned. Uncle Milo taught us several Italian dishes, which are now the highlights of my culinary repertoire.

I was thrilled early on in our relationship when I learned my ex-husband cooked like an angel. Maybe that was part of why I married him. Watching Thierry bent over a cutting block made my knees weak. Eating his coq au vin was on par with multiple orgasms. His love of cooking and my gluttony accounted for significant parts of our relationship. Of course, banging the cook while a cassoulet baked in the oven was not so bad either. I remember sitting on the granite-topped island in our kitchen in France, my legs wrapped around Thierry's waist, and his pumping buttocks reflected in the stainless-steel doors of the refrigerator. Now, his second wife is enjoying all his kitchen talents. If he is still true to form, he's probably *heating up* other women's kitchens in addition to his own.

Tonight's dinner is pizza from scratch. As soon as I get home, I mix the dough, stretching, kneading, and stroking until I have the pliability I want. In my Instapot, I simmer tomatoes and herbs. The pressure cooker produces a near copy of Uncle Milo's rich marinara, thick and slick with olive oil, that he simmers all day on the stovetop. While the dough rises and the sauce cooks, I run to Publix for artichoke hearts, fresh mozzarella, mushrooms, olives, basil, pepperoni, sausage, anchovies, spinach, and two bottles of Italian wines. I know what Justin looks like naked, but I don't know what he likes on a pizza.

My cousin, Tony, still complains when his mother loads a pie with vegetable toppings. He picks off the mushrooms and peppers until the crust is only covered with sauce and cheese. "It's a pizza, Mom. Not a salad!"

A few minutes before seven, I fire up the grill and roll out the dough into four rounds, ready to be personally topped. Justin arrives on time wearing a comfortable pair of jeans that sit snugly on his slim hips and a soft T-shirt stretching across his hard chest. He looks so damn sackable I can barely stop myself from dragging him into the bedroom.

He pulls me close enough to feel the beat of his pulse, smell the spiciness of his skin, and taste the sugar of his breath. "What's for dinner?"

"It's create-your-own-pizza night. I made the dough and sauce. You get to choose your own toppings."

"The twins would be in heaven with this."

Juno and Bella rise from their dog beds in the living room and come to greet him. "I meant to ask you the last time I was here what happened with the other dogs?"

"Felix, the black male, went to his new home right after the Meet and Greet. A couple I met there fell in love with Lady, and her adoption was completed a week later. Now I have just my two dogs since you adopted Fancy."

I have not been asked to foster any more greyhounds, and I wonder if Debbie has banned me from the rescue group. Would she be that vindictive because Justin preferred me to her?

I hold up a chilled bottle of Prosecco in one hand and room-temperature Chianti in the other. "Which one do you want?"

"I'll open that one." He unfastens the Prosecco's wire cap and works the cork with his thumbs. It pops and flies across the room, bouncing off the countertop. A diaphanous mist spirals from the neck as he pours the bubbling wine into tall glasses and hands me one.

I take a sip, savoring its crisp bubbliness. "How are Fancy and the girls doing?"

"It's like I have three daughters. I'm worried about the dog having separation anxiety on Monday when Eden and Savanna go to school. Hopefully, with Cecilia letting her out in the yard during the day, she'll be content to wait until they get home. I'll let you know how it goes."

We personalize our individual rounds of dough with the various toppings. Justin lays pepperoni edge to edge and sticks out his tongue with distaste when I offer him anchovies. After grilling our pizzas, we take seats in the dining room.

"Be careful," I warn him. "It's still hot."

"Why is it the things I love keep hurting me?" I give him a sharp look while he blows on the slice in his hand. "I mean the things I love to eat. Either they burn the roof of my mouth or aren't healthy for me."

I take a bite and then hold my mouth open. "Hot. Hot. Hot."

"I see you're one of those do-as-I-say-not-do as-I-do people."

My smile becomes a sly grin. "Maybe I just like to put hot things in my mouth."

He shakes his head and clicks his tongue against his teeth. "I've been warned about girls like you."

"What warning was that?"

"You're all quiet class and beauty, but then you like to talk dirty and get me into trouble."

"That's me. Nothing but trouble."

He cocks his head, his eyes assessing. "But trouble can be a whole lot of fun."

Over dinner, we learn more about each other. Justin's sister, who also lives in Coral Springs, is his twin. "Does your sister have twins like you do?"

"No, she has a girl who is a year older than Eden and Savanna and a boy who is five."

Justin also attended top-notch private schools in Fort Lauderdale and graduated from the University of Florida. Recently, his parents retired to The Villages, a community for older adults in central Florida. In contrast, I grew up with my aunt and uncle, attended public schools, and never went to college. We were raised in different environments with different life experiences, but here we are, sharing our histories, homemade pizza, and a pleasant evening. By the time the food is consumed, the wine has me loose-limbed and relaxed.

Justin polishes off the last bite of his second pizza. "That was great. I've never had it grilled before. How did you find the time to get everything ready?"

"It's called multitasking. I can get a lot done if a sexy guy is coming over for dinner. Are you ready for dessert?"

A tiny, knowing smile plays over his mouth. His eyes devour me with a hunger so intense I wonder if a more attractive woman lurks behind my chair. "Actually, I'm looking forward to getting you into bed and showing you *my* multitasking skills."

I stand, stack his plate on mine, and head to the kitchen. He joins me and places the wine glasses and empty pizza platter in the sink. I furiously scrape leftover toppings into a plastic container to get to my bedroom as soon as possible. Justin presses himself into my backside. His fingers skim the nape of my neck and trace the edge of my earlobe. He wraps both arms around my body and envelopes me until I feel like I'm merged into the cavity of his ribcage. All thoughts about cleaning the kitchen disappear as a trail of fire burns when his hand slides upward from my waist and lingers on my breast.

"Annie." He exhales. "I want to go slow with you and take my time in your bed, but I want you right here."

Over the last four years, I have dragged around my recollections of Thierry like a stuffed animal carried by a toddler. It's time to replace them. Tonight, I want the new and improved version of kitchen sex with Justin.

He shifts behind me. The hardness of his erection presses into the base of my spine. Sensation spikes between my legs. My breath comes out in shallow pants. I'm so swollen it feels like a fist is clenched between my thighs. "Do it here. Now. Please."

He bends me forward over the countertop. The ogee edge bites into my abdomen as I rest on my elbows. He lifts the tiered skirt of my sherbet-colored Olivia Rubin sundress until the fabric bunches on my back.

"Jesus, I love the way your ass looks." With one hand, he palms my behind, exposed by a white lace thong.

I shiver and suck in a breath with the hiss of his zipper and the crinkling of a torn wrapper. The sounds are so anticipatory and arousing. My forehead dips to the backs of my hands. Instead of pushing my thong down my legs, he slides the thin strip to one side, and his penis touches me.

"Spread your feet a little."

He teases my slick flesh. Holding my hips, he positions himself and slides partway into my body. "God, you feel better than I remember. So tight."

He kisses the exposed skin between my shoulder blades. I arch my back and push my bottom into him. He moves the tip of his cock in and out, testing, preparing me.

He whispers, "Ready?"

"Yes."

He presses farther inside, thick and enormous, until he's buried deep. I tighten around him. His thighs slap the back of mine as he plunges hard and fast with long, smooth strokes. At this angle, his cock slides back and forth across my G-spot, turning me into an orgasm waiting to happen.

A cry escapes my mouth.

"You like this?" There is a sound of satisfaction and pride in his voice.

I whimper and nod.

He drives slowly, with even thrusts, making soft sounds of effort like he wants to pound into me but doesn't. Instead, he eases the weight of his body off mine, slides his hand down my thigh, and lifts my knee to the countertop. With gentle pressure between my shoulder blades, he urges my head and upper body to drop then he starts again. With me positioned this way, he hits the perfect place, like I've been custom-designed for him.

"Harder," I moan, so close, so very close.

His fingers dig into my waist as his speed increases. "Too hard?"

"Perfect."

The first deep tremor ripples. Justin maintains his pace. Another tremor follows and then the dam breaks. A searing orgasm burns through my veins and flashes across my skin, reverberating through every nerve ending in my body.

I'm not a screamer. Until now.

When I go quiet, his sharp, quick grunts are the only sounds. Though the intensity of my orgasm abates, Justin doesn't stop. He slows, inhales a ragged breath, and moves faster than before. A low groan tears from his throat when I squeeze him, triggering one last thrust for his release. Everything stills except for my wild beating heart and his sharp, uneven pants. After a time, he steadies me, pulls himself out of my body, and helps me put both feet on the floor.

Then he mutters, "Fuck!"

I look at him over my shoulder. "What's wrong?"

There's a trapped, panicky look in his eyes. "The condom broke. I'm so sorry, Annie."

Cold grips my spine with what this means so early in our relationship.

CHAPTER 22

THIERRY ALSO SAID he was sorry on the awful day I was served with divorce papers. At the time, his mistress was five months pregnant.

Wiping away bitter tears, I said to him, "But you said you didn't want children."

"True, Cherie. But now I am having a son."

"We can stay married, and I'll help raise the boy." Being a stepmother would be fantastic.

But Thierry wanted his child to be born in wedlock. To have an illegitimate heir would break his parents' hearts. Three short months later, at age twenty-six, I was a homeless divorcee. My only consolation in suffering this horrific and humiliating end to my marriage was in knowing my ex-husband would always be a philanderer. Having him break my heart once was better than repeated sufferings.

As I face Justin, a trickle of semen dampens my thong and runs down my leg.

He drops the ripped condom in a nearby trashcan and zips his jeans, his face dark with concern. "You wouldn't happen to have a Plan B pill handy?"

"No."

He checks his pockets for his wallet and keys. "I'll be right back."

"Where are you going?"

"There's CVS not too far from here."

"Wait," I grab his arm to stop him. "Don't go."

"We can't rely on you just finishing your period or expecting it in the next couple days."

"That's not it. Can we sit and talk?"

"We will when I get back." He walks a couple steps away, then returns with measured strides. "You need to understand. I love my daughters, but I don't want another unwanted pregnancy to complicate our future."

Whose future he's referring to? His and his daughters? Or his and mine?

"Trust me, Justin. There's nothing to worry about. Just sit down. We *need* to talk."

No conversation ever ends well that starts with that sentence. His face hardens, and his jaw tendons look like ribbons under the skin. Without thinking, I place a hand on my abdomen. Justin's eyes follow the movement, and the color drains from his face.

"Are you already pregnant?" His lips become a tight, thin line, as if the words he does not want to say are trying to force their way out. Then they do. "It's not mine. That first condom didn't break."

The implied accusation and insult slap me like a strong gust of wind on a wet winter's day. His expression looks like someone closing up a house in the presence of imminent danger. Doors are slammed shut and locked. The lights are extinguished and curtains drawn. Shutters are pulled and latched over windows. Before my eyes, Justin becomes a stranger to me.

"I'm not pregnant. Just give me a chance to explain."

Deaf to anything I say, Justin walks to the front door and throws it open. "I'm getting that pill. Afterward, we'll talk."

"No. I don't need it, and I won't take it." The Plan B pill is not cheap. I can't have him spend fifty dollars for nothing. Besides, what effect might it have on me?

"I don't care what you think you do or don't need. To protect us both, I'm buying it, and I expect you to take it. Do you hear me?"

"Loud and clear." A hairline crack in our relationship opens with a razor-thin edge and then rapidly drops into a deep chasm. Justin's behavior is typical of how my father has dealt with me over the years. I don't need another man in my life who won't listen or talk to me in times of stress. "Either stay and talk to me or don't bother coming back."

He steps outside. "If you won't take the pill, don't track me down months from now with a paternity suit. I'll fight it!"

"No problem. I won't call you or change my mind."

"I mean it, Annie. I won't be forced to raise more children I didn't plan for."

His words chill me, but I beg instead. "Please, just come inside so we can talk."

"Not until I'm sure I can't be stuck with another unwanted pregnancy." He tips his chin up, looking mutinously stubborn and implacable. "What's your decision? Will you take the pill?"

"No."

He stares at me, then turns and heads to his car.

I grab onto the door handle for support. "For the record, my only concern with a broken condom is a possible STD. What I wanted to tell you in a rational conversation was that in high school, I had uterine cancer and a hysterectomy."

He spins around, a look of disbelief then horror crosses his face.

I close the door.

CHAPTER 23

SECONDS AFTER LOCKING the deadbolt comes the sound of knocking. Leaning against the door, I'm grateful there's no glass for him to see me.

"Annie? Open up. Please. I'm sorry. I didn't know." He keeps knocking and rings the doorbell.

I turn off the outside lights on the porch, plunging him into darkness. Juno and Bella know something is amiss. They rise from their dog beds and lean against my legs, offering canine support and emotional closeness. As my Velcro dogs, they sense the pang of sadness slicing through me.

My phone vibrates on the kitchen counter. I hit the ignore button, sending Justin's call to voicemail. Then, I shut the blinds facing the back patio and check that the French doors are locked, in case he attempts to enter through the backyard. I hope the dogs don't have to pee. If he finds me outside the house, and pleads his case, I won't have the strength or will to resist him.

My phone dings with a text. I wait in my dark bedroom with the greyhounds for the doorbell to stop ringing, the knocking to cease, and the phone to no longer send out alerts. After a few more minutes of silence, I go to the front window and peek between the blind slats. The brake lights of Justin's car brighten as he turns from the driveway onto the street. After watching until he's out of sight, the dogs and I go to the kitchen door, but they're reluctant to go outside without me.

118

"C'mon. We'll all go out."

I lead Juno and Bella to the backyard and walk them to the far fence line. Palm fronds rustle in the dark evening. Insects drone. Birds call to each other. A soft, humid breeze sways the branches of the date palms lining the rear of the property. A small iguana runs up one trunk and disappears into the pinecone-like crown, where new branches sprout with a minty lemon scent. On our return to the house, the dogs stop and squat on the grass, inches from the concrete patio.

I silence my phone, put away the leftovers, and clean up the kitchen. The dogs and I head to my bedroom for an early night. After I finish in the bathroom, Juno and Bella stand next to my bed as if to say: *You need us.*

"Okay, you can sleep with me."

I pat the mattress, and they jump up. It takes a while for all of us to secure a position, even though it won't matter. At some point during the night, I'll be clinging to a sliver of the king-sized bed.

"Good night, girls, and thank you." Each receives a kiss on the head before the light is extinguished.

My dreams are vivid and exhausting. At times, my subconscious says: *This isn't real. Wake up.* Twice, I open my eyes in the dark room, readjust the pillow, and scoot a fifty-pound animal to the other side of the mattress before toppling into another ravine of disturbing experiences, familiar faces, and unlikely strangers.

My father figures prominently in the first dream. We have just endured a long separation. Either I was confined in a concentration camp, or he was forced to spend a year with children in an elementary school. It's hard to tell which one of us suffered more. He throws his arms wide in greeting, but my feet are mired in something sticky like the ground is covered in industrial-strength glue pads. Eventually, he becomes impatient with my slow progress and walks away without a backward glance.

In the next dream, Thierry is the main character. I'm in the stands at the final LNB Pro tournament. His team won, and he was chosen as the MVP. While accepting the award, he thanks his beloved wife for her support and points to the stands. The camera pans in my direction. I smile and blow a kiss. But on the giant video screen above the court is a blond woman seated in another row, holding a little boy. The child has Thierry's coal-black hair and waves at his daddy.

The last one is the worst. As I hold a sleeping newborn, Justin and the girls stand beside my hospital bed. A bright fluorescent light hums and buzzes overhead, and an IV machine beeps incessantly. The only one smiling is me despite hurting all over. I ask why they have such glum faces, and Justin holds up a mirror. All the hair on my head is gone, and I have no eyebrows or eyelashes. He lifts the infant from my arms and tells his crying daughters to say their final goodbyes. Justin, Eden, Savanna, and the infant leave as doctors and nurses fill the room.

I roll out of bed at four, tired of tormented dreams, twisted sheets, tossing and turning. Juno and Bella snooze on. With my head feeling like pizza dough someone has over-kneaded, I take aspirin and drink a defibrillator in a mug. Sufficiently caffeinated, I'm finally ready to check my phone.

There are two missed calls from Justin and a slew of text messages.

Justin: Please open the door and let me in

Justin: I'm sorry. I should have let you talk

Justin: I'm sorry. I panicked

In the verbal messages, his voice is layered with regret and remorse. The second message came a few minutes after the first. Justin speaks softly yet formally, like he's giving a legal deposition and must carefully choose his words. "Please answer your phone. I don't want to leave things this way. I said some things I shouldn't have. I know you're not that kind of woman. I really care about you. Call me as soon as you get this message."

The earnestness in his tone conveys a barely perceptible plea. *He didn't know.* Justin married pregnant Lucy when their relationship was strained, and he likely carries baggage related to trust and honesty, too.

With my second cup of coffee, I sit in the living room and stare out the front window to the east. Inhaling the aroma of pungent but sweet black coffee, I watch the sun come up, feeling like a fragile teacup that had been dropped onto a hard floor. Shards prick my skin with tiny cuts while a large fragment lodges in my chest.

My issues, of course, started with my father, who always viewed me as a piece of unwanted property he inherited but couldn't let go. Instead, he was a neglectful and inattentive owner, paying my aunt and uncle to be his property managers.

My ex-husband lavishly spent money on me instead of being faithful. His generosity was a substitute for love and respect. This became obvious when he was under a marriage-ending time constraint. My lawyer negotiated a well-funded settlement and hefty alimony payments in exchange for an expedited divorce. Today, I live off the money earned from my modeling and graphic design work. Meanwhile, Thierry's money accumulates in accounts set up by my financial advisor for my future goal.

Justin said I'm perfect and elegant and beautiful. Flattery is nice, but I need someone who will be a strong tether when life spins out of control. Someone who will listen when I want to talk, and who will encourage and support my long-term plans. After learning about his marriage and seeing him with his children, I had hoped Justin might be that particular person.

A man who would love and accept me as a barren cancer risk.

CHAPTER 24

AT NINE-THIRTY, the sound of typewriter keys signals a text on my phone.

Justin: You awake?

Five minutes pass. During that time, I stare at the message and debate whether to answer or ignore it, but something has me typing a text back to him.

Annie: Yes

The little dots immediately appear with the formation of his return message.

Justin: Talk or text

Texting will allow me to formulate answers, then delete or revise them. Talking is not an option at this time. Any emotion in my voice might betray my feelings.

Annie: Text

Justin: I'm sorry

Annie: I know

Justin: I acted like a parent not a boyfriend. It's not an excuse. Just an explanation

Frankie once told me of a rough patch in her marriage when she treated Dale like another child instead of a man. "Let's face it. Men suck at housework and taking care of kids. I had to make a choice between accepting his way of doing things, yelling at him for his incompetence, or doing everything myself. In the end, I decided he was a great husband and father and deserves for me to treat him like one. It doesn't matter if he can't fold laundry worth shit."

Justin has spent the last four years dealing with twin girls at home and men on the job. The only adult females regularly in his life are Cecilia and his sister. In one of our conversations, he admitted he's not had much female companionship except for relatives since his wife died. I decide he's worth an explanation.

Annie: I understand why it happened

Justin: Good. Will you help me understand what you went through?

Despite his empathetic question, a self-protective instinct triggers my typed response.

Annie: Why?

Justin: Because I care about you

My cancer declaration had to have been like a bomb detonating in his face. He could have left and never contacted me again. Instead, he wanted me to let him in last night, and this morning, he's reaching out again.

Annie: It's hard

Justin: Give me what you can

The microphone icon will make it easier to speak the messages, instead of typing them. But I'll need to proof them for crazy autocorrect errors before hitting the send button. Whether it's texting or talking, that period of my life is still a painful topic. Dragging the experiences of a hysterectomy followed by chemo out for discussion is difficult. I usually keep them hidden. Just thinking about using words to describe their impact causes a bitter and acidic swirl to agitate my stomach.

Annie: In my junior year of high school, my abdomen swelled overnight. Someone started the rumor I was pregnant

Months before the surgery, students at my high school laughed, whispered, and pointed at me—their thin but pregnant-looking classmate. Some didn't care if I heard their comments.

"Who would want to have sex with her?"

"It would be like fucking a hole in a board."

Should I tell him the awful things that happened to my aunt, uncle, and cousin? One day, I was called into the main office, and a guidance counselor asked about my condition. Despite insisting I wasn't pregnant, social services contacted Aunt Linda. They investigated because of suspected sexual abuse by Uncle Milo or my cousin, Tony, who is three years older than me. There was talk about removing me from their home and putting me in emergency foster care. The case was closed after I was examined by a gynecologist. Since this part of the story involves my family, it's theirs to share with Justin, not mine. Some time passed while I decided this.

Justin: Still there?

Annie: Yes

Justin: Your family didn't notice anything wrong?

Annie: As soon as my aunt found out she took me to a doctor

Crying with the trauma of a first-time pelvic exam and bleeding all over the table, I kept apologizing to Aunt Linda. The doctor confirmed I wasn't pregnant. And still a virgin. The almost nonstop spotting wasn't an extended period as I thought it was.

Annie: A fast growing tumor was in my uterus. A biopsy detected cancer cells. The safest thing to do was a hysterectomy

Justin: You were 16?

Annie: Almost 17. I had chemo after the surgery. It was really hard losing my hair

Justin: Is that why you keep it short?

Annie: I started to grow it back when chemo ended. Three years later my annual lab work came back positive

Justin: The cancer returned?

Annie: Follow-up tests since then have all been negative but I keep my hair short just in case

Justin: That's understandable

Annie: But there are no promises the cancer won't come back somewhere else

The anniversaries of my surgery or annual exams stir up anxiety for me. Simple aches and pains are also triggers. Is that a regular headache or the start of a brain tumor? Is my stomach upset from something I ate or is it cancer?

Justin: How do you cope with the fear?

Annie: My family and online support groups. I also focus on wellness and staying healthy

Justin: Counseling?

Annie: Early on. The best thing for me was when I was scouted by a modeling agent. I never returned to regular high school classes and kept myself busy with travel and work

Justin: Your husband knew about your medical history?

Annie: He did and was fine with it

Until my marriage ended, I didn't fully realize what my permanent infertility meant to Thierry. I could never change my mind. But he could.

Justin: I'm sorry you went through all that

Annie: Thank you

Justin: You're such an fantastic woman. I'm just grateful you're interested in me. I hope you'll give me another chance

Annie: I want to. I really do. But I need some time

He does not respond right away. Maybe he's uncertain if this relationship should continue. I'm a liability, a risk that comes with additional stresses and fears. Is he considering the possible ramifications to him and his children of letting an infertile cancer survivor into their lives?

Justin: We'll keep in touch

Annie: I'll text you later

Justin: I'll be waiting

CHAPTER 25

DURING THE NEXT week, I texted and talked to a dozen people, but none of them was Justin. One phone call is from my father.

"Annie, I'm letting you know I've purchased a condo in Palm Beach. I'm not moving in until I have the kitchen and bathrooms updated. I'll call you again when I get to Florida."

At the end of our conversation, I asked him for the address of his new home and checked the listing on the Realtor.Com website. The sales price is almost seven hundred thousand dollars for a two-bedroom, two-bath unit in a small multi-unit structure built in 1985. The building is directly on the beach and also has an unobstructed view of the Intracoastal Waterway across Ocean Drive. The location with front and back water accounts for the high cost, but how can Dennis afford such a property, including the renovations? Barbara must have left him better off than he initially told me.

I call my cousin to discuss my current situation with Justin and to seek her advice.

Frankie asks, "Are you going to see him again?"

"I don't know if I should."

"Are you still worried that you like his daughters more than him?"

"No, at least, I don't think so."

But out in public, I catch myself watching mothers holding onto small children, toddlers sitting in strollers, infants swaddled in snuggly carriers. I drive past elementary schools with the same lustful longing of a man in a midlife crisis checking out much younger women. What if Eden and Savanna are more important to my relationship with Justin than he is?

"You're doing it again," says Frankie.

"Doing what?"

"You're breaking up with a perfectly nice man when the relationship moves from attraction to intimacy."

"What are you talking about? Justin and I have already been intimate."

"Physically, yes. But when your emotions start becoming involved, all he has to do or say is one little thing to give you an excuse to back away."

I open my mouth to refute her but stop. All my life, and especially after the divorce, I've guarded my feelings. Every little girl abandoned by a father and every ex-wife discarded by a husband has a chipped and fragile heart she protects with the ferocity of a mother tiger. When feelings intensify in a relationship, and the risks play out in emotional extremes, I distance myself to lessen the pain.

Frankie continues. "You need to give him another chance. Like he said, he didn't know about your hysterectomy. He wouldn't have been so insistent about the Plan B pill if he did. You have to remember that when it comes to men, we need to cut them a little slack. It's not that we're better than they are. It's just that they're not as good as us, especially when it comes to sensitivity and intuition."

I spend the day thinking about contacting Justin when I receive an unexpected text on Sunday afternoon.

Unknown number: Hi Annie it's Eden and Savannah that's not how to spell my name I didn't do it the phone did

It takes me a moment to figure out the girls are using their voices to text a message to me, minus the punctuation. This isn't Justin's number, so are they contacting me on Cecilia's phone or someone else's?

128

Annie: Hi. Whose phone are you using?

Unknown number: Look she answered lemme see it's my turn now tell her about our own phone hey Annie Daddy got us a phone we called Grandma but we want to try texting with you let's ask Daddy how we can face time with Annie wait a minute you have to say goodbye bye Annie

The call disconnects. Minutes later a new text appears with Justin's number.

Justin: I hope you don't mind the girls contacting you with their new cell phone

Annie: I don't. How is everyone doing

Justin: We're all good

Annie: You broke down and bought them a phone

Justin: It's what they wanted for their birthday

Annie: When is their birthday?

Justin: Wednesday. I made a deal with them. I'd get them a phone this weekend if I didn't have to throw a party. Cecilia and I are taking them to dinner and a movie later today

Annie: And they agreed????

Justin: They really wanted a phone and a party but I gave them the choice of either not both

He didn't invite me to join them, and that's fine with me. I'm not ready to become integral to their family celebrations. Still, I would like to wish the girls a happy birthday.

Annie: May I give them a present?

Justin: You already did. Fancy. But they wouldn't say no to more gifts. How are you doing

Annie: Better

Justin: I promise to restrict on how often the girls can contact you. Do you prefer a phone call, an illegible text, or FaceTime?

Annie: Perhaps phone calls or FaceTime until they figure out how to text a little better. They can call once a day if that's all right

Justin: I'll let them know. Thanks

Annie: OK. Bye

It seems he's leaving any further contact up to me. The next hurdle I need to cross is what to buy soon-to-be eight-year-old twins for their birthday. I emailed a designer I know at Versace and asked for a contact who deals with children's clothing. A day later, I purchase two jungle print pleated skirts with a Greek key design on elastic waistbands and two white T-shirts with the Versace logo printed in ombré colors across the front. The clothes will be airmailed to me from Milan. I also pick up two gift cards at Pet Supermarket.

The girls call once a day, sometimes using FaceTime. We talk about Fancy and school. The evening before their birthday, I ask, "Are you excited to turn eight tomorrow?"

Instead of answering with gleeful excitement, they both become somber. Eden says, "Our mommy died the day after our birthday."

Savanna's voice quivers. "She would have given us each a new phone, a big party with other kids, games, and lots of presents." Soft weeping follows her words.

"Don't cry," Eden says to her sister, even though her voice sounds full of tears too.

I softly say, "I'm sorry your mother died so close to your birthday. Mine did, too."

The girls are silent for a moment as if digesting this piece of information. Eden's face fills the phone screen. "Your mommy died too?"

"Yes, she did. You don't remember much about your mom because you were only three years old, but I was even younger when I lost mine."

"Were you a baby?" Eden asks.

I have a moment's hesitation about discussing this with the twins, but who else can relate except another motherless child? I want them to understand that time only blunts the pain of loss but doesn't erase it. "Yes. I had just been born. Even though it happened a long time ago, I still feel a little sad on my birthday since that's the day my mother died. I never knew her, but I really miss her. That's normal, and sometimes crying helps me feel better."

Savanna's face takes over the screen. "Did your daddy have to take care of you by himself like ours?"

A double whammy of grief wraps its lethargic arms around me, slumping my shoulders. "No. I didn't have a great dad like you. Mine didn't know what to do with a tiny baby, so my aunt and uncle took care of me."

"For how long?" both girls ask in unison.

"Until I graduated from high school." With the phone held at arm's length, both of their shocked expressions are visible, but I don't want to discuss my disaster of a father with first graders. "You two are lucky to have such a wonderful daddy and a grandmother who cares for you so much. I was lucky to have my Aunt Linda and Uncle Milo. They had a boy and a girl who were older than me. So I was able to grow up in a family with kids who were like my brother and sister."

The conversation ends with me wishing them a happy birthday tomorrow and a hint about having a present for them as soon as it arrives. They question me, but I tell them they'll have to wait. After disconnecting the call, I sit with the phone lying on my chest while reclining on the sofa. The house is quiet. My thoughts center on my dead mother, and numbing grief swamps me.

I never considered the parallels between my life and the twins' lives. Of course, there is one glaring exception. They have a father as the central figure. Putting a hand to the base of my throat, a tiny mouse-like squeak escapes me at the thought of Justin. I wait for an epiphany to show me what to do about our stalled, or possibly ended, relationship. Why was I so attracted to him when he was not my usual type? Why had I leapfrogged past several conventional stages between meeting a guy and having sex with him? I'd never done that before.

After deliberating on this for a while, I make a decision. I'm not going to be a broken bird anymore. Risking my heart means it might break again, but God knows it's been broken a hell of a lot already, and if I'm honest with myself, it will probably happen again. I don't want to be so afraid of pain that I push away an opportunity to have a husband, children, and a family when it's right in front of me. I hope I'm ready for whatever happens.

CHAPTER 26

ON THE DAY of the girls' birthday, the clothes arrive on my doorstep. Each outfit is wrapped in a separate gift box. I wasn't expecting the fancy packaging, although I told Ilaria, the woman in Versace's children's division, about the twins. She included a birthday message and a discount coupon. I doubt Justin will be purchasing designer duds for his daughters, so I keep the coupon. Since Christmas is less than three months away and if the girls like the clothes, I will buy more in the future. Of course, that depends on their father and me still being in a relationship. I text Justin on Wednesday after the package arrives.

Annie: Hi. I have presents for the girls. When would be a good time to drop them off?

I hope he'll let me to give them to Eden and Savanna in person and not leave them on the doorstep. I don't hear back from him until after four in the afternoon.

Justin: Can you come around five-thirty?

Annie: See you then

In the gathering darkness that evening, I knock on Justin's front door, and a girl's voice says, "Just a minute."

When the door finally opens, the twins bounce on the sill with Justin behind them. Fancy's muzzle clears the side, her nostrils moving as she sniffs the air. When she realizes it's me, small whines and sounds of excitement emanate from her.

Here is an opportunity to remind these first-time dog owners of what to do when someone familiar comes to the door. "Tell her to sit and be calm before you invite me inside. You girls will need to settle down too if you want her to do the same thing. I'll wait."

The girls have Fancy sit, and Justin smirks at me. "Don't I count? I'm excited to see you, too."

He comes forward on the doorsill, which makes him several inches taller than me. Placing his hand on the nape of my neck, he kisses me—in front of his daughters. When I glance to my right, they stare at us, googly-eyed. They've never seen their father kiss me before. Or maybe they've never seen their father kiss any woman. Fancy has never seen me kiss a man either, which may explain why the twins and their dog all have open-mouthed expressions.

Justin steps back, and I move inside. When I do, Fancy strains against the leash to come closer to me. "Don't let her loose yet," I instruct. "I'm going to ignore her."

"Why?" Eden asks.

"I don't want her excited when she can finally greet me. That's when she'll forget what she's been taught." I glance down at Fancy and point to her feet. "What's that?"

The greyhound's nails are painted a sparkly pink color. The twins raise their hands for me to see their fingernails are sparkly pink, too.

Eden asks, "Do you like it? We gave each other manicures."

Savanna adds, "Daddy said he didn't want us to do his nails, so we did Fancy's instead. She likes them."

"You all look very pretty and girly." I give each of them a gift box. "Happy birthday. These are for you."

We head into the living room, where Fancy can watch us, and I can keep an eye on her. The girls remove the pink polka dot wrapping paper. When the Versace logo on the box is exposed, Justin narrows his eyes at me. The greyhound lies on the rug, so I stand, pet her, and unclip the leash. The twins open the boxes, squeal, and gush upon seeing the clothing. Fancy pokes her nose into the tissue paper and sniffs.

"Thank you, Annie. Thanks so much."

"There are gift cards for Pet Supermarket in the boxes, so you can buy something for Fancy since her birthday is next month."

The girls hold the shirts to their chests and the skirts at their waist. "Let's go try them on."

After they race from the room with the dog on their heels, Justin pockets the gift cards. Picking up the lid, he once again eyes the embossed logo. "Are these the real thing?"

"I called someone I know and had them sent from Milan. Is that okay?"

There's a too-long pause while his face is a vacant mask. "Um, I've never bought the girls designer clothes before."

"Are you afraid they'll expect couture in the future?"

"I just hope they don't expect it for all their clothes."

At that moment, Eden and Savanna return wearing the T-shirts and skirts that fit but are a little large on their slender frames. "How do we look, Annie?"

I tuck Savanna's shirt into the skirt's elastic waistband. "You look great. I wasn't sure what size to get, but I think this works and you'll be able to wear the skirt for a while. Listen, I want to tell you about these clothes." The girls stop twirling and flaring the skirts out around them. Even Fancy sits down and looks at me like I'm about to impart crucial information. "Have you ever heard about Versace?"

They shake their heads.

"Gianni Versace was a famous clothes designer from Italy. After he died, his sister took over the company. I've worked for her in the past and know some people there. When I heard it was your birthday, I called a friend and asked if they had any children's clothes I could buy. They sent me these skirts and T-shirts from their samples." I don't share with them or their father the deep discount I received, which covered most of the shipping costs.

"What Annie is telling you is that these clothes are really special," Justin adds. "You need to be extra careful with them because you won't get more." The girls finger the fabric of their garments with reverent awe. "Hang them up and put on your play clothes."

After they leave, I stand. "Thank you. I enjoyed getting them birthday presents."

"No, I should thank you. Those are really nice gifts you gave them."

I glance at my watch. "Well, I should go so you can have dinner."

"I was going to order pizza, because I'm part of a video conference at seven tonight. I need to be home for that."

"Can we go out and have pizza with Annie?" Eden enters the room and stands behind me.

"Yeah, can we?" Savanna adds, moving to my side and slipping her hand in mine.

I look at Justin, unsure what to say or do.

"Please, pretty please," the girls beg.

He looks at me, raising his eyebrows in question. "It's up to Annie."

"Can we go have pizza with you?" Savanna asks, pressing closer against me.

"Daddy will pay," Eden adds to sweeten the deal.

Fancy also leans her body against the front of my thighs, giving me an idea. "How about we get pizza and take Fancy to a dog park? I bet she would like to run and stretch her legs."

"Can you eat food inside a dog park?" Justin asks.

"No. But there are two parks across the street from each other by the Coral Springs Sportsplex. We'll eat at the one with picnic tables then go across the street and let Fancy loose at the other one for dogs."

The girls and their greyhound prance in happy agreement with the plan.

Justin says, "Well, then let me buy the pizza."

"We'll need to hurry because the dog park closes at eight."

Justin calls in a Domino's order, which is ready for pickup when we arrive. I buy sodas for all of us, to the girls' delight. At the park, we share our pizza crusts with Fancy, who is kept leashed to the picnic table. At seven-thirty, I drive across the street to Dr. Paul's Dog Care Center Dog Park, named after a local veterinarian who unexpectedly passed away. The girls and I watch Fancy race around the near-empty area. When a maintenance worker comes to lock up, we're the last ones to leave. We stop at Cherry Smash, a local ice cream shop just a couple miles from the twins' home. Sitting outside at a metal bistro table, Fancy finishes the remnants of our cones.

I hope Justin doesn't mind his daughters returning home at their bedroom time sweaty, excited, and full of sugar. He's waiting for us but not upset when Eden and Savanna recount topping off our evening with ice cream. "Looks like everyone had a good time. Remember you have school tomorrow. Get in the bathroom and take quick showers."

"Do we have to?" Eden asks.

"If you don't, your beds will stink."

The sisters share a quick glance. "We're okay with that."

"Then let me say it in another way. Thank Annie then go take a shower."

After gushing thank yous and hugs, the girls head to their room and bathroom. As soon as they're gone, Justin pulls me into his arms, and a dam of longing bursts inside me. He does not hug me like he's thanking me for giving his kids birthday presents and taking them out of the house while he has to work. It is nowhere near that polite. Instead, it's an I-can't-believe you're-here and a you-matter-to-me kind of hug. I embrace him tightly with the same degree of feeling, then step backward, thrilled to the core.

His eyes drop to the pulse point in my neck, and his smile is crooked and mischievous. He knows what a hug from him does to me. "I take it you four girls had a good time."

My gaze strays to the greyhound sprawled in her dog bed in the family room. "We did. I hope the twins can fall asleep."

He shrugs one shoulder. "They're entitled to a little sugar and excitement on their birthday, although tomorrow morning will be hell for all of us."

"Do you want me to help get them up and ready for school?"

His eyes stare with wicked intent running through them. "Are you asking to spend the night?"

"No, I was offering to come back here in the morning."

"Thanks, but I got this. If we run late, I can call Cecilia."

I had forgotten their grandmother is two houses away and ready to lend a helping hand at any moment. I bite my lip then decide to say what's on my mind, hoping I don't sound presumptuous. I also don't want to give Justin the mistaken impression that I value his daughters more than him. "The girls and I talked about other things they could do with me, like getting manicures and pedicures, going to a fashion show, and clothes shopping. You know, things you or Cecilia don't do with them."

With quiet wonder, he asks, "You would want to do that?"

"I'd love to. I really enjoy their company. I was thinking they're not too young to get involved with dog rescue. Perhaps they can learn to train Fancy as a therapy dog, or they can volunteer at a local shelter. I'd be happy to help with that too."

"And what about me?"

I laugh. "What about you?"

"Are you dumping me for my kids?"

I squeeze my arms tighter around his neck. "Never! You are a package deal. I just don't want the kids to feel neglected because of how much I want to be their hot dad."

Justin nuzzles the side of my neck. "How hot am I?"

"You're sweet and kind hot; smart and sensible hot; patient and thoughtful hot; strong and gentlemanly hot." I palm the front of his pants.

"And that's without even mentioning what you do to me with this." We kiss with our tongues, exploring, teasing and swirling like crazy. I'm lost in sensation. Everything disappears but his sounds, his scent, his taste, and the feel of him against my body. My brain focuses on his hand on my bottom, his mouth on mine, and his erection pressing against me.

"We're done!"

The cry from the back of the house causes us to spring apart. I run my hand over my short hair, panting from heat and longing. Justin bends forward at the waist with his hands gripping his hips.

"Dad! Are you coming to tuck us in?"

"Hang on. I'll be right there." He straightens and shakes his head. "With kids like mine, who needs a cold shower?"

"Will I see you this weekend?" I pick up my purse from a nearby table.

"Plan on it."

CHAPTER 27

STARTING THAT WEEKEND, Justin, the twins, and I form a schedule. On Saturdays, the girls and I take Fancy to a dog park in the morning followed by lunch. We did experience a scary incident where Fancy zipped out of the gate with a group of exiting dogs. Luckily, she stayed with them until Eden brought her back into the enclosure.

As a result of this, I bought a GPS tracker for her. After attaching the small device to her collar, I instructed Eden and Savanna in its use. "This will locate her anywhere in the world. I bought a twelve-month subscription of monitoring for you, but after that you need to save your Christmas and birthday money to pay for next year. Will you do that?"

"We will." They nod.

I placed the eight-inch charger cable back in the box. "Don't lose this. The battery is good for only a few days then you'll need to charge it, just like you do with your phone. Keep it with Fancy's dog food. Then you'll always remember where it is."

I set up the app on their phone and mine. We practice viewing the live tracking which isn't very exciting since Fancy is sitting beside us. Later, at a dog park, we watch her movements and the activity monitoring.

"This is so cool," Eden coos.

"Remember, this is just a tool to use in case she gets lost. You still need to be careful with her since she can be killed or injured when she's on the loose."

On Saturday nights, the twins are either with Justin's sister or Cecilia. He always leaves my house in the wee hours of Sunday morning to be at home regardless of when his daughters return.

Since getting all my recent foster dogs adopted, Debbie Hale-Brown has not contacted me about providing a temporary home for another greyhound, not have I reached out to her. My excuse is because I'm scheduled to be in Spain for a photo shoot at the end of the month. But, not having heard from the rescue group concerns me. I find it hard to believe that no former racers have been turned over to the organization despite the imminent closing of all dogtracks in Florida by the end of 2020.

The weekend before I leave for Madrid, Frankie is having a birthday party for Jonas, who turns two. She urges me to ask Justin and the girls to come. "Tell them it'll be a casual family gathering. The only kids will be mine and Dale's brother's two girls who are close to the Eden and Savanna's age. They can all play together."

I call Justin. "How would you and the girls like to go to a birthday party for my cousin's two-year-old son this coming Saturday afternoon? There'll be a bunch of people there you don't know, several squealing girls running around, and my family will be delighted to embarrass me in front of you or embarrass you in front of me. It'll be awful. What do you think? Do you want to go?"

"That's next Saturday, huh?"

"You've got plans already, right?"

Justin clears his throat. "Actually, I was going to ask if you wanted to go to my sister's house next Sunday for a surprise birthday party."

"Whose birthday?"

"Mine."

"Yours?" I rub my temple. Didn't he say it was a surprise party?

"And my twin sister's."

"Justin, let me explain a basic rule about surprise parties to you. They work better when the birthday boy and girl don't know about them."

"Yeah, but it's tough to do that nowadays with cell phones and kids who can't keep a secret."

I laugh. "Does you sister know?"

"I'm not sure."

"It's at her house, but she doesn't know there's to be a party there?"

"She and her husband are going away for a romantic weekend. My parents are driving down to take care of their kids. Mom is planning the party, but I assume my brother-in-law is in on the surprise. I've been asked to pick Gretchen and Heath up at the airport and stay for dinner afterward. I knew something was up when I learned lots of other people are coming."

"Did the twins let it slip?"

"The text messages to my mom on their phone did that."

"Ah, I see."

"There will be a bunch of people there that neither you nor I know. My mom will probably rope you into helping in the kitchen, and my dad will talk your ear off about how much he hates living in a retirement community. Oh, and Cecilia will be coming with a friend. I suspect it's someone from her Mah Jongg group. Are you interested in coming to *my* party on Sunday after I go to yours on Saturday or do you have other plans?"

While I dread Justin attending my family event, the anticipation of meeting his parents and sister thrills me. I wonder if he feels the same. "You're sure about this?"

"I want you to meet my family, and I'd like to meet yours. These are the people you grew up with, right?"

"Yes. The party is being given by my cousin, Frankie." I list the family members who will be there, including Dale's divorced brother, Dean, and his daughters. "My cousin, Tony, will be the only one not there. He's stationed with the Air Force in Guam."

"Well, I guess we're on for two family get-togethers this weekend. Just remember to be surprised at mine."

I pick Justin and the girls up in my SUV on Saturday with two dog crates in the rear. Juno and Bella are coming to the party since Aunt Linda will take them home with her and dog-sit while I'm away.

When Eden spots my dogs, she asks, "Annie, can Fancy come too?"

"I'm sorry but I don't have room for another plastic dog crate in the back."

"She can sit with us," Eden suggests.

"We can't do that. It's not safe. If we have an accident, she could get thrown around and badly injured. Did you buy a seatbelt harness for her?"

The girls look at their dad, who says, "No. I guess we should have gotten one."

"Then Fancy will have to stay home today," I say.

Disappointment tugs down the corners of the girls' mouths.

When we arrive at Frankie's house, all her in-laws are there. It has been over a year since I've seen Dale's brother, Dean. He used to look like a lumberjack in a fairy tale with a bushy beard that covered his face like wall-to-wall carpeting. More muscular and taller than his father and brother, I could envision him carrying logs under each arm without throwing out his back. However, after a contentious two-year battle with his ex-wife over money and child custody, he's whittled to a husk of his former self.

I introduce Justin and his daughters to everyone. Within minutes of meeting, Natalie, Eden, Savanna, and Dean's two daughters fling their arms around each other, giggle, squeal, and disappear down the bedroom hallway. My two female greyhounds join the girls like they are all a group of women heading to the ladies' room.

Dale and Dean maneuver Justin to a cooler full of ice and beer. Frankie's mother-in-law sits at the kitchen island, which is covered with chips, dip, a platter of veggies, and various other finger foods. Dawn grazes while her husband, Roger, claims the recliner in the family room and channel surfs the big screen TV.

With everyone occupied, Frankie pulls me into her bedroom with the birthday boy, Jonas, planted on her hip. "Justin's hot and well-built. I can see why you're attracted to him. I would lick that if I was still single."

"Frankie!" I glance over my shoulder to make sure no one overheard her.

"What? You're right. He's very doable. Yeah, he shaves his head because he's going bald, but the look works on him. The twins are darling too with all that red hair and freckles. We better get back out there before Dale finds out Justin's an engineer and asks him to soup up our riding lawn mower."

When I approach the knot of men around the beer cooler, Justin says to Dean and Dale, "When the girls were small, I would put them in a double stroller and run at night."

"On purpose?" Frankie's husband asks.

"Well, I couldn't always get to the gym, and it helped put them to sleep. Besides, jogging in the evening relaxed me."

Dale drains his beer. "The only reason I would run at night is if zombies were chasing me."

Just as I am about to drag Justin away from the never-intentionally-exercise group, the front door opens. Aunt Linda walks in followed by Uncle Milo. I halt in walking toward them.

My father enters the house, looking around with an aloof and arrogant expression.

CHAPTER 28

WHAT IS DENNIS doing here? Every hair on my body stands on end, signaling a possible threat. Maybe my panic shows in my clenched jaw, darting eye movements, or the tension in my shoulders. Whatever it is, Dennis picks up on it, and in a few long, purposeful steps, he's in front of me, looming to his full height.

In a loud, jovial voice, he says, "Annemarie, it's so good to see you again." He bends forward, and it appears he's kissing my cheek, but instead, he whispers, "Stop looking at me like I'm shit on your shoe."

His breath has the nasty botanical smell of gin. I step back, making no false gesture of physical affection. "What a surprise to see you here."

Aunt Linda wraps an arm around my waist and smiles, but her eyes are pinched at the corners. "We were about to leave the house when Denny showed up. You didn't tell us his wife died and he's moving back to the area."

"I told Frankie."

"Well, the least we could do is invite him to come with us to a family celebration and hope it'll take his mind off his grief."

I stop myself from saying aloud that a couple of G and T's beat us to it.

"Is this your Aunt Linda and Uncle Milo?" Justin stands on my other side, clueless to the drama.

In his deep, mellow voice, which often quiets conversations around him, Dennis says, "The lovely lady is indeed her Aunt Linda, but I am Annemarie's *father*, Dennis Warden. And you are?"

He stares at my aristocratic father like he's a mangy stray in need of a flea bath. "I'm Justin Stabler. Annie has told me all about you."

Dennis appears taken aback by the coolness of Justin's tone since strangers are usually somewhat star-struck upon first meeting him. I smile in shameful satisfaction and fall slightly in love.

Uncle Milo joins our awkward quartet and extends his hand. "Hello, there. I'm Annie's Uncle Milo. My daughter tells me that you're her new boyfriend. It's nice to meet you."

Justin gives him a warm handshake. "I'm happy to meet you too, sir. She's told me a lot of wonderful things about you and your wife."

I peek at my father. He is an expert in bland smiles and rigid self-control, but I detect tiny cracks in the façade. His lack of warmth and paternal absenteeism may not matter to society sycophants, but here, among family and friends, he *is* barely one step above shit on my shoe.

Dennis claps Milo on the shoulder. "Where can a man get a drink around here?"

My uncle flashes him a tight smile. "I'll show you where they usually put the cooler."

My father's eyes widen at the mention of camping equipment instead of a fully stocked bar staffed by a mixologist. Still, he follows Uncle Milo out of the foyer.

After they leave, my aunt smiles at Justin. "I'm so glad you could come. Frankie insisted Annie invite you. Are your daughters here?"

"They disappeared with Dean's girls and Natalie. I think they're in a bedroom somewhere."

"I'll go find them." Linda bites her lip. "I'm sorry, Annie, about surprising you with Denny. When he found out you were going to be here today, he asked if he could come. I didn't feel comfortable saying, 'No, your daughter doesn't want to see you.'"

I hug my aunt. "That's okay. It looks like he's going to be out of his element and more uncomfortable this afternoon than I am."

"Well, it's about time." She squeezes my arm and leaves.

I take Justin's hand and lead him to Frankie and Dale's bedroom. At the foot of their king-sized bed, I turn, wrap my arms around his neck, and kiss him. "Thank you."

"For what?"

"For not treating my father like he's royalty."

"I remember you telling me about him and he recently made you cry. He's lucky I'm at least civil to him."

"You don't think I'm like my dad, do you?"

Justin kisses me. "No, you're way prettier." He puts his hands on my cheeks and kisses me again. "And sweeter." He looks deep into my eyes. "And more wonderful in every way possible."

I hug him close while battling tears. After a minute, we part, and Justin says, "Ready to rejoin the party?"

I nod.

The men are in the family room, occupying every seat, including the raised hearth of the never-used fireplace. Everyone has a beer except Dennis, who is drinking a glass of wine.

Dale says to his father, "C'mon, Dad, the only time you killed a deer was with a Ford station wagon."

Roger harrumphs and raises the footrest of the recliner. "Maybe so, but I used to go hunting with my father when we lived in Pennsylvania."

Dean laughs. "Grandpa told us he took you duck hunting, but it was only a couple of times because you hated getting up at the crack of dawn and freezing your ass off."

The doorbell rings, and Frankie calls from the kitchen, "Dale, the pizzas are here. Everybody else head to the patio."

Aunt Linda emerges from the back hall with Jonas, the five little girls, and my two greyhounds. Roger, Dean, and Dennis stand. Instead of heading outside, my father detours to the kitchen counter and tops off his glass of Chianti. Juno and Bella come to my side, waiting for me to signal them to stay in the house or go outside. Dale passes us with a stack of pizza boxes in his arms. Dennis spots my dogs and approaches.

"Are these two yours, Annemarie?" His speech now has the sonorous over-deliberation of a practiced drunk.

"Yes."

He runs one hand down Juno's back. "This one has nice balance."

Eden and Savanna grab their father's hands. "Are you coming, Daddy?"

Dennis raises one eyebrow. "These are your children, Justin?"

"Yes. Eden and Savanna, this is Annie's father. Say hello to Mr. Warden."

"Hello," Savanna says in a shy voice.

"Hello, Mr. Warden." Eden's eyes fix on the tall man. "Why didn't you take care of Annie when she was growing up? Our mommy died too, but Daddy didn't give us to somebody else."

CHAPTER 29

OH, MY GOD. I love her!

Dennis inhales sharply, then scrutinizes the little girl with his usual imperious expression. "I don't think that is any of your business, young lady."

"Yes, it is. Annie is our friend, and it makes her sad that her mommy died, and her daddy left her alone."

Frankie pops her head into the house. "Are you guys coming?"

Dennis does not answer Eden but heads out to the patio. The birthday lunch consists of three distinct groups of conversation. There is a steady stream of mindless chatter from all the kids except little Jonas. The women talk about domestic issues while I smile and nod. The men, except for my father, discuss sports and their jobs.

Until recently, I had been a cliché at these family gatherings being that I was the only unmarried woman in the group. The one dumped by her ex-husband for a new and improved model. The one still dealing with daddy issues. For these reasons, I kept myself emotionally hollow to avoid the pain of heartbreak, while still hoping for my father's attention to fill the empty places inside. Barbara once told me he showed their friends some of my magazine photos that he downloaded to his phone. But he never shared his approval and pride with me. In fact, the tables might now be turned. He may need me and the rest of the family to fill the hole in *his* life.

Natalie wails, "Not that one, Mommy! I want the same size!"

Frankie only ordered one cheese pizza for the kids, and the last slice is significantly smaller than the others. "Can someone explain to me why they can't cut equal pieces? Are they deliberately trying to ruin every family dinner?"

Natalie's wails become louder as her mother tries to appease her with a bigger slice from another pie with the pepperoni removed. Dennis keeps refilling his wine glass from a bottle on the table. Has he ever eaten takeout pizza and consumed grocery store wine with squalling children and people whose annual salary is less than what his friends pay for a car.

By the time the pizza is finished, the candles blown out, and the cake cut, my father has crossed the line into drunkenness. He stumbles into Milo when rising from his chair. "Sorry. Caught my foot."

Foot, my ass. The lone slice of pizza he put on his plate is still there, minus only one bite. However, the wine bottle closest to him is empty. He sways from side to side as he moves toward the swimming pool. Thank goodness, the kiddie gate surrounds it, preventing him or any of the children from falling into the water.

Savanna pulls on my arm, and in a loud stage whisper, asks, "What's wrong with Mr. Warden?"

What do I to say? Has she ever seen someone who has had too much to drink?

Before I can speak, Eden answers, "He's drunk."

Should I try to coax Dennis into the house to lie down? Considering his mood and his feelings toward me, pushing him would likely result in the obnoxious and granite stubbornness of the inebriated. He slowly walks to the screen door and stands with his hands braced on the pool enclosure, facing the backyard and the lake beyond it.

"It's time for Jonas to open his presents," Aunt Linda trills in a saccharine falsetto. "Let's get everything put inside. C'mon, girls, you can help."

While everyone carries some piece of detritus from the meal into the house, my father unlatches the pool enclosure door and steps outside. Should I stay outside and watch him in case he falls into the lake?

Aunt Linda moves next to me and lays her head on my arm. "Don't worry about Denny. People like him always land on their feet. It's everyone else who suffers. I issued the invitation because I thought with his wife passing, he might want to be a part of our family again."

"You're too kind and generous for an asshole like him. But I love you for trying."

I check on my father from various doors and windows while Jonas opens his gifts. When the cleanup begins, Dennis reenters the house and plops down on the living room sofa. With his head back and mouth open, he falls into a stupor with the erratic snores of an asthmatic greyhound.

Dale empties the garbage, and Uncle Milo follows him out to the garage. Dean and Justin begin a Nintendo game on the Wii console in the family room. Roger settles himself on the recliner, and Jonas sits on the floor with several of his birthday presents. The girls return to Natalie's bedroom, where their high-pitched voices sound like they're all speaking at the same time. Dawn, Linda, and Frankie wash glasses and utensils. I leash Juno and Bella for a walk around the block.

Upon my return, Frankie's voice is louder than usual. "Where's Jonas? Has anyone seen him?"

Roger says, "He was here playing with his toys a few minutes ago."

"Maybe he's with the girls. I'll check." Linda heads down the hall.

Dale walks toward the main bedroom. "He might have climbed onto our bed to take a nap."

Dean and Justin pause their game, unsure what to do. But they do know that playing Nintendo while everyone else searches is not an option. People start calling the little boy's name. The tension mounts when no one can locate Jonas.

"Check under furniture and in closets," Frankie instructs. "When he's tired, he'll crawl somewhere and fall asleep."

Dennis continues to slumber on the sofa, and Uncle Milo checks behind it. Despite knowing how cautious Frankie is about pool safety, I go outside to the patio. The kiddie gate is undisturbed, and only the automatic pool cleaner moves in the crystal blue water with chugging sounds. After looking around the deck, I turn to go inside when my eye catches on the door leading out here from the pool bath. It is slightly ajar.

With a ragged breath, I shudder and recall Dennis opening the screen door to the backyard. I race to it and find that, not only is it not locked, but it isn't latched either. I push it wide open and run down the sloping lawn. Without thinking, I splash into the lake with my sandals and long sundress, calling for Jonas, sweeping the water with my arms and feet. After slogging through the muddy bottom for the width of the yard, I raise my head and look farther along the shoreline to the neighboring property. My heart stops when I spot a neon-yellow plastic kayak tied to a stake and floating partially in the water.

The toddler is in chest-deep water next to the boat. Strings of brown and green algae hang off his wet head.

"Jonas!" I scream and run through the muddy shallows as fast as I can.

He gives me a toothy grin and holds up his pudgy little hands. Clingy strands of vegetation coat his fingers. "'Ee."

I half-sit, half-fall beside him, my white eyelet dress floating around us like a shroud. Smiling through the tears flooding my eyes, I pick the stubborn algae from his fingers. "I see, you silly boy."

He claps his hands to reward my efforts. "Keen."

"Yes, you're clean now. Except for this." I smooth my hand over his dark hair to dislodge more wet strands and hold out my arms. He throws his sturdy thirty-pound, wet toddler body at me. Struggling to my feet, I heft him onto my hip.

Frankie and Dale's neighbor has a chain link fence and hedge along his property line down to the water, so I slosh through the shallows to reach my cousin's yard. I struggle partway up the low, grassy slope in my dripping dress and slippery sandals, hefting a sopping Jonas. Dale bellows a panicked shout and runs toward us from the side yard. He stays upright until he is five feet away. Like a runner stealing second base, his feet suddenly slide ahead of his torso. He skids past us into the lake and disappears under the water.

Jonas laughs and points his index finger. "Dada."

I nod. "That's your daddy all right."

Dale emerges wetter and muddier than either Jonas or me. He lifts his son from my arms and peppers his face with kisses. Not all the wetness running down his cheeks is from the lake.

"Thank you, Annie. Thank you for saving him."

"It's more like I found him rather than saved him. He was sitting in the water by your neighbor's kayak."

Dale swings a meaty arm around my shoulders, pulls me tight against his chest, and kisses my head. "But you found him before something bad happened. Thank you."

Like swamp creatures, we climb the rest of the way up the sloped lawn, with dripping clothes. Our shoes make squelching, fart sounds, which makes Jonas laugh. By the time we are near the pool enclosure, people spill out of the house.

Frankie pushes her way through them to get to us first. "Oh, my God! Oh, my God!"

Aunt Linda rushes forward with a beach towel. Instead of wrapping it around her grandson, she throws it over my shoulders with a pointed look at my chest. Perfectly revealed through the thin fabric of my bodice are the dark circles of my nipples. My wet skin and bikini panties are outlined against the tissue paper thinless of my soaked sundress. Justin shoulders his way to my side, puts his arm around me, and ushers me across the patio.

I point to the pool bath. "Let me go in there to dry off. Will you ask Aunt Linda or Frankie if they can find me something to wear?"

Thirty minutes later, Jonas is bathed and napping. Dale is clean and dressed in fresh clothing. I'm wearing one of my cousin's T-shirts, a pair of leggings, and Dale's flip-flops, which are closer in size to my feet than any shoes Frankie owns. Roger, Dawn, Dean, and his children have departed. Although no one points the finger at Dennis for leaving the screen door unlatched and unlocked, I'm sure my aunt will tear him a new one on the drive back to their house. I can see the anger bubbling beneath the surface with her noisy breaths, flinty eyes, and flaring nostrils. Dennis appears clueless to the angry grandmother landslide he is about to be hit with.

After loading the dog crates, a carton of supplies, and my two greyhounds into the back of Milo's van, I say to Linda, "I give you permission to let him have it. Just don't scare the dogs, okay?"

She nods, still too angry to speak, and climbs inside. Dennis is pale and snarly with purple shadows under his eyes and likely in the initial throes of a hangover. He gives me a half-hearted wave when I icily say goodbye to him.

I whisper to Uncle Milo before he slides behind the steering wheel. "Call me if you need bail money."

Frankie hugs, kisses, and thanks me again. While Justin gets the girls strapped into the backseat of my SUV, my cousin stands in front of me with her face set, her eyes red-rimmed from crying, but her mouth firm. "I owe you, Annie."

"No, you don't. It was pure luck that I found him first."

"I'm sorry, but I'm not buying that. You were the one fated to save my baby."

"Well, I'm glad the little guy will be fine. This is a story we can tell every year on his birthday to embarrass him." I speak in a light-hearted tone to relieve some of the anguish still darkening Frankie's coffee-colored eyes.

She grips my elbow. "I mean it about owing you. Whenever you're ready, I'm in."

My heart thumps, and my hands tremble. "Really? What about Dale?"

"We talked while Mom cleaned up Jonas. He's onboard too."

"You're sure?"

"We both are. Saving our son today was the sign we needed."

CHAPTER 30

FOUR YEARS AGO, I used my divorce settlement to fund oocyte cryopreservation or freezing of my eggs. Although I no longer have a uterus, I have two intact ovaries. When I had my hysterectomy, harvesting my eggs was not given as an option. At the time, motherhood was the farthest thing from my seventeen-year-old mind.

I asked the doctor about having a child in the future, and he shook his head. "That won't be possible, but you can always adopt one. There are many children out there who need a loving parent."

I knew about all greyhounds literally dying for a home after their racing careers ended. That day, I vowed to adopt them as my children. In my immature naiveté, I also thought adopting a motherless human child would be as easy as rescuing a homeless dog. Later, I learned about the long and challenging process when I was overwhelmed with a desire for a child.

After hitting me with the bombshell of his impending fatherhood, I argued with Thierry about staying married and doing surrogacy to have our own baby. However, undergoing the IVF procedure did not interest him when he had a son due in a few months. Or maybe he did not want *me* to be the mother of his child. So, I negotiated a hefty settlement in exchange for the quickie divorce and began the process of IVF.

My follicle count, or ovarian volume, was checked and judged likely for a successful retrieval. I underwent an ultrasound to determine the condition and location of my ovaries, as they sometimes move after a hysterectomy. After getting the green light, my hormone levels were monitored to establish when egg stimulation and retrieval could be scheduled.

On the day of the procedure, Aunt Linda drove me to the clinic. A nurse administered intravenous sedation and pain medication. The entire process took less than thirty minutes. The doctor extracted a dozen viable eggs. These were handed off to an embryologist for freezing. Just to be sure, I underwent a second procedure, and had my eggs frozen at a different facility in another state. I wanted an extra measure of security by having multiple embryos ready when I was.

I would find a man who will agree to father my child in my ideal plan. We would marry or only co-parent. Lately, I have pictured Justin as that man. The day the condom broke, and he panicked about a possible impregnation, was an awakening for me. But I've been reluctant to bring up the subject with him. The lizard part of my brain that holds onto every fear and worry keeps poking me to ask him. If he says he doesn't want more children, every minute I spend with him is a delay in finding a man who will be a caring father to my frozen embryos. I set my thirty-fifth birthday as the deadline to find that remarkable man or use an anonymous sperm donor.

My mind is still reeling from Frankie's surrogacy declaration when Justin and the girls pick me up at my house the following afternoon. In the car are his sister, Gretchen, and her husband, Heath. They had flown to the Bahamas and stayed at the Atlantis Resort on Paradise Island for a three-day holiday.

Gretchen is a pretty, blond woman who looks like someone cast for the role of a kindergarten teacher or an RN, which happens to be her profession. Her weekend vacation was mostly spent outside because her nose and cheeks are lightly sunburned. She has an infectious grin that scrunches her green eyes nearly shut. Justin's brother-in-law, Heath, has black hair that is thick and messy and brushes the tops of his ears. His face is narrow, and his jaw sharp. He wears tortoiseshell glasses with large lenses that dwarf his face. I'm unable to determine Gretchen's or Heath's height since both are seated in the backseat when I'm introduced. Eden and Savanna are squeezed together between them and share the middle seatbelt.

I feel a bit awkward taking the spacious front seat. "I should have driven myself."

"It's okay," Gretchen says. "Heath moved back here with us girls when we got to your house, and we don't have far to go."

I was hired for a photo shoot at the Atlantis Resort about ten years ago and recall the tropical destination well. I twist to face the rear seat. "Did you guys try the water slide that looks like a Mayan temple?"

Gretchen says, "Heath went down it a couple times. I chickened out."

"Do they still have sharks swimming around the tube at the bottom?"

Gretchen shudders. "That's why I passed on it."

"C'mon, honey," her husband chides. "There were little kids going through it. You were safe."

"No, thank you."

No cars are parked on the street in their neighborhood, only in the neighbors' driveways. Justin and Heath retrieve wheeled suitcases from the BMW's trunk. I check my handbag, making sure I have the two presents. Inside are wireless charging docks for the birthday brother and sister. Eden and Savanna each grab one of my hands.

Gretchen approaches the front door.

Her husband steps aside and extends his hand. "After you, Justin."

Eden and Savanna giggle. As soon as Justin and Gretchen enter the house, there is a loud chorus of happy birthdays.

Eden grins up at me. "It's a surprise party for daddy and Aunt G."

"It is?" I respond with wide-eyed innocence. "Did you know about it?"

The two redheads nod and Savanna says, "Nana told us we had to keep it a secret."

We wait to enter the house as a contingent of people surround Justin and his sister a few feet inside the door. Finally, the girls and I step inside. An older woman skirts around the congestion and approaches. She is petite with a big smile and head full of greying brown hair. This must be Justin's mother, who retired as a high school principal. I close the door behind me.

"Hi, Nana!" the twins call out loudly to be heard above the other voices filling the space.

"Look how big you girls are getting. Well, you just had a birthday too." After hugging her granddaughters, the woman straightens with a pleasant smile. When her head tilts back to look at my face, she struggles to not show surprise. She wasn't expecting her son's new girlfriend to be so tall. "Hi, I'm Estelle. You must be Annie. It's so nice to meet you."

"Thank you for the invitation. I wasn't expecting a surprise party."

"I hope you don't mind it's not going to be a quiet family dinner tonight."

"Not at all. Is there anything I can do?" I remember Justin's warning about his mother roping me into kitchen duty.

The foyer and living room begin to empty as people move to the patio and other rooms of the house. Estelle takes my hand and leads me past the dining room to the kitchen. "Do you know Cecilia, Justin's mother-in-law?"

"Yes."

"She said the two of you would help me set up the appetizer trays, but she's not here yet. Do you mind getting started without her?"

"Not at all. Just don't ask me to cook anything to put on them."

"No. No. It's all prepared. If you could lay the appetizers out to look pretty that would be great."

Estelle has Alexa notify her when the crab puffs need to come out of the oven, when the pastry crust of pigs in a blanket is baked to perfection, and when the air fryer needs to be refilled with more mozzarella sticks. She has the ruthless time management of an educator who spent decades attuned to bells signaling the start and end of the school day and changing classes.

Estelle delights in having me reach items on high shelves. Her every move in the kitchen is calculated, and she delegates tasks with gentle firmness and the right amount of instructions. She makes the most of our private time together by delicately asking questions, but I don't feel like I'm being interrogated or judged by my boyfriend's mother.

Different children run in and out of the room as we work, snatching up the finger foods and creating blank spaces on the trays I fill. The ever-changing groups of mischief-makers run and chase each other with unsupervised abandon, making it clear their parents are busy with the party.

"There!" Estelle announces at last. "Let's get everything on the tables outside. This should hold the hungry horde until the rest of the food arrives."

She had ordered platters from Ethos, a nearby Greek restaurant, to be delivered in an hour. Although Estelle kept me busy in the kitchen, I wondered why Justin never came to find out where I was. We exit through open sliding doors to a large patio. I look for him, but he is not in sight. Estelle and I deposit the platters on folding tables lining one wall. We struggle to work our way back through the throng of hungry partygoers who descend upon the food.

Estelle hugs me after one more trip with the last of the appetizers. "Thank you for your help. Don't worry about dinner setup or cleaning. I've got that handled with other volunteers. Get yourself a drink and go mingle."

On the patio is a table with plastic cups and napkins. Soft drinks and bottles of water nestle in a giant vat of ice. An older man resembling Justin is behind a portable bar, handing out beer, pouring wine, and mixing drinks. The one major difference between this man and his son is that he doesn't shave his head. A corona of curly gray hair circles the back of his scalp from ear to ear.

When I sidle up to the counter, he glances up and smiles. "You must be Annie."

"How did you know?"

"My son told me to look for the most beautiful woman to grace the inside of a fashion magazine."

I smooth my hands down the wide legs of the black Donna Karan jumpsuit I donned today. I took special care with my appearance, including wearing more makeup than usual. "Justin goes a little overboard with his compliments."

His father's green eyes sparkle. "No, he doesn't. I agree with him. By the way, my name is Tom. What can I get you to drink?"

"White wine." I turn away slightly and glance around the patio. "Have you seen Justin? I was helping Estelle in the kitchen."

Tom hands me a filled plastic flute and rises on his toes. "He was here not too long ago, but I don't see him now. Maybe he's out front with some of his buddies from high school who Estelle invited."

I raise my wine in salute. "Thanks. It's wonderful to meet you. I'll walk around and see if I can find him."

I stroll along the length of the patio, smiling and nodding to strangers. Gretchen is surrounded by several women who titter like schoolgirls.

I reenter the house, and someone calls out. "Annie! Over here."

Dammit! I plaster on a smile and head toward the family room. "Hello."

Cecilia pats the sofa cushion beside her. "Have a seat."

I hesitate. "I'm looking for Justin. Have you seen him?"

The twins' grandmother wears a white top with embroidery in a matching design to her polyester pants and sensible sandals that could be used for hiking. She brushes away a lock of flyaway grayish-red hair that dances across her cheek. Cecilia has a good figure and attractive features. I can't understand why she chooses to dress so matronly. Justin said his mother-in-law is only in her late fifties. Is she resigned to looking like a traditional grandmother since her daughter's death?

Cecilia smiles at me like someone demanded it of her. "Spare me just a few minutes. We haven't seen each other since you relented and gave Eden and Savanna the dog. You can see now that your *concerns* were groundless."

Whoa. Is Cecilia conveniently forgetting that I canceled the adoption because of her contentiousness with Justin? With great reluctance, I sit beside her but on the cushion's front edge to aid in my quick getaway when needed.

And I do not doubt that I will. Cecilia makes me bite my tongue so often it won't take long for a deep groove to form in it.

"It is a good home for Fancy now that *everyone* is getting along." Justin said his mother-in-law was bringing a female acquaintance to the party. Why isn't she sitting here keeping Cecilia company? "I was told you were bringing a friend. Where is she?"

Cecilia stares over my shoulder with a fixed expression. I turn my head, but no one is there.

"She went to use the bathroom." Cecilia latches onto my free hand as if to hold me in place. "Stay here until she returns. The twins have been telling me about the adventures they've been having with you."

"We only eat fast food outside and visit dog parks with Fancy. I wouldn't call those *adventures.*"

"They say you'll be helping them train Fancy to be a therapy dog."

"No. I won't be training her or them. There's a program that does that. I just volunteered to take them."

"How do you know if Fancy will work out as a therapy dog?"

"I don't. Not until she successfully completes an AKC Canine Good Citizen Test. Although, I'm sure she'll pass since it assesses manners every dog should have. And she does."

Cecilia rubs her forehead as if confused by what I said. "What kind of *manners* are you talking about?"

"Things like coming when called, sitting, laying down, staying, and being friendly with unknown people and other dogs. After she demonstrates these behaviors, she and the girls will prepare for therapy dog training."

"And they allow young children do this?"

"There's no minimum age for handlers who pass the test."

"The girls have to be tested too?" Cecilia's eyes widen as if I'm suggesting they train to fight forest fires.

"Yes. But after completing the program they'll have to be accompanied by an adult on visitations until they're eighteen years old. I know they'll be wonderful dog handlers, especially with children in hospitals and schools, or elderly folks in nursing homes. Since they need service hours to graduate from high school, volunteering with Fancy would give them an advantage on college admission applications. Not many children start community service while they're still in elementary school."

"Well, when you put it like that..." Cecilia shrugs one shoulder. "Still, the dog might not be suitable, and the girls may find they don't like being around children with issues and old people."

What a negative, judgmental pain-in-the-ass Cecilia is. "Anything's possible. I really need to find Justin now."

I half-rise from the sofa, disengaging my hand. But Cecilia grabs my arm throwing me slightly off-balance. Some wine sloshes out of the glass and onto my pants leg.

"No, don't go yet," she commands.

I slip from her grasp and stand. "I need to get something to eat before this wine goes to my head. Would you like me to bring you back a plate of appetizers?"

She spits out, "I'm not helpless, you know. If I want something to eat, I can get it. I can also do anything with my grandchildren they want to do."

A toddler drunkenly runs into the room, chased by a young woman who scoops him up and then spins him in a circle. "Where do you think you're going buddy-boy? It's time for a poopy diaper change."

When the mother sees us, she apologizes and hustles away. I follow her and the squirming child from the room.

Behind me, Cecilia says, "Justin went into one of the bedrooms across from the living room."

Why didn't she tell me that before?

A hallway runs from front to back on the other side of the house. An open door on the right end shows an empty bathroom. A closed metal door at the other end likely leads to the garage. Three doors line the middle of the wall; one fully open, one slightly ajar, and one tightly shut.

I peek into the first room where two boys are vroom-vrooming with dozens of Matchbox cars on a rug imprinted with roads, intersections, and buildings. Then I push the partially open door to the next room. Several girls, including Eden and Savanna, play with dolls and a large dollhouse on a low table.

Eden looks up. "Hi, Annie, do you wanna play?"

"Um, I would, but I'm looking for your dad. Do you know where he is?"

She shakes her head and returns to dressing the baby doll in her lap.

Behind the door of the last room, I hear the low murmur of adult voices. I lightly tap on the wood.

Justin calls out, "Who is it?"

"It's Annie." I crack the door open. "Can I come in?"

Justin leans his bottom against the top of a large wooden desk, his hands wrapped around the beveled edge. Debbie Hale-Brown has her arms wrapped around his neck and her mouth on his.

CHAPTER 31

JUSTIN JERKS UPRIGHT, pulling Debbie's arms off him. His eyes widen in guilty panic. Then he steps sideways, his gaze never leaving my face. "It's not what you think, Annie. Believe me."

He reaches my side and places a firm hand on my elbow. There's a smear of Debbie's hot pink lipstick on his upper lip. His fingers tighten around my arm. Either he is trying to hold me in place or conveying the earnestness of his denial.

I blink and turn my attention to Debbie. A giant smirk stretches her mouth. For some strange reason, Justin's steady touch calms me in this awful and awkward situation. I say nothing, waiting for biblical pain to flood my body. Instead, kaleidoscopic images click into place to form a complete geometric picture.

I direct my words to Debbie. "Did you plan this?"

She tosses an extension lock of blond hair over her shoulder. "Of course not. These things just happen sometimes."

"Bullshit!" Justin's hand releases on my arm and slides around my waist, but I don't look at him. "I'll tell you what I think happened here. First, Cecilia invited you to this party. Then she agreed to keep me occupied, so you could give Justin some cooked-up story, probably about a problem with Fancy's adoption paperwork."

Debbie's smug expression deserts her. She crosses her arms over her chest and works to maintain her fading smile.

Justin's shoulder brushes mine, but I maintain eye contact with Debbie. "While Cecilia holds me hostage in another room, you set this little scenario in motion. When I'm finally able to get away from her, she directs me to door number three. After I knock and identify myself, you throw yourself at Justin and kiss him. How am I doing so far?"

Debbie shakes her head. "You're way off base."

"I understand why you agreed to participate in the charade, but the big question is why did Cecilia engineer it in the first place." This time I turn to face Justin. "You mentioned a while back that she was afraid her granddaughters would prefer me to her. I wonder if the time I've been spending with them on Saturdays has her worried, and she decided to try and break us up."

Justin scratches at his whiskered jaw. "I can't believe she would do that."

I'm shocked he hasn't worked it out for himself. After all, he's the one who told me Cecilia had been threatened by *his* relationship with Lucy and now mine with the girls. "Think about it, Justin. She wants you to be with someone like Debbie who isn't interested in your children, and who they don't particularly like. With you involved in that kind of relationship, Cecilia will end up being the stronger mother figure for the girls."

"She's right."

Standing in the hallway behind us is his mother, Estelle.

Justin gapes at her. "Mom?"

"It's no surprise Cecilia is jealous of Annie. The same thing happened with me."

"It did?"

Estelle gives him a stiff nod. "Sure, she spent more time with the girls because I was working, and she wasn't. But she also knew when there were school holidays, and they could visit with me and your father. Those were always the times she enrolled them in classes or programs they couldn't miss.

At the most, we were able to get them overnight, or on a weekend, two or three times a year."

"Why didn't you say anything?"

"I didn't want to create more stress in your life. Cecilia lived so close to you while we were all the way down in Fort Lauderdale. As a single parent with two toddlers, you were dependent on her, but I could see what she was doing. She doesn't like to share. I believe what Annie says is true."

"What's going on?" Justin's sister, Gretchen, crowds into the hallway behind her mother. "Is there a problem?" She leans sideways to look past her mother and brother at Debbie. "Who are you?"

Justin's voice is clipped and brisk. "She's someone from the greyhound rescue group who dropped off some paperwork, but she's leaving now."

Gretchen's sharp green eyes, so much like her twin's, move from the lipstick smear on her brother's upper lip to Debbie's hot pink mouth. Half-smiling, I wipe off the evidence with my thumb.

Debbie picks up a folder off the desk, loops a knockoff Louis Vuitton purse over her shoulder, and avoids eye contact with anyone. "Excuse me."

We part like the Red Sea, allowing her to exit between us.

Gretchen looks at her mother, Justin, and me. "I expect one of you to fill me in later, but right now I came to tell you the Greek food has been delivered. Mom, where do you want to put it?"

When Gretchen and Estelle leave, Justin tugs me farther into the office and shuts the door. One of his hands cups my head as the other winds tighter around my waist. We stand nose to nose, stomach to stomach, and toe to toe.

"Kiss the taste of that woman off me," he murmurs. "Please."

I raise my index finger, warding off his mouth from mine. "First, tell me you weren't kissing her back."

"I wasn't kissing *her* at all."

"Tell me she isn't your other girlfriend."

"She's nothing to me. You are my *only* girlfriend."

"Tell me you believe what I said about Cecilia."

Time grinds to a halt as his eyes shift sideways. "I'm having a hard time with that."

I drop my arms from around his shoulders and step back. "You don't believe either me or your mother?"

"Cecilia is just not that smart or devious. Yes, she wants to be a big part of Eden and Savanna's lives, but she wouldn't deliberately throw another woman at me."

"Then how did Debbie know to show up here?"

He rubs his face like he wants to scrape off any lingering skin cells not belonging to him. "She went by my house, but no one was home. Cecilia was pulling out of her drive, and Debbie stopped her. Her story is that she spilled a drink on the original paperwork and needed it re-signed, so Cecilia offered to show her the way here. Cecilia was just trying to be helpful but fell for that woman's lies."

"Well, Debbie wasn't involved in making sure the twins were always tied up during the times your mother had school vacation."

He sighs. "I know that's what Mom thinks, but it's just not true. The girls were premature and involved in a lot of different therapy programs as babies. Cecilia handled most of the appointments while Lucy and I worked. They started preschool at age four and the only time they could do things like dance classes, gymnastics, and swimming lessons was on weekends and during the summer."

"Then why have they been able to do things with me on Saturdays?"

"We decided at the start of this school year to focus on getting a dog, so they didn't sign up for any classes. My parents moved to The Villages after Mom retired, and they're too far away for weekend or overnight visits. But now that I know how they feel, I'll make sure during Christmas or next summer that Eden and Savanna spend more time with them."

All his explanations are reasonable. Except in my heart, I'm certain Cecilia is behind the curtain, like the Wizard of Oz, manipulating people to her advantage. Why can't he see it? He's the one who warned me about her.

"Annie?"

I put a lazy hand on the back of Justin's neck and kiss him. When our lips meet, the concerns in my head disappear. His whiskered face feels rough, but his lips are velvety soft. In the past, it was always easy for me to stop kissing someone, even Thierry, but it isn't like that with Justin. He's magnetic, making it difficult for me to pull my lips away, and addictive, making me want more. When he's not kissing me, I'm like a junkie looking for my next hit from him.

A gentle tapping sounds on the closed door. It cracks open, and Gretchen says, "Annie? Justin? Dinner's ready. You can bang the living daylights out of each other after we blow out the candles."

CHAPTER 32

ON MONDAY, I catch a non-stop flight from Fort Lauderdale to Spain shortly before noon. The twelve-hour ride will deposit me in Madrid on the morning of the following day. When I scheduled the trip months earlier, I tacked on a couple extra days for sightseeing as well as an upgrade to a first-class seat. Thierry taught me that spending the extra money on international flights is worth every penny.

My plan for the additional time is to visit the Prado art museum to see its collection of masterpieces by Renaissance and Baroque masters, like Bosch's Garden of Earthly Delights and the vast number of Goya's artwork. Also on my list of must-sees is the Royal Palace of King Philip V, with more paintings by Goya, Caravaggio, and Velazquez.

After the *Debbie Incident*, I'm still unsettled by Justin's failure to see Cecilia's role in it. When we left the office and rejoined the partygoers scattered among tables on the screened patio, Cecilia sat with perfect posture, socializing with guests seated around her. She was close enough for me to overhear her chattiness with a slight hint of bitchiness. She acted like there had been no drama created by her machinations of Debbie, Justin, and me. During the meal, a strange sensation burned in my chest. I pushed the delicious falafel, Greek salad, and moussaka around my plate. I had no appetite.

Justin whispered in my ear, "Don't you like Greek food?"

"I love it, but I think something disagreed with me."

Since then, I've been asking myself if I'm falling for a different kind of Mr. Wrong. One who will not necessarily cheat on me, but in a confrontation, he'll take another woman's side over mine. Is the Debbie debacle another conflict with Cecilia in which I limp away battle-scarred and scared? At what point will I tire of skirmishes with her? Because of her history with the family and her physical closeness, will the week away from Justin be good or bad for our relationship?

The flight attendant interrupts my pre-takeoff musing, to ask if I'd like a glass of champagne. Years ago, I learned they only serve the good stuff when the jet is in the air. "Is it the usual swill-on-the-ground?"

He nods with a resigned expression. "I'm afraid so."

"I'll wait."

Hours later, as the cabin lights dim, I stretch out on the elongated seat with my blanket and pillow. Despite my conscious decision to enjoy the diversion of the trip, my unconscious brain is filled with endless and exhausting dreams. I wake up from them disoriented until I realize I'm in a plane hurtling through the sky at over five hundred miles an hour. I adjust my position but fall into the same canyon of disturbing scenarios involving Justin, Cecilia, Debbie, and the twins. When the lights come on with the smell of freshly brewed coffee and reheated pork products, I rouse myself and sit up. Although my dreams were vivid at the time, all I am left with is a lingering feeling of frustration. After landing at Barajas International Airport, I texted Justin.

Annie: Just landed. How is everything and everyone?

I don't expect a reply since it is three a.m. in Florida. I clear customs, claim my luggage, and travel to the hotel. In my room, I stare out the window at the weak light pouring onto the wet sidewalk from a shop across the street. Raindrops slide down the glass, inches from my nose, smearing the usually vivid Spanish colors into an abstract landscape.

By the following day, Justin had not texted me back yet. The photographer, his assistants, and all the models meet in the lobby. I'm older than the other three girls by about eight years. Outside the large plate glass windows, yesterday's heavy rain lifts to a light drizzle, but fat, gray clouds hang in swells over the city like dirty meringue. The photographer describes the scenes in his *brief*, which is the concept and story he devised. He mostly plans outdoor shoots since we will be wearing the designer's spring clothing line. He does not offer alternate indoor locations if the weather continues to be wet and cold. Throughout the day, the other models and I do our best to appear comfortable in thin, lightweight garments while posing in fifty- to sixty-degree temperatures and light rain. The fashion stylist and the HMUAs, hair and makeup artists, are driven crazy with constant repairs.

When I complained, the photographer's assistant said, "We planned this because costs and tourists drop at the end of October making the shoot less expensive, but we didn't count on the weather being this bad."

"I understand, but why didn't someone figure out what do to in case the rain doesn't let up?"

The young woman shrugged. "The weather report didn't indicate that it would last this long."

Back in my hotel room at the end of the day, I read the text Justin finally sent me.

Justin: Glad to hear you arrived safe. We had to take Fancy to an emergency vet. She wagged her tail and hit it on the corner of a kitchen cabinet. Blood everywhere. The place looked like a slaughterhouse. Freaked me and the girls out. Cecilia blames you for not cautioning us about this but how were you to know this would happen

Annie: Is she okay now? And the girls? You?

I don't get a return message until the next morning due to the time difference.

Justin: We panicked at first. Cecilia recommended I call Debbie and ask what to do. She met us at the vet's office and handled everything since you weren't here

Oh, no! This is the worst-case scenario for me. I'm unable to do anything, and Cecelia knows it. Later, as my hair and makeup are done in a cold tent, my phone dings with another text.

Justin: Don't worry about Debbie. I thanked her for her help but said I wasn't interested in a romantic relationship with anyone but you

His words are reassuring, but being over four thousand miles away leaves me feeling as helpless as a fish at the end of a line. With Cecilia and Debbie working to drive a wedge between Justin and me, how long will he remain committed to our relationship?

By the third day of what was supposed to be a two-day shoot, the photographer decided to amend his *brief* to focus on spring showers. At one point, a teenage model and I lean against a stone wall as a freezing, hard drizzle drips down our faces like tears. My hair lies flat on my head in wet commas. I'm shivering so hard I can barely sustain the pose.

"Jesus Christ! Can't you hold still long enough for me to get a decent shot?" He shakes his head, covered by a slouchy hipster beanie, lowers the camera with hands inside fingerless workout gloves, and turns his leather-jacketed back to me. "Why did the client insist on this old model and one who just started her period?"

His assistant catches my eye and mouths, "*Sorry.*"

The young girl beside me hangs her head, shivering and whimpering. I stomp to the photographer as he hands his camera to the assistant holding a large golf umbrella over his head. The heat of my anger warms me. I grab the collar of his leather jacket and strip it down his arms in one fluid movement before he turns around.

"Hey!" he yells.

I knock the umbrella out of the assistant's hand, sending it bouncing across the cobblestones. Then I catch hold of the photographer's knitted beanie and fling it over my shoulder.

"What the *fuck* do you think you're doing?"

"I'm making sure you work under the same conditions you're forcing on us. Let's see how good your pictures are when you're too cold and wet to hold the camera steady."

"You're fired!"

"Fine." I stand nose-to-nose with the cheap asshole. "I'll just go call Frida and tell her how you're treating the models on *her* photo shoot."

I can't believe I'm standing my ground with a well-known photographer. I have never done this before. Unlike the other models who are in the early stages of their careers, I can afford to be defiant. Despite this, I'm as shaky from the cold as from my audacity. I'm taking a risk that he doesn't find out if this *old model* is friends with the Dior designer and has her number in her phone. I need him to fall for my bluff.

The chilliness in his pale blue eyes remains as he picks up his jacket. "Robbie!"

His assistant returns with the umbrella held aloft again. "Yes?"

"Find me a dry place to finish this goddamn shoot today."

Inside the changing tent, I rifle through my bag and pull out my phone, needing to call a taxi to take me back to the hotel. I want it waiting outside as soon as I change into my street clothes and gather my belongings.

Another assistant rushes to my side. "Don't call Frida! We're going to revise the brief to interior locations."

I smile to myself. The photographer's assistants are in a panic that I'll complain to the client. "I've got to tell her I've been fired, so she can find you another model."

The woman covers my phone with her hand. "No, don't. I'm sure Paul didn't mean it. Let me talk with him. Get changed, and I'll be right back."

My work on this photoshoot continues, but each day when I return to the hotel, I take a hot shower, call room service for dinner, and fall into bed. Never before was I too tired to explore foreign cities in my free time. Am I getting too old for this kind of work?

By the last day, everyone is exhausted, frustrated, and sick, including me. I have only one day for sightseeing. Instead of visiting the museums, I spend the hours until my flight home in my hotel room, consuming cold remedies, zinc, and vitamin C.

At *la farmacia*, I buy disposable face masks and nitrile gloves to wear as a courtesy to those seated around me at the airport and on the plane. But my coughing and nose blowing still results in looks of disgust from fellow passengers. By the time the plane lands, my chest aches, and I am light-headed from the effort of pulling enough air into my lungs. Heat flushes my neck and, on the way to baggage claim, I am forced to sit at a gate for several minutes or risk falling flat on my face.

I weave through travelers with the single-minded purpose of getting home to bed. I heft my suitcase off the conveyor, and run through the automatic doors, bumping into a businessman on his cell phone. Walking to the Uber pickup lane, I strip off my mask and suck in the humid gasoline fumes of a South Florida airport. At my house, I give the Uber driver a hefty tip. Still, it is not nearly enough compensation for a major disinfection of his vehicle.

I undress and fall into bed. This has to be a terrible, incurable disease, ravaging and assaulting my body, and not just a bad cold. I wake up from a short nap and contact Aunt Linda.

"Will you (cough) be able to keep June and Bella (sneeze) a little longer?"

"That's not a problem. Is there anything I can do for you, honey?"

"Just stay away. You don't want to come down with what I have."

Other than a couple trips to the bathroom and replenishing my water glass, I remain in bed for two days. Justin contacts me when my stash of tissues is gone, and I'm forced to blow my nose with toilet paper. When that runs low, I will be shit out of luck, literally and figuratively.

"You sound horrible," he says.

"I feel (cough) even worse."

"I'll stop over after work."

"No (cough). I don't want you to get this and give it (hack phlegm) to the girls."

"Is there anything you need?"

"I downloaded the Publix app on my phone today (cough and hack) to order some supplies (sneezing fit)." I fall back on my pillows, weak and exhausted.

"Listen. Don't try talking any more. Text me what you need, and I'll bring it to you."

Thirty minutes go by before I can work up enough energy to send him a message.

Annie: OJ, honey, Kleenex (lots), toilet paper, chicken soup, Tylenol AM/PM, decaffeinated tea, menthol cough drops, nasal decongestant. Ring the doorbell when you get here and leave it on the front step

Justin: I should be there around 6:30. Unlock the door or leave me a key. I'm coming in

Annie: You'll get sick then I'll feel even worse

Justin: I'll be fine

I drag myself out of bed, unlock the front door, and leave a small paper bag hanging from the knob with a note saying: USE THESE! I INSIST! Inside are a disposable mask and gloves.

It's close to seven p.m. when he calls out, "I'm here."

There's a rustling in the kitchen with the refrigerator door opening and closing. He enters my bedroom wearing a mask but no gloves. I'm buried under my duvet with only my eyes and the top of my head with unshampooed hair showing. "Thank you (cough). I'll get everything later."

He says nothing but walks into the bathroom and turns on the shower. Upon his return, he strips the duvet and sheet off me.

"Hey!" I grab for them but fail. He lifts me into his arms like he's carrying a wounded warrior off the battlefield, and deposits me in front of the shower. He pulls my T-shirt over my head. "Get in there while I change the bed."

"You don't know where the (hack) sheets are?"

Pulling my pajama shorts down my legs, he says, "Don't worry, I'll find them after checking through your drawers."

"They're (cough) not in a drawer."

"Then I'll have a chance to check out your panties and sex toys first." He opens the shower and pushes me inside.

I luxuriate for a long time in the steamy enclosure, sitting on a teak stool and letting the hot water beat on my head and back. I shampoo my hair and wash myself, standing only to rinse off.

Justin returns and stares at me through the fogged door. "Are you okay?"

"I'm going to set up house in here. I can breathe for the first time in days."

"C'mon out. I'll dry you off. I have some Panera soup heating."

I lift my head. "Not Campbell's in a can?"

"I bought you the good stuff."

A short time later, I'm propped up in a freshly made bed, sipping hot chicken and rice soup from a mug after downing a decongestant with cold orange juice.

Justin sits on the end of the bed. "How do you feel?"

"Like I might want to live again (tiny cough)."

"You should have called me to come over as soon as you got back."

"I didn't want to infect you."

Or have him see me looking like this. Some women can pee, vomit, and fart in front of their boyfriends or husbands, but I'm not one of them. Although Justin is intimately acquainted with all my body parts, he doesn't need to see, hear, or smell how they function.

"Why didn't you have your aunt or cousin help out?"

I polish off the soup then blow my nose. "I didn't want to pass this onto them either(cough)."

"You're lucky your cold didn't turn into pneumonia."

"I know." I hand him the empty mug. "What the girls and Fancy up to?"

Since tomorrow is Halloween, we talk about the girls' costumes. Since they were three years old, Cecilia (who else?) has made their outfits based on twin cuteness, such as Thing 1 and Thing 2 from Dr. Suess' *Cat in the Hat,* Alice in Wonderland and the Queen of Hearts, and the good and bad witches from *The Wizard of Oz.* This year, they will be the sisters in *Frozen.*

Justin says, "I hope I don't bring the wrong kids home. There'll probably be dozens of Elsas and Annas out there. Next year Eden and Savanna want to figure out costumes where Fancy can take part."

After he leaves, I swallow two Tylenol PM tablets and sleep until morning. I wake up no longer feeling like a sodden pile of wet laundry and call Aunt Linda.

"You sound a lot better," she says. "How do you feel?"

"I'm still a bit congested and tired, but I'm on the mend. How about I come and get Juno and Bella tomorrow?"

"That's fine, but they're welcome to stay longer if needed. Uh, Annie…" There is stiffness in her voice that draws my attention. "Dennis left here a little while ago. He came with a suitcase expecting we would put him up for a few days."

"I thought he was staying at his condo while it was being remodeled."

"His contractor found mold in the walls of both bathrooms. He was forced to move out until an abatement team can remediate the problem. After what happened with Jonas, I just can't have him here with me right now. I'm sorry."

"Don't be sorry. You did nothing wrong. I already told him he can't stay with me. If he has enough money to buy a beachfront condo and have it remodeled, he can get himself a hotel room."

"I did tell him you're sick which is why your dogs are still with me. I don't know if I convinced him not to show up on your doorstep or not. I said he should call you first. Have you heard from him?"

"No. Maybe he found another place to hang out and someone else to mooch off."

I am on my laptop catching up on emails when my doorbell rings. Since I didn't enter the Publishers Clearing House sweepstakes, I doubt it's a manic group with balloons and a giant cardboard check for me. Maybe it's some young, white-shirted Jehovah's Witnesses on bikes. I might have invited them in for a drink, if I wasn't involved with Justin.

The doorbell rings again. Wishing it was the sweepstakes people or the missionaries, but knowing who it more likely is, I put down my laptop and stand up from the sofa.

CHAPTER 33

WITH A RESIGNED sigh, I fling the door wide. "Dennis, what are you doing here?"

He has two Rimowa aluminum roller cases in his hands. "I have no doubt Linda has already called you, so you know why I'm here. May I come in?"

I hold my ground. "I already said you can't stay with me."

"It's only for a few days."

"I'm just getting over being sick (fake cough). You should get a hotel room, one close to your condo so you can oversee the remodeling. This is too far away, and I haven't had a chance to disinfect the place yet."

"I don't want to stay at a hotel."

I lean against the doorframe with my arms crossed. "Why not? I'm sure Barbara left you enough money to pay for a room."

Dennis' shoulders slump at the mention of his dead wife's name. A morose expression drags down his features as if he's clawing at his cheeks. He stares at me with the blank, sedated look of a recent trauma victim. His aura of handsomeness and mature allure deserts him. A carnival guesser would have put him at least ten years older than his actual age.

"You're right, Annemarie. I can afford a hotel. It's just that I need…" A self-pitying sob cracks his voice. "Why did she have to die and leave me alone?"

Dennis closes his eyes tight and clamps a hand over his mouth to hold back his emotions. Before my eyes is the physical manifestation of a grieving man. I know the feeling well. Your body aches with it. It messes up your digestive system, sleep patterns, and the ability to hold a conversation without crying. I wouldn't wish it on my worst enemy—including my father. Since I was an infant when his brother and my mother died, I never saw Dennis grieve for anyone until now.

I take hold of his wrist. "Come in."

He allows me to lead him inside. When I release him, he stumbles on his long legs like a newborn colt standing for the first time. With an arm around his waist, I maneuver him onto one of the dining room chairs. I'm not sure he could navigate the step down to the living room sofa without falling. He sits sideways with his elbow on the tabletop, his hand covering his face. I sit across from him and wait. Dennis looks like he's been running on emotion and alcohol since Barbara's death six weeks ago. He knuckles the last few tears off his cheeks but says nothing.

To fill the awkward silence, I say, "I didn't realize you felt so strongly about her." I can't say the word *love* because I'm not sure he is capable of that emotion for his dead wife. He certainly has never expressed or displayed it for a living daughter.

His voice emerges rough with anger. "I begged her not to have another surgery. She had a bad reaction to anesthesia the last time. But did she listen to me or consider my future without her? No!"

His rapid switch from numbing grief to visceral anger catches me off guard. I imagine he mostly stays angry because it's a familiar and energizing feeling for him.

He lifts his head and looks at me. "I know I have no right to ask anything of you despite you being my daughter. But I'm asking, no, I'm begging you to let me stay. I don't want to be alone right now."

"You were alone in your condo until the mold abatement forced you to leave."

"No, I wasn't. The workmen were there during the day along with the interior designer. I have two friends who also live in the building, and I would spend evenings with them. There were people around me, except when I was sleeping."

"Why don't you stay with those friends then?"

He pinches the bridge of his aquiline nose as he inhales deeply. "My friends are generous with their evenings, but I cannot sleep in their homes."

I sense there's more to that story but don't ask. I've heard and read about the excesses of the Palm Beach mega-rich with their mansions, yachts, and private jets. The dark side involves drugs, sex, and vulgar consumption. Models are often recruited as *party girls* for events catering to the wealthy. When I was younger, I avoided them at all costs. To these VIPs, I was only a potential hookup, and nothing more.

My father continues his argument for staying with me. "I realize I am a huge imposition to you, but you have the room, and I could help out with your dogs when you get them back from Linda."

"Frankly, I don't trust you to take care of my dogs. If you would get drunk at a party for a two-year-old and leave an outside door open, how do I know you won't do the same thing here and put my dogs in danger?"

His chest expands with a deep inhale. "I feel terrible about what happened and have apologized to both Frankie and Linda. I haven't been around small children in a long time, so I forgot how careful you need to be."

"You haven't been around dogs either. If you leave a door or a gate open, they'll take off too." I want Dennis to know I'm immune to his apologies and explanations. I've been inoculated from excuses for his neglectful behavior.

"I may not be familiar with children, but I remember how to ensure that greyhounds do not get loose. I can promise it won't happen, but if you don't give me a chance to prove it then there's nothing more to say." He pushes himself to his feet,. His voice is a world-weary monotone. "I'll be on my way."

"Wait." I stare through the glass tabletop at my bare feet to avoid seeing a flash of triumph or glee on Dennis' face. "You can stay here for a few days but there are conditions."

"Such as?"

I raise my eyes. "You need to stop anesthetizing yourself with alcohol. I know you've always been a social drinker but at Frankie's house you were drunk and even the kids knew it. When you cross that line, you're more likely to be careless. Can you promise me that won't happen while you're here?"

A variety of emotions flicker across his face. Embarrassment and humiliation accompany his loss of pride. My haughty, arrogant father does not want me to see him in this weakened state. Nor does he want me lecturing him or setting conditions regarding his behavior.

His Adam's apple pops in his elongated neck like a small creature being swallowed by a snake. "I will curtail my intake of spirits while staying under your roof."

"Also, I won't be your servant. With Barbara, you were waited on by her staff, but here you're on your own. You can have whatever food is in the kitchen, but I'm not going to cook and serve meals or pick up after you."

He arches his eyebrows. "I don't expect you to do that. Anything else?"

"I can't think of anything else right now."

"I do have a favor to ask."

Here it comes. Is he going to ask me for a loan? Will he insist I install blackout curtains on his bedroom windows? Does he want me to stock the kitchen with bizarre or expensive foods?

"May I walk Juno and Bella when they return?"

I stare at him agog. "You *want* to walk my dogs?"

Dennis' upper lip curls in disdain. "Why do you find that so hard to believe?"

I shrug. "I don't know. I thought you weren't interested in them anymore."

"I may not have been around greyhounds for a number of years, but I'd still enjoy exercising them." He looks off past my shoulder. "Barbara was a wonderful woman, caring and loving with people. Our only issue of contention was her insistence on no pets of any kind, especially dogs. I've missed them. I can assure you they will be safe under my supervision."

I stand. "Then let me show you to your room."

CHAPTER 34

MY HOUSEGUEST WILL not be staying for only a few days. The abatement team found that Dennis' condo is not the only one with mold issues. The problem is so widespread the entire building, with eight individually owned units, must be evacuated. It will take several weeks until the property is deemed safe for occupation.

I'm not raising a stink about his extended occupation because he's been a rather pleasant houseguest. Dennis cooks dinner every night for the two of us. Although his menu is limited to grilled meats and salads, it is very tasty and it means I don't have to prepare anything. His bedroom is kept tidy. He does his own laundry and spends most afternoons away from home. What has melted my heart is how he is with Juno and Bella. The morning after they returned home from Linda's house, Dennis puts their leashes on and heads out the front door.

I look up from my breakfast oatmeal. "Are you taking them for a walk?"

"What tipped you off?" He stops. "Do I have your permission?"

"Just let me know when you leave with them, okay?"

The front door opens again more than an hour later, and Dennis appears happier than I have seen him in years. Juno and Bella spend the day with me in my office, but after another long walk in the evening, they curl up with him on the sofa while he watches TV or reads. This soon becomes our new routine.

Today when he comes home from their morning exercise, he asks, "What are the names of your neighbors who live in the unusual round house?"

Because my street is not in a development or gated community, builders and homeowners had free rein to construct whatever house style they could get the planning commission to approve. We have ranches, typical Florida CBC block homes, McMansions, bungalows, and the one geodesic dome to which Dennis refers.

"Do you mean Elf and Ramp?"

"Not the dogs' names. What are the names of the people?"

"How the hell should I know? I've only met them once, but I see their dogs all the time."

"They told me a coyote has been sighted in the area. We likely won't have to worry about leaving Juno and Bella unattended in the backyard, but they're warning neighbors who have cats or small dogs." To my amazement, Dennis kneels in front of my greyhounds, nuzzles their faces, and croons, "I won't let a mangy coyote hurt my beautiful girls. No, I won't."

I always thought my father viewed dogs as a commodity to breed, train, and sell. This is the first time I've seen him treat them as creatures with dignity, intelligence, and big hearts. If Dennis had not hung out with racetrack workers and high society all his adult life, he might have realized the wonderfulness of dogs in comparison to humans a long time ago.

The most significant handicap to having my father as a live-in is finding a place to be intimate with Justin. We don't use his house because of his eagle-eyed neighbor/mother-in-law. I would not put it past her to use her key to sneak in and catch us in the act.

This is our second sexless weekend, and I'm checking out graveyards, parking lots, and storage sheds. After dinner on Sunday at the Royal Pig Pub in downtown Fort Lauderdale, Justin asks, "Do you mind if we stop at the construction site so I can pick up some paperwork for a bridge restoration I'm overseeing?"

"Not at all. Tell me what you're doing to the bridge."

He gives me a wry grin that is now as familiar to me as my hands. "Never ask an engineer to tell you about their latest project. But you asked for it, so here goes. The first span across the New River was built in the early 1900s. Later it was changed from a fixed bridge to a drawbridge and has been widened four times since. Although over thirty thousand vehicles cross it every day, it's not been upgraded or refurbished for over thirty-eight years."

"How much more has to be done?"

"We'll be finished later this year. We've replaced all the electrical, mechanical, hydraulic, and emergency response systems. We've renovated the bridge tender house, are putting noise-reducing wheel paths on the deck and adding underdeck lighting to illuminate the Riverwalk underneath it. We're also upgrading the walk ramp on the south side to comply with ADA requirements."

A few minutes later, he stops the car outside a tall chain-link fence and unlocks a heavy-duty padlock. After pulling through, he exits the car again and locks the gate behind us. He parks close to a grey metal construction trailer.

Holding onto his arm, I cautiously walk over the bumpy, debris-strewn ground to the temporary office. "This looks like a shipping container."

"It is one. They don't have a lot of bells and whistles inside, but they're heavy duty, weather-proof and theft-resistent."

Justin unlocks the door. He watches me climb the wooden stairs, his eyes roving over me from top-to-bottom. A shiver runs down my back and echoes through my body as his gaze lingers on places that are not quite proper. He winks, and I shiver before stepping into the dark interior. He flips on the lights and an air conditioning unit kicks on. Several desks line the walls of the spare and bare, but surprisingly neat, trailer.

He walks around a desk and sinks into a chair that squeaks as he gets comfortable. Pushing back farther, he beckons to me.

I stand between him and the desk. "Is there something you want to show me?"

His lips curve into a devilish grin. He pats the open seat between his thighs. "Put your foot up here." When I do, he runs his fingers up and down my shin. Looking up at me through his lashes, he says, "Did you wear this dress to drive me crazy?"

Maybe the thought was in my mind when I put on this H&M backless mini dress with a deep V-neck, long puffy sleeves, and ruffles. "Is it working?"

One of his hands wraps my ankle. The other one drifts up the back of my calf, along the underside of my thigh where his fingertips trace the crack of my ass. I am unable to pull away because of his tight grip on my ankle.

"I like when you wear a thong." He looks up at me, running his fingers between the fabric and my flesh. He continues forward until he finds my center. One finger slips inside. His thumb circles my clit. With his eyes locked on mine, he whispers, "I've sat in this chair for hours and imagined fucking you here."

Sucking in a breath, I lean back, resting my hands on the desktop. He slides his finger a little deeper, and his thumb teases me in tight, light flicks.

Justin leans forward and presses his mouth to my kneecap. "See the file cabinet behind me?"

I lift my eyes to the low grey metal box, not unlike the shipping container we're in, and nod.

"Picture yourself bent over it and me taking you from behind."

My straight leg trembles and I stagger slightly. Justin withdraws his fingers, stands, and pushes the chair out of the way. "Which is it?" he whispers against my mouth. "Desk or file?"

My nipples harden. "We'll start with your desk."

The clink of his belt buckle is followed by the scratch of his zipper. He kisses me lightly, then passionately, drawing my tongue into his mouth. We do not break contact as he presses me backward onto the desktop. His hands slide down my legs then draw my knees up. Encircling my ankles, he lifts them to his shoulders. Lust narrows his jade-green eyes and parts his lips. He pauses before reaching between us to guide his cock. I moan and the metal desk squeals when he pulls my hips forward and thrusts inside. His rhythm, the angle, and the position are perfect. I screw my eyes shut as a delicious cry of delight escapes my lips.

What would my response be if this wasn't a Sunday evening on a closed construction site, but a regular weekday with dozens of male workmen outside? I imagine that is the situation we're in—where any moment the door might open, and we'll be caught. I do not feel any inhibitions, just plenty of novelty and excitement.

Justin's big chest expands, and he pulls air into his powerful lungs. His thrusts punctuate his words. "You…like…this…don't…you?"

Is he inside my head and picturing himself in the same sexual fantasy?

He growls, "Let it go, sweetheart. Let me see it. I want to feel it."

Justin's steady rhythm and verbal demands send me over the edge. When I come back to earth, I blink, and stare up at an acoustical tile ceiling. Justin pulls out and eases my legs down to the floor. He spins me around to face the file cabinet and pushes between my shoulder blades to lower my upper body. I place my palms flat on the metal top.

He leans over me and whispers in my ear. "Don't move. I'm not done with you yet."

Closing my eyes, I hold my breath as he lifts my skirt over my hips.

Cupping my ass with one hand, he moves the thong to the side. His cock slides inside, deep, long, and smooth. The aftershocks of my orgasm still tingle at the base of my spine. Blood beats like a drum between my legs, and I arch against him. Holding my hips, he pumps into me as his breathing quickens to sharp, irregular gasps.

"Oh God!" He shudders and comes.

Later, using tissues from his desk drawer, we clean up and fix our clothes. Justin puts a hand on my waist, and I rest mine on his shoulders. His kiss is gentle but thorough as we lazily explore each other's mouths. Tender and unhurried, we melt into each other in this stark, male-dominated workspace. With our faces inches apart, we shyly smile, our foreheads touching.

"You know what?" he says.

"What?"

"I'm going to have a tough time working at this desk without thinking about your legs covering my ears."

"You say that like it's a bad thing."

Justin laughs. "It's not. Trust me. But the pictures in my head will play hell with my concentration while I work."

"Maybe you should have thought of that before bringing me here. But now we know you've got mad skills on office furniture."

He frames my face with his hands like he always does. "As long as you have a houseguest, we're going to be forced to find a bunch of different surfaces and places to test my mad skills."

CHAPTER 35

I BECOME JUSTIN'S copilot on wild adventures of locating spots to have sex without paying for a hotel room. And without getting caught. The cover of darkness is more secure, but we also risk daylight trysts in unlikely places. A facsimile bed is created in my large SUV with the back two rows of seats folded flat, a thick comforter, a sheet, and two pillows. We discover that the parking lot at Target isn't as busy as Walmart and a whole lot classier.

The upper deck of the airport parking garage provides enough vehicles that Justin's car is not conspicuous when backed into a space. With the foldout sunscreen covering his windshield, we are not interrupted by anyone returning to their vehicle or pulling in next to us. One night, we park on the street behind his house, skulk through his backyard, and make love on his pool patio. The neighbor lets out his dog and the yappy terrier barks at us until its owner yells, "Pickles! Get in here." We could have gone into the house and not turned on any lights but outside in the cool night air is much more exciting.

These thrilling sex-capades are thanks to Cecilia who insists we spend as much free time together as possible. But everything comes at a price. My Saturday mornings with Fancy and the twins came to a halt while I was in Spain followed by recovering from my cold for two weeks. At that time, Cecilia convinced her granddaughters to enroll in a class at the Coral Springs

Museum of Art. However, she neglected to inform them and their father that the class runs from ten to noon every Saturday for six weeks.

When I call to schedule our first Saturday outing in over a month, Eden says, "We can't go because of our art class. Grandma didn't tell us there are six classes. She says we need to finish since she paid for them."

In a slightly weepy voice, Savanna adds, "Don't be mad."

"I'm not mad." *At you.* "Your grandmother probably forgot about our Girls' Day." *Like hell she did.* "We can take Fancy out after you get home from your class."

We still go to the dog park, but sometimes vary our routine. I may bring Juno and Bella, and we will hike through parks with each of us walking a leashed greyhound. We take Fancy for walks along city streets and at strip malls. Sometimes we shop at Pet Smart or Pet Supermarket. Often we stop for drinks and snacks at local restaurants with pet-friendly outdoor dining areas. Fancy is well-behaved and friendly with a variety of people and their pets.

Justin and I have talked more about enrolling the girls and the greyhound in the therapy dog program. He is all for it but wants to wait until Fancy has been with them for a while and his daughters are a little older.

For a Saturday in November, I bought a one-day pass for the dog beach in Hollywood. "Let's see if Fancy likes the sand and water. If she does, we can get an annual pass and come more often."

"It's a long way from home," Eden says after the sixty-minute drive.

That's true. The twins and I live in the northwest sector of the county. This dog beach is in the southeast corner. All the other canine-friendly beaches are restricted to residents of the city where the beach is located, but it turns out we have nothing to worry about. Fancy is not a beach baby. The shifting of the sand on the way to the shoreline makes her uneasy.

"What's wrong?" Savanna asks when I take control of the leash as Fancy skitters and balks.

"She's not used to walking on a soft surface. Let's head to the water where the sand is packed down."

If anything, that's worse. The noise, as well as the ebb and flow of the waves coming ashore, spook her. She watches the water like it's a wet predator sneaking in for an attack and then retreating. After fifteen minutes, we leave the beach and head to the parking lot. As soon as Fancy's feet hit the pavement, she visibly relaxes.

"She doesn't like swimming pools either," Eden announces.

"She doesn't?"

The little girl shakes her head. "We begged her to get in with us, but she kept barking like she was telling us to get out of the water. When Daddy opened the door, she ran into the house and wouldn't come outside."

"Will she be like that when she needs a bath?" Savanna asks.

"Remember, I told you that you'll only need to give Fancy a bath if she gets dirty or smells. I'm sure she's never been in a pool or bathtub before which may be why she's so skittish at the beach. The best way to bathe her is to tie her in the backyard or on the patio and slowly pour a bucket of warm water over her. Then shampoo her, being careful around her eyes, and rinse her off with another bucket of warm water. You can dry her with big towels or let her run around in the sun."

"Is that what you do with Juno and Bella?"

I place my hand on Savanna's coppery head. "To tell you the truth, I've never given them a bath. I've talked with other greyhound owners who only wash their dogs if they've rolled in something nasty."

Eden looks at me with such a comical expression that I want to hug her. "What nasty things do they roll in?"

"You don't have to worry. Dogs that live near wooded areas will roll in deer or fox poop. Remember they were originally used for hunting, so they do that to disguise their smell."

The girls emit watery snorts of horror and disgust. Upon arrival back at their house, we tell Justin about our non-day at the beach.

Eden checks Fancy's front paws for any lingering grains of sand between her pads. "She hated walking on the beach."

Savanna sits on the carpet next to her sister. "She doesn't like the ocean either."

"Is bathing her going to be problem?" Justin asks me.

Before I can answer, Eden says, "Annie doesn't wash Juno and Bella."

This time, I instruct Justin on the hygiene requirements of greyhounds. When I finish, he looks like he's been handed a gift. "Great! A female in this house that doesn't need her hair washed." He runs his hand over his bald pate. "And she doesn't need it cut either."

Eden emits a squeal of exasperation. "Daddy! We keep telling you to let us have short hair. We can take care of it then. Even Carl at Just Kids said that."

I raise my eyebrows at Justin. He turns and focuses on the girls and dog on the floor. All I see is his profile, the strong line of his jaw, and tension bunching his shoulders. Is short hair on a female a problem for him?

"Don't you think so, Annie?"

Eden's question snaps me back to reality. "What?"

"Don't you think it's easier when a girl has short hair?"

Justin shoots me a micro look that contains a macro message. It's obviously one of those unspoken parental communications. "Well, not always."

"Why not?" Savanna asks.

"For one thing, you need to have it cut more often and can't pull it into a ponytail, pigtails, or a bun if you're having a bad hair day. Plus, you're limited to just one hairstyle." I light-heartedly wave jazz hands on either side of my ears. "This is it for me. I can't look any different unless I grow it out or wear a wig. I have to shampoo, condition, and style my hair every day when it's this short."

"Every day?" The twins reply in shocked unison.

"When my hair was this long," I tap the outside edges of my palms against my jawline. "I only had to wash it twice a week. In high school when my hair was as long as yours, I only did it once a week. I know it's harder to work with long hair, but taking care of short hair requires a lot more time and money."

My eyes shift in a quick glance to Justin. The ghost of a smile curves his mouth. I exhale with relief. I gave his daughters an acceptable explanation, but my reprieve will be short-lived. Very soon, I need to tell him something that will determine the future of our relationship.

I am in love with him.

My spark of attraction has flamed into a fire. I find him endlessly fascinating and enjoy every minute we are together. When I recall the bliss of making love to him my insides clench with need. My biological clock ticks loud in my subconscious, energized by fantasies involving his sperm. He is a perfect husband and father candidate.

Justin not only says the right things, but he does the right things too. He married his pregnant girlfriend at a time when their relationship spiraled downward. Thierry did too, but he was married to me at the time. Justin is raising his daughters as a single father rather than handing them off to a relative like my father did. He readily admits when he is wrong, says he's sorry, and means it. Getting my father or ex-husband to apologize would be like getting a celebrity to publicly admit to plastic surgery.

Justin is secure enough to ask me to choose the wine at restaurants. "Since you lived in France, you're a better wine connoisseur than me."

I'm not, but he says my judgment is better than his. He doesn't insist on knowing my political affiliation or who I voted for in the last election. He is interested in my work as a graphic designer without being patronizing because he designs much larger and more functional projects. He is pleasant to the waitstaff at restaurants even when they screw up our orders. He does not act bitter or weird about being a widower. Despite not knowing the number of zeroes in my bank balance, he has not urged me to get a college degree claiming I am not a success without one. Justin also hasn't quizzed me about my finances either. One of my internet dates spent the evening trying to convince me to finance his latest project.

Justin drives an expensive car but does not consider it more valuable than his messy kids. His appetite for making love mirrors mine and he is the best lover I have ever had. Often, I want him again as soon as we finish. He may not have any hair on his head, but I love the feel of his scalp and face stubble between my thighs. He is thoughtful, chivalrous, and the kind of man I always dreamed about and lusted after since we met.

The big question for me is: When will be the perfect time for me to tell him all this?

CHAPTER 36

I HAVE TWO invitations for Thanksgiving. One is at Aunt Linda's where I have celebrated every holiday except when I was married to Thierry. My cousin, Tony, whom I haven't seen since last year, will be in town. This year, he's bringing his fiancée who is also in the Air Force and stationed in Guam.

The second invitation is from Justin by way of his sister. "Gretchen and my mom want you to know you're welcome at our dinner if you don't have other plans. I warned them you may be expected to eat with your own family."

My father is invited to a dinner hosted by one of his Palm Beach society friends. I don't know who is more relieved—me, him, or Aunt Linda. When she extended the invitation to Dennis and me, I asked her, "Are you sure you want him there?"

Her sigh carried a heavy load over the phone line. "Frankie and I will keep an eye on him and Jonas." Several days later when I called with the RSVP for me only, she said, "Am I a terrible person for feeling relieved Denny isn't coming?"

"Not unless I'm as terrible as you. He's not been any trouble as a houseguest, but it would be awkward for all of us to have him there after what happened."

"You know, it's always been a struggle for me to be around him. I can never forget how miserable he made my sister. Besides, he's so been distant with our side of the family ever since your mother's death."

I know what she means. Even now, interactions with my father are pleasant but not without effort. We're like two strangers at a bus stop who start talking, but when the bus is late, we're obligated to keep the conversation going rather than sit in uncomfortable silence.

Shortly before noon, I arrive at the three-bedroom, two-bath house where I grew up. My contribution today is an over-sized pecan pie and an equally large pumpkin pie that I purchased at BJ's. The usual group who gathers for monthly dinners at Frankie's house is in attendance, including her brother-in-law. His daughters are with his ex-wife's family.

My cousin, Tony, jumps up from the sofa when I enter the living room. His hair is military close-cropped with only a hint of its dark curls. His cheekbones slant downward across his angular face. I still envy his full red lips, which look like he's been eating juicy strawberries. His almost-black eyes are alert and all too keen. He wraps me in muscular, tanned arms, extending beyond his black T-shirt's short sleeves.

With his face buried in the crook of my neck, he says, "Eiffel, it's so great to see you again."

I smack his muscle-hard back when he says the nickname he bestowed on me as a teenager. Every time I'm in Paris now, I send him selfies with the iconic landmark in the background. Our embrace includes rocking side-to-side. Tony loves good hugs more than I do.

I kiss his forehead. "I missed you, Ant." Although his nickname is often used for guys named Antonio or Anthony, I started calling my cousin this when I towered over him as a teenager.

He releases me. "I want to introduce you to my fiancée. Yo! Come meet my cousin." I elbowed Tony hard in the ribs and he rubs the spot. "Hey, what's that for?"

"You don't call for a lady by saying *Yo*. Shame on you."

A short, curvy woman with dark eyes slips against Tony's side. A tiny gap between her two front teeth gives her an innocent elfin look. Rapunzel-like ropes of inky licorice hair cascade over her shoulders and down her back.

He slings his meaty arm around her. "This is my cousin, Annie, who grew up with me and Frankie. And, this lovely lady, who I can't wait to marry is *Yohanna* Rivera."

My cheeks explode with heat as Tony's merry eyes glisten with amusement. I bend forward and embrace the much shorter woman, surreptitiously sliding my hand over her silky locks. That's when I can tell that her curves are comprised of defined muscles. I wonder if she acquired them on the job or if she regularly engages in some kind of competitive sport.

I stand back and give her my brightest smile. "Welcome to the family. As someone who was informally adopted by them, I can assure you they're wonderful and will love you with all their hearts. Of course, you'll fit in much better than me."

"Why?" A frown creases Yohanna's forehead.

I move to stand on Tony's other side, drape my arm across his other shoulder, and rest my chin on his head. "They can look you in the eye without having to tilt their heads back."

When the ten adults and two children sit at the dining room table, extended with two extra leaves, a feast spans the center section. Dishes of sliced turkey, ham, mashed potatoes, sweet potatoes, and stuffing are passed up and down its length along with Dawn's green bean and mushroom soup casserole, Uncle Milo's rigatoni, and Frankie's cranberry and orange relish. Dale ladles gravy from a soup tureen rather than a gravy boat.

Yohanna says to Linda, "This turkey is delicious. What's your secret?"

Tony laughs aloud. "Mom's secret is someone else cooks it."

Other humorous family anecdotes are shared with Yohanna. Frankie recounts not finding the usual Playboy magazine collection hidden in Tony's bedroom but several of her mother's romance novels.

"Hey," says her brother. "It was a good education into how women think."

"Baloney!" Frankie retorts. "You were reading them because they had sex in them."

Linda shakes her head. "I kept those because they were my favorites. I ended up having to throw them out because…well, you know why."

The table erupts with loud noises of disgust and fake gagging.

Tony points his fork at his sister. "Let's talk about why skipped your college classes for a week because of a two black eyes." He turns to his fiancée. "Frankie bought an ab roller. You know, one of those waste-of-money home exercisers with two handles and a wheel."

"Shut up, Tony," Frankie threatens.

Dale pauses from shoveling mashed potatoes into his mouth. "No, go ahead. I've never heard this story."

"She started rolling and, at some point, her arms gave out. She hit her forehead so hard on the wheel it gave her two black eyes. Mom let her stay home from school for a week."

I bite my lip as Aunt Linda exchanges a knowing glance with me. She allowed her daughter to remain housebound for fear of having the Department of Children's Services show up on her doorstep again. She had been warned that if any other allegations of abuse were reported about her family, even if they were groundless, the case would be investigated thoroughly.

By the time Frankie returned to the college campus any residual bruising was easily covered by makeup, but once again I felt the burdensome weight of bringing the family into the DCF spotlight. Although more humorous stories follow, I do not participate in the hilarity. I leave soon after my pies are served, and the dishes cleaned up. Since Dennis departed from my house to join his friends before I left home, I need to get back to my dogs.

I give Yohanna a hug. "It was wonderful meeting you. I'm so glad you're joining our crazy family."

"Everyone has been great. Keep the date in April open for our wedding in San Antonio."

"I will."

When I say goodbye to Tony, I whisper in his ear, "You picked a good one, Ant."

"I know. She's small but mighty and will keep me in line."

Shortly after I arrive home, Justin calls. "Guess what? My parents took the girls with them to their house for two days. I'll drive to The Villages on Sunday morning to pick them up. I was thinking you could spend tonight, tomorrow, and Saturday with me."

"What about Cecilia?"

"That's the other good news. Her sister is visiting from Orlando and the two of them are headed to a timeshare in the Keys for a few days. If you stay here with me, we can go anywhere except a mall on Black Friday and wake up together every morning."

"Is there going to be sex?" I ask in a teasing voice. "I would really only be interested if there's sex."

"I promise you'll get three meals a day, all the wine you can drink, and hours of my mind-blowing lovemaking."

"Be right there."

In no time, I'm packed, including food and beds for Juno and Bella. Justin and I agreed to treat them to a two-day visit with Fancy. I text my father with my revised plans.

Annie: I am spending the weekend with Justin. The dogs will be with me. We'll be home Sunday morning

Dennis: I've been invited for a quick cruise to the Bahamas on a friend's yacht. I'll be home soon to pack. Be back on Tuesday

Okay, he wins in the weekend-with-the-rich-and-famous category, but I win in the weekend-with-a-hot-guy category. For the first time since I started coming to his house, I enter Justin's bedroom to hang up my clothes. A queen-size mattress is covered with a color-blocked bedspread and sits on the frame of a metal four-poster. A long light wood dresser with nine drawers matches the two nightstands. The decorating is not what draws me up short.

On every flat surface are photographs of Justin and Lucy.

When I halt after a few steps into the room, he bumps into my back. "What's wrong?"

I turn to face him. "Is this where we're going to sleep?"

His slow smile is a parody of a sexy leer. "For a few hours."

"Justin, I'm serious."

"About what?"

My sigh carries weary resignation. "The pictures."

He leans to the side as his eyes travel around the room. "Oh. I forgot about them." He steps around me and places my bag upright against the dresser. "I'll put them away. I should have done it before now."

Justin sweeps the frames into his hands, opens a cabinet door in one of the nightstands, and dumps them inside. They are now out of sight but not out of my mind. I can't begrudge the twins having visual cues of the woman who gave birth to them, but shouldn't a widower have banished the photographic remembrances of his dead wife by now, especially the pictures in his bedroom? Justin no doubt grieved Lucy's loss for some time. After the flowers died, the empty casseroles returned, and the sympathy cards discarded, it was appropriate for him to keep pictures of her around, to talk about her, and to recall the good times. But he's in a relationship with a new woman, and overlooking the photos in the bedroom where he plans to make love to me is disconcerting.

I unpack my toiletries in the bathroom and hang up my clothes. Two closets straddle each side of a short hallway to the ensuite bath. I breathe a sigh of relief. The inside of the one Justin directs me to use only contains boxes of Christmas decorations, tax returns, and empty clothes hangers.

After letting my dogs explore their new surroundings, Justin and I relax on the family room sectional. He leans back against the squeaky leather and crosses his arms behind his head. "Are you hungry?"

"A little. But not for Thanksgiving leftovers."

"I'm not sure what is in the refrigerator but let's see what we can put together."

We assemble a charcuterie tray of cheese cubes, olives, grapes, crackers, almonds, baby gherkins, ham, and salami. While I lay out the food, Justin opens and pours wine into two goblets.

He clinks his glass against mine. "Cheers. Nothing says weekend party like deli meats and cheese."

Our two-day and three-night weekend date turns into playing house with three female greyhounds. They are only slightly less demanding than real children. On the first night, Fancy wanders the house and returns to bark at Justin several times.

"Why is she doing this? She never barks when the girls are here."

"That's why she's doing it. She gets a lot of attention from them and wants you to bring them home. We'll need to exercise her more to tire her out and play with her like they do."

Juno and Bella stare at me and emit soft whines and groans. Justin's lean, handsome face tightens with these additional canine sound effects. "What's wrong with them now? Do they want to go back to your house?"

"I think they'd do the same thing there. They miss my father."

"Are we that boring?"

"No, just not as attentive to them."

Frequent long walks and play times settle the dogs, allowing us to have frequent and long play times, too. I enjoy every minute of cooking and eating with him, both of us exercising the dogs and watching movies, showering together, and making love in a real bed again. I thought my mattress was heaven, but that's before I laid on Justin's memory foam with him. I am going to miss spending an entire weekend on his hard body and in his soft bed.

Despite all this wonderfulness, in the back of my mind is the need to tell him I love him and the hope that he'll say the words first or right after I do.

CHAPTER 37

THE CHRISTMAS HOLIDAY is fast approaching. My father moves back into his condo the second week of December, sending Juno and Bella into a canine funk for several days. The twins' art class at the museum concludes but Cecilia and I continue playing tug of war with their free time. I don't create too much of a fuss since Justin is caught in the middle. As a result, I spend only one weekend afternoon with the girls when I help the Stablers put up their Christmas tree and decorations.

After hauling out boxes of ornaments, stockings, and wreaths from the bedroom closet, Justin and I erect the artificial tree. An hour later, Cecilia arrives with a Tupperware container of sugar cookies for the girls to decorate. Our ornament helpers abandon us and dance into the kitchen ahead of their grandmother. Fancy rises from her dog bed to join them.

Cecilia flashes a disingenuous little smile, more at me than Justin. "You two can finish the tree, can't you? It's too tall for the children to reach most of the branches anyway."

Justin's rueful smile catches my eye. "Sorry about that. I thought she was coming over later. Yesterday, they baked the cookies and made the frosting but ran out of time to decorate. I guess she wanted to make sure it didn't happen again."

Over Alexa playing Christmas music in the background are snippets of Cecilia's instructions on using royal icing to outline and fill in the designs on the cookies. Justin and I finish decorating the tree, speaking very little.

I wave goodbye to everyone in the kitchen. "I'm leaving now."

Cecilia presses a small paper plate into my hand with three cookies covered with clear plastic wrap. "We made these for you."

Savanna points to one particularly well-decorated cookie with white icing and silvery nonpareils. "I did the angel."

Eden licks a dab of red off her finger. "Mine is the Santa."

This cookie is indicative of someone more interested in eating than decorating. The last one is an evil-grinning, green Grinch. When I look at Cecilia, she cocks her head with a twitch of her mouth which passes for a smile. An hour later, my phone dings with a text from her.

Cecilia: Just so you know, I am very upset to find my daughter's pictures missing. You may have replaced her in Justin's bed but you will never replace her in the twins' lives. I'll see to that.

I don't say anything to Justin until we get together on the weekend to wrap Christmas presents for his daughters that he had delivered to my house. He covers the packages with holiday-themed paper while I handle the ribbons and gift bags. Many of them come in twos while others are meant to be shared.

He hands me the last box containing a kit for making cake pops. "This may be the first year since the girls were toddlers that they'll come up empty handed from snooping around my house or Cecilia's for their presents."

The mention of his mother-in-law's name reminds me of the text I received from her. "I want to show you something Cecilia sent me."

After reading the message, his eyes darken, and his face becomes stormy. "She noticed the photos of Lucy were gone when we put the empty boxes of decorations back in the bedroom closet. She asked to speak to me outside so the girls wouldn't hear. I made the mistake of telling her the pictures made you uncomfortable."

"Dammit, Justin, why did you say that? I'm already walking on thin ice with her."

"I wasn't thinking. Hell, it's been four years. I'm entitled to a relationship with another woman." His anger dissipates as quickly as it rises. "Don't worry. It's nothing. She'll be fine."

"I'm not sure she'll ever be fine with *me*. I'm replacing her daughter in…" My index finger taps his rock-hard bicep. "…your bed and with your kids."

"Can you believe she was shocked when I told her you spent the weekend with me? What does she think we've doing the last three months? Holding hands?"

I clench my fingers together with an audible sigh. Cecilia's hostility is a complication our delicate new relationship doesn't need. She has no qualms throwing around her opinions about me, asking pointed questions neither Justin nor the twins can or want to answer, and digging up flaws for their exposure. Will the Stablers eventually see me through her lens finder? After all, I'm the outsider, and she's the relative who has played a significant role in their lives. Will her perspective become theirs as she continues to shine a harsh light on me?

Justin throws an arm over my shoulder and tips me toward him. "Don't be upset. She'll come around."

I straighten, which pushes me away from him. "And what if she doesn't?"

"She'll have to. I'm not giving you up because Cecilia doesn't want me having sex." He winks, laughs, and kisses me. "Besides with your father back in his condo, we'll have full use of your house and bed again."

"You mentioned having the girls visit your parents during Christmas break. Will we be able to spend time at your house while they're gone?"

There's an awkward silence until he responds. "That weekend after Thanksgiving was kind of unusual because not only were Eden and Savanna out of town, but so was Cecilia. I don't know when that'll ever happen again."

I pause with my mouth slightly open. "Are you telling me I can't spend the night at your house when the girls are gone because your mother-in-law would disapprove?"

"You know how nosey she is. I don't want her noting when you arrive and leave. Or worse, coming over and interrupting with any flimsy excuse she can think of."

"Do you think she would barge in on us?"

"No. We've already established that she can only use her key and come in without calling in an emergency. But…" He wipes his hand across his mouth. "It's just awkward knowing she's two doors away. Watching the house. Noting when cars come and go and lights go off."

I study his face with its stubbly skin and the mouth I have kissed hundreds of times. His dancing green eyes are now somewhat duller. He looks miserable, and then it hits me. "Are you saying if Cecilia *thinks* we're making love in your house, you might not be able to perform?"

He shrugs.

"Justin, we've had sex at the airport garage, on your patio, in parking lots, and a construction trailer. The possibility of getting caught in those places never had a negative effect on you."

I stay silent while he twists in the wind to formulate a reply. "I don't *think* it would happen, but I don't want to take the chance."

I am in shock.

Is Cecilia's influence so pervasive that it clings to the walls of the Stablers' lives like a slimy black leech? Have I underestimated her? If her presence in a nearby house can affect Justin sexually, what other power does she have? Despite my best efforts, am I fighting a battle I can never win and wasting my time pursuing a more committed relationship with this man?

CHAPTER 38

THE TWINS CALL me the week before Christmas. "Hi, Annie." Eden speaks first. "We need a favor."

"What is it?"

"We want to buy a present for Grandma this weekend, but Daddy can't take us, and she can't go because her toilet needs fixed."

Justin is unavailable on Saturday because of the grand opening ceremony and press conference with city officials for the completed bridge project. In one of our nightly phone calls, he complained about his required attendance. "I drew the short straw for the department and have to be the bobble-head nodding behind the politicians while they speak."

Savanna's slightly higher-pitched voice comes on the line. "Daddy gave us money. Can you take us? Then Grandma won't know what we buy."

"Sure."

"Let me tell her what else," Eden says. Her voice is faint until she wrests the phone from her sister. Her next words are loud and clear. "Daddy said we need to get a haircut. We want one like yours."

Small warning bells go off in the back of my mind. "Did your father agree to that?"

"He said we need it trimmed. A kid in first grade has lice. I think it's Presley. He's always scratching his head." Twin noises of disgust emanate from my phone.

Years ago, an extreme haircut was the most effective lice treatment, but times have changed with over-the-counter medication. Perhaps Justin feels shorter hair would make applying the medication and shampooing easier. "You need to have your dad let me know how short it should be."

"Okay, we will."

On Friday, Cecilia calls me. "Hello, Annie. I appreciate you taking the girls for their haircut tomorrow."

"I don't mind. When is their appointment?"

Cecilia informs me they are scheduled for ten A.M. and gives me directions to the kiddie salon. "They'll be at my house. You can pick them up at nine-thirty. I don't want Carl to rush because you're late, and he has his next haircut waiting. I'd take them myself, but I'm expecting a plumber in the morning. Why can't tradespeople narrow their time to less than a four-hour window? As professionals, they should know how long it takes to fix something. Instead, they hold customers hostage like we have nothing better to do than wait around for them to show up."

By Saturday morning, I still have yet to hear from Justin about the haircut. I called him from my house before leaving to pick up the girls. But I was sent to voicemail. He likely has his phone on vibrate or mute to not interrupt the ceremony. "Hi. I know where and when to take the girls for their hair appointment but not how much to get cut off. Let me know before their ten o'clock appointment."

At Cecilia's house, the twins exit the front door as soon as I park in the driveway. "Annie! We're ready! Let's go! This is gonna be so much fun!"

Both girls are dressed in the Versace skirts I gave them for their birthday. Instead of the white T-shirts that came with the outfit, they wear long-sleeved, black tops since the temperature overnight dropped into the low seventies. They clap, jump, and dance like we're headed to Disney World, not a hair appointment and the mall. After making sure they're buckled into the backseat, I turn toward Cecilia who hugs her cardigan-covered arms tight against her body. She frees one arm, gives me a dismissive wave that doubles as a farewell, and disappears into her house.

At the salon, Carl is a short, middle-aged guy with a gingery beard that covers his face like shag carpet, and a long, droopy mustache that twitches above his friendly, white-toothed grin. He reminds me of the bandy-legged cartoon outlaw, Yosemite Sam, who uses a set of portable steps to mount his horse. When I come forward with the girls, I get that familiar gazing-at-a-skyscraper look from him.

I shake his hand. "Hi, I'm Annie, a friend of the family. The twins' grandmother asked me to bring them in today for a haircut."

"It's nice to meet you." In addition to my height, Carl checks out my hair. When I catch him appraising my head, his cheeks redden to match his mustache. "Sorry, occupational hazard. You have a beautiful skull and features for that style. Whoever cuts your hair does a really good job."

"Thank you."

Eden is already in the adjustable chair. Carl fastens a pint-sized plastic cape printed with under-the-sea cartoon creatures around her. "Are we doing the usual trimming of the ends?"

Eden turns her head toward us. "We need it shorter because someone in our class has lice."

He nods. "You won't be the first ones. How much should we take off?"

Carl and I confer with the girls and settle on shoulder length. They can still pull it into a ponytail or pigtails and there will be less bulk for them to struggle with. "I've suggested this to their grandmother in the past, but she was resistant to having more than an inch cut off. I'm glad head lice affected the length this time. After the cut, she'll know I was right all along."

Carl dampens Eden's hair with a spray bottle, massages in a product formulated for curls, and then gets to work with his scissors. Savanna waits by my side making comments.

"Daddy will be *so* happy with our hair."

"It was okay for Mommy to have long hair. Hers wasn't curly like ours."

"Maybe Eden and I can do each other's hair when it's shorter instead of Daddy."

By the time Carl finishes with Eden, I'm happy with our decision. When her hair is pulled straight, it reaches the middle of her back, but as soon as it is released from the comb, it springs up to her shoulders. Also, her hair no longer lies flat on her skull like a helmet then mushrooms out. From the center part, it spirals in loose curls, framing her face with soft ringlets.

The hairdresser spins her around to face the mirror. He fluffs the curls. "With less weight, your hair is more curly than frizzy. What do you think?"

Eden clasps her hands together and squeals. "I love it! How does it look, Annie?"

"It's fabulous!"

Savanna runs to the chair. "Do mine now!"

Carl whips the cape off Eden with a flourish. She runs to me and shakes her head from side to side. "Do you really like it?"

"I do. You look elegant and beautiful." I recall the adjectives Justin used to describe me. I'll tell him to use the same words when Eden asks if he likes the hairstyle. And she will.

After Savanna is done, Eden hands over an envelope to Carl. He opens it at the register, and by the expression on his face, I can tell something is not right. "Is it the wrong amount?"

"Well, today's haircut was a bit more than their usual trim, but that's okay." He opens the register drawer and slips the bills inside.

I lean over the counter and speak in a low voice. "Are you going to use your tip to cover the difference?"

"Eden and Savanna are repeat customers, so it's no big deal." I reach into my purse, but he waves me off. "You don't have to do this."

I place a twenty-dollar bill on the countertop. "Yes, I do. Thank you for taking extra time today. You did a beautiful job."

At the mall, we stop at the food court since it is lunchtime then head to Macy's. With my help and suggestions, the girls buy Cecilia a necklace with a pendant spelling out Love You Way More, a five-piece miniature Versace fragrance gift set, and a blush pink Calvin Klein zippered hoodie. I kick in a few extra dollars so they can spend all the money Justin gave them for the three gifts.

On our way out of the store, I asked, "Do you want to stop and see Santa?"

The girls look at me like I have a boa constrictor draped around my neck.

"Annie! We're too old for Santa." Eden puts enough admonition in her voice for me to realize my faux pas.

"Grandma told us last year he wasn't real." Savanna sounds a little wistful.

To drive her point home, Eden adds, "Remember we're big girls who can have our hair the way we want it."

When I check my watch, I'm surprised it is three o'clock already. "Let me call your dad so he'll know we're on our way."

The phone rings then my call goes to voice mail. I leave a brief message.

"Maybe he's putting Christmas lights on the house," Eden offers as an explanation.

Savanna pushes open the glass exit door. "Or he's outside with Fancy."

I hold the heavy door for them. "You're right. He probably couldn't get to his phone or doesn't have it on him. I guess we'll just surprise him when we get there."

CHAPTER 39

WHEN WE ARRIVE at the twins' house, it is difficult to determine if anyone is home since Justin always parks in the garage and no lights are turned on inside yet. I ring the doorbell as Eden and Savanna chatter behind me.

Suddenly, Justin flings open the door and yells, "Where the *hell* have you been?"

His eyes are flinty-hard and angry. In his hand is a tumbler half-filled with amber liquid. The twins go still and silent while pressing against the back of me.

"What's wrong?" I only saw him this upset during the broken condom incident. His barely checked fury is that of a generally placid man pushed to his limit.

"What isn't wrong? This morning some asshole who's texting and not paying attention bumps into me as I'm getting my phone out of my pocket. Guess whose phone goes flying into the New River? I go to Cecilia's house after the ceremony, which takes hours longer than it needs to be, but no one's there. I can't call her because I don't have a *fucking* phone!"

Twin gasps occur behind me. I am just as surprised to hear Justin use foul language in front of his daughters. Or has he forgotten they are behind me?

"Then I remember the girls are with you. So, I come into the house and find the well-trained dog you had us adopt pissed on the carpet, shit right where I stepped, and chewed the door frame to the backyard."

I slow my breathing to speak in a calm voice. "I'm sorry you had such a bad day. Didn't Cecilia come over to let Fancy out at noon?"

"Obviously not. I've been waiting for you to get back, so I can go to the Verizon store. Why did it take so long to get Cecilia's gift?"

"We did more than just shop. I took the girls to their hair appointment, and we had lunch too."

"What do you mean you took them for a haircut? Cecilia always does that."

"She had a plumber coming this morning."

Justin continues to stand in the doorway while the girls and I wait outside on the front step. "Why didn't anyone tell me this?"

"I thought you knew." Now I'm a little irritated by his attitude. Why do I have to explain myself when I'm the one who did him and Cecilia a favor? "I tried calling you this morning about the hair appointment."

"What time was that?"

"Around nine, I think."

A look of intense aggravation crosses his face. His arm jerks and some of the booze in his glass sloshes onto the welcome mat. "Great! That was probably the call I was trying to answer when my phone fell."

Wait a minute. Is Justin saying what I think he's saying? I straighten to my full height and stare directly into his eyes. I want him to know I have boundaries not to be crossed. "Are you blaming *me* for losing your phone?"

The aggression drains from his features and a flush creeps up his neck. "No, of course, not."

Maybe because her father's voice modulates into his normal speaking tone, or maybe because I'm standing up to him, or maybe because she's tired of being ignored, but Eden chooses that moment to pop out from behind me. "Daddy, look at my new haircut."

Justin's gaze turns away from me and focuses on his daughter. His mouth falls open, his eyes bulge slightly, and his body tenses into immobility. A breath of coldness makes me alert.

"What the—" Justin bites off the last word by gritting his teeth together. His eyes blaze with fury. "Get in the house!"

"But, Daddy, don't I look pretty?"

God bless Eden for trying to brazen it out. Meanwhile, Savanna's head is buried in the small of my back. Either the girls have never seen this side of their father before or his volcanic reaction is something they have dealt with in the past. Whichever it is, I will not let them handle his temper alone this time.

I spread my feet apart and brace myself. "Girls, go back to my car."

I don't need to repeat the command. The rapid scurry of footsteps and soft weeping accompanies the slamming of a door.

Justin's eyes narrow to slits, and he looks like he's about to detonate. "Those are my daughters!"

"And the only way you're getting close to them until you calm down is by beating me into unconsciousness."

We square off in a stare-down. Blood pounds through my body. I fist my hands to stop the quivering. I am a mother bear, furious on behalf of his children and ready to go into combat if necessary. I'm not sure how long our battle of wills lasts. I know from canine behavior that prolonged eye contact is a stand-off with the possibility of aggression. The dog who looks away first is the submissive one. I hate being put in this position, but for the twins' sake, I am prepared to face any confrontation.

At last, Justin inhales a deep breath, expanding his chest. We maintain visual contact, but his green eyes no longer shoot fiery red daggers at me. "I would *never* physically hurt my daughters or any female."

His words offer a balm to my fear for the girls, but the generality of saying *any female,* rather than being specific to me, fills my heart with setting concrete. "What about Fancy?"

He draws his eyebrows together. "What about her?"

"Is she okay?"

"I yelled, but I didn't touch her. Do you want to see for yourself? I put her in the girls' room."

"No, I believe you."

As we talk, Justin's anger drains away starting with his tight mouth loosening, his neck and shoulders relaxing, and the knotted muscles in his arms easing. "Can I go apologize to my daughters now?"

I step to the side. Justin brushes past me, emptying his tumbler into the shrubs. At my car, he motions for one of the girls to lower the window. I guess they locked the doors. The glass slides down and Justin leans forward, speaking softly. I can't hear what he says, but the girl closest to him nods. There is more discussion between him and his daughters. Eventually the door opens, and Eden emerges first. Justin hugs her then Savanna exits the car. He sets his empty glass on the roof to wipe his more emotional daughter's tear-stained cheeks.

They walk toward me when Eden stops. "We forgot grandma's presents!"

She reaches into the open back door and retrieves the bag with the hoodie, which also contains the two smaller gifts. She skips ahead of Justin who walks together with her sister. "Guess what? Daddy likes our hair, but he'll have to get used to it."

I smile with delight and relief. "I knew he would."

"Thank you for taking us shopping and for our haircut today, Annie." She leans her shoulder into me.

Squeezing her little body against me, I say, "You're very welcome."

Eden heads into the house. Savanna slips her hand from her father's and wraps her arms around my hips. "Thank you."

Unlike her sister, she does not specify the reasons for her gratitude. But when I look into her eyes which are still shiny tears, I'm certain her thankfulness is not for the same thing as Eden.

Justin touches her shoulder. "Fancy has been waiting for you. Go say hi to her, so I can talk with Annie." He watches Savanna through the open front door and waits. Then he steps closer to me. I smile but he doesn't. In a low voice, more menacing than when he shouted, he says, "Don't think because you can't have children that you can have mine."

My chest implodes with a pain as sharp as if I have been stabbed. Justin turns away from me, moves inside his house, and closes the door. I look at the barred entrance, and reality slams into my face like the flat side of a shovel. I am still as delusional about men and their love and respect as the day Thierry told me his mistress was five months pregnant. When I can catch my breath, I head to my car with feet made of lead.

I turn on the engine and back out of the driveway. The magnified sounds of the tires and engine alert me that the back door is still open. I stop, open the driver's side door, and put one foot on the street. The car moves ahead, scraping my shoe against the asphalt. Jamming my foot on the brake again, I push the gearshift into the parked position. Keeping one hand on the car's body for support, I walk around the hood to the rear passenger door and shut it. Sunlight glints on the glass. Justin's tumbler is on the roof, although it slid closer to the hatchback. I want to hurl the lead crystal to the pavement, shattering it into dozens of sparkly pieces, but my numb brain still thinks about kids in bare feet or dogs out for walks. Instead, I carry it with me. With each return step, my body folds in on itself until I'm walking like an arthritic old woman. I flip the glass onto the passenger seat beside my purse.

Functioning on autopilot, I drive home without crashing into a palm tree or concrete wall. I let the dogs out, feed them an early supper, and curl up on the sofa.

My right eye throbs with pain, like a nail being driven into the iris. Maybe it's the first sign of a growing brain tumor. Tiny shards prick at various spots from my head to my feet, but the worst one is lodged where my heart used to be.

CHAPTER 40

I WAKE UP on Sunday morning with dry eyes. I still have not cried although I've been vacillating between anger and pain since leaving Justin's house. The only aching part of me is my stomach. It feels raw and wounded. Is that why I keep rubbing my abdomen, or is it because of Justin's reminder that I will never feel life growing in there? Tears spring to my eyes, but never enough to overflow.

Maybe he feels I am not good enough to love and be a stepmother to his daughters, although it is obvious, I am good enough to fuck. How could I have been so gullible? I must admit Justin never made me any promises. He never told me he loved me and, thank God, I never said the words to him. I close my eyes and heave a sigh ragged with regret. I am grateful for the fury that clogs my throat and prevents me from weeping. It helps mask the hurt. From experience, I know one needs to cry out the pain to begin healing. But right now, my anger allows me to ignore my stupidity.

I received an unexpected text later in the day.

Cecilia: I knew you could not be trusted.

Annie: What are you referring to

Cecilia: You know.

Annie: I don't

Cecilia: You should

If she referring to the twins' new hairstyle, I choose not to respond. Arguing with Cecilia would be an exercise in frustration and futility, like disagreeing with a government employee or an angry toddler. Christmas is two days away, and my dining room table is stacked with the girls' presents. I also purchased several for them including jewelry-making kits, a children's book titled *A Greyhound's Tale: Running for Glory, Walking for Home*, and aqua-colored Chloe skinny jeans. I wrapped them in the same paper used to cover the presents from their father and grandmother. Then I tucked them in the pile, hoping they won't be noticed until it is too late.

Hopefully, Justin will neglect to check the tags before the twins open them on Christmas morning. If he does spot the ones I bought, will he cull them before they're put under the tree? I'm anxious because he hasn't contacted me about picking up the kids' gifts, and I refuse to remind him they are at my house.

Finally, his text chimes on my phone the afternoon of Christmas Eve. I'm surprised he waited this long. Did he forget? What would he do if I was unavailable or refused him access? He probably knows I would never allow that to happen for the girls' sake.

Justin: Sorry I waited so late. When can I pick up the twins' presents

An emotion as mean as a box of rattlesnakes at a revival meeting runs through me. I do not reply until he sends a second text.

Justin: Are you there

Annie: Yes

No little dots appear indicating a reply being typed. He must be thinking about my lack of response.

Justin: When will it be convenient for me to stop by

Again, I wait to respond until I see him typing then quickly send out my text.

Annie: Whenever

His dots stop then disappear. A short while later they resume.

Justin: I'm headed home from work. I can be there in twenty minutes

Annie: Fine

Justin: C U soon

No, you won't. I send the dogs out to the backyard. With the front door open, I cart the presents out of my front entrance and neatly stack them beside the door. Back inside, I wait for his arrival. From my office I watch his car pull into my driveway on my phone's Ring app.

After parking at the front entrance, Justin hesitates half in and out of his car. He stares at the pile of wrapped gifts and then scans the windows and door. Slowly he stands, his eyes on the house, and pulls his phone from his pocket.

"Hello," I answer.

"Annie? What's going on?"

"The girls' presents are on the porch."

"I know. I can see them. I thought we could talk."

"There's nothing to say."

"I think it's best for us to talk about what happened on Saturday."

"And *I* think it's best if we don't see each other anymore."

Justin leans against his car and drops his head. "I never meant to hurt you."

"And I've never understood when a man says that to me. You knew those words would wound me and you said them anyway."

He raises his head and looks directly at the Ring doorbell. Then he turns around with his back to the door and puts his elbows on the car roof. "I was frustrated and a bit drunk. I didn't mean it. You can't be mad at me because of that."

"When what you say or do hurts me, *you* don't get to decide how I feel."

He nods his head, the phone still pressed to his ear. "You're right. I'm sorry for what I said and how it hurt you. I was wrong."

"Thank you. Good-bye."

"Wait!" Justin spins around, facing the house again. "Don't hang up!"

"What now?"

"Are you telling me that's it? We're done?"

"Yes." The word catches in my throat. Justin staggers slightly, and I gather my courage. "I want you to pick up the presents and leave. Don't text me and don't call me. Please respect my decision to end things between us. I'd rather miss you than hate you."

I disconnect, but Justin continues to stare at my house, the phone against his ear. It seems to take forever. Finally, he lays his phone on the roof of his car and rubs his fists under his eyes.

Is he crying? I rise from my desk chair.

Just as I reconsider my decision, he pulls out his key fob, presses a button, and the trunk lid pops open. With his head down, he gathers presents in his arms and stows them in the back. He completes the job in three quick trips. At the driver's door, he plucks his new phone off the roof, gets behind the steering wheel, and drives away.

I sit down on my desk chair again, weeping and wailing in his wake.

CHAPTER 41

MY FATHER DEPARTS on the weekend prior to Christmas Day for a ski vacation at a friend's house in Aspen. I wonder if his *friend* is female, owns the yacht on which he sailed after Thanksgiving, and is a possible candidate for Wife Number Three. I welcome not having to spend the holiday with him as this will be a difficult Christmas for me. I'm not ready to let my family know my relationship with Justin officially ended the day before. I plan to act like nothing has changed.

But I am no more than six feet inside the door before Frankie says, "What happened? Who died?"

"What are you talking about? No one died."

"Well, I can tell something's wrong. You have that I'm-never-getting-laid-again look."

Without warning, tears seep from my eyes. "Dammit! I thought I had my shit together."

Frankie tugs the handles of the gift bags I'm carrying out of my hands and yells, "Dale, come here!"

I turn around, not wanting him to see my face.

Behind us, her husband says in a bright, cheery voice, "Whaddya need?"

"Take these." Then Frankie wraps an arm around my waist, propelling me to the front door. "Put the presents under the tree. Annie and I are going for a walk."

"Is the car broken?"

Frankie rolls her eyes. "No."

"Then what's the problem?"

Over her shoulder, she says, "Annie and I need a few minutes of alone time."

"Are you trying to keep me out of the loop?"

"Yes, dear, I am."

The crinkle of wrapping paper and the rustle of tissue paper sounds behind us. "I'll hold down the fort, but don't forget—" In a voice reminiscent of Jack Nicholson in *A Few Good Men,* Dale barks, "*You can't keep me out of the loop. I am the loop.*"

Frankie prods me ahead of her. "I know. I'll tell you all about it later."

"Okay. Love you, babe."

We stop at my car so I can pull tissues from a storage compartment. "The wine I bought is still in here."

"We'll get it when we come back."

We head down the street from the house to a small children's park. I dab at my eyelashes along the way. "This is why I hate crying. Once I start, I can't stop. The worst part is that it doesn't make me feel better."

We sit on a bench far enough away from several small children and their parents. One mother spots Frankie and waves.

She returns the greeting. "Hi, Magda."

I sniff to hold back more tears. "I wonder if her family celebrated Christmas really early or they have plans for later today."

"Neither. That's Magda Silverstein." Frankie twists her body toward me. "Now tell me what happened."

I relate Saturday's events, followed by Justin coming to my house yesterday. "I cried off and on all night. I feel like I'm broken inside."

Frankie pats my knee. "That's because you are. Listen to me, Annie. I know you better than you know yourself. You may feel horrible right now but you are brave and strong. All at the same time."

"No, I'm not."

"Yes, you are!" She grips my hands in hers. "You've always been my hero. As a kid, you never whined or acted pathetic because you didn't have a mother and your father couldn't be bothered with you. Instead, you adopted my family as your own like it was no big deal. You had cancer at an age when no teenager should have to deal with such a life-altering illness. Then a year later you're off to Europe modeling in runway shows. Your asshole of a husband dumps you in the worst way possible and what do you do? Take him to the cleaners and create a new life for yourself. You are the most courageous and resilient person I know."

I am speechless. I never knew Frankie viewed me this way.

"This breakup with Justin is *nothing* compared to what you've survived in the past. I expect you'll thrive from this experience once you get over the heartbreak. But let me ask you a question. Are you really finished with him?"

I blow my nose and nod.

"What about Eden and Savanna?"

"They're the other reason my heart is broken. I don't want them to think this is their fault."

"Maybe you can work out a way to keep in contact with them even if you and Justin are no longer seeing each other."

Of course, Cecilia will nix that idea. She's probably celebrating the end of our romantic relationship with rum-laced egg nog and Christmas cookies. "I don't know if Justin will agree to that." I slump against the back of the bench and sigh. "Why do I get involved with emotionally unavailable men and try to make them love me? You'd think after what I went through with my dad and Thierry, I would be better prepared."

Frankie offers suggestions, comfort, and assurances that everything will work out for the best. Then Dale sends an SOS text to her phone. "Uh-oh, the fort is under attack and needs reinforcements."

On the walk back, I say, "You know, maybe I should save myself from all this drama and forget about ever finding love."

"Stop it!" Frankie pulls me to a halt. "Everyone's heart gets bruised, and more than once, but they still keep beating. Forgiving people who hurt you is pure selfishness. The bastards may not deserve it, but you do it anyway, so *you'll* be happy again. Not them."

Since Frankie's family celebrated Christmas Eve with Dale's parents and their other Forbes relatives, only Uncle Milo, Aunt Linda, and I are at my cousin's house today. This holiday won't be as enjoyable as in the past, but I'm determined not to allow my sadness to affect the rest of the gathering.

Just like with my cousin, as soon as Linda sees me, she asks, "What's wrong?"

I close my eyes, resigned to recounting the breakup with Justin again. Before I can say anything, Frankie intervenes. "We'll talk about it later. No sense letting an outsider ruin our family holiday."

Aunt Linda's eyes widen. "Oh, no, Annie! Did you breakup with Justin?"

I nod.

"I don't understand," she says. "He seemed like a really nice guy."

"No! He's an asshole." Frankie takes Linda and me by the hand, leading us to the family room. "There will be no more talking about this today. We're going to have ourselves a merry little Christmas, dammit!"

Later in the afternoon, I gather the gifts I received, wish everyone a happy holiday and my thanks. When I open the car door, my phone rings.

The twins' faces appear on the screen.

CHAPTER 42

"MERRY—" I HALT my cheery greeting with a good look at the girls. They appear distraught, and their cheeks glisten with tears. "What's wrong?"

Eden speaks first. "Daddy said we broke up with you."

I don't want to say the wrong thing here. ""Your dad and I won't be dating any more, but it's his decision whether I keep in touch with you or not."

Savanna squeezes more of her face into the screen. "Are you mad because we got you in trouble?"

"What do you mean?"

The two girls face each other, communicating something with their eyes before turning back to the screen. Eden sighs. "Nobody has lice at school."

It takes me a moment to process what this means. "Did you lie so you could get your hair cut shorter?"

Their two heads nod, and Savanna whispers, "We're sorry."

The children shouldn't feel responsible for the breakup. Their new hairstyle is only a small catalyst for ending a physical relationship in which I gave more of my heart than I got in return. "You did *not* get me into trouble."

Eden says, "Grandma says you're too pre-presum…it's a big word I can't say. Daddy told her you aren't pushy. You know all about hair and clothes and makeup because you have your picture in magazines."

"Are you *really* a model?" Savanna's voice has the awestruck tone of a child meeting a superhero.

I don't want these young and impressionable girls to have a false impression. For many models, being on a magazine cover or in print ads has the exact opposite effect of what most people think. It is not an ego trip because we don't look that way in real life. With hair and makeup, lighting, digital manipulation, and learning how to pose to the best advantage, we create an illusion to draw attention to the product being sold. Most models are insecure people, hyper-aware of their imperfections. I would hate for the twins to admire me for the photographed fantasy that someone else put together.

"I get paid to sell things. I'm like a real-life clothes hanger. Because I'm tall and skinny people notice what I'm wearing and not me. I modeled more when I was younger, but now, I mostly work on my computer designing advertisements."

Eden says, "If you're not in trouble, why can't we see you?"

"Like I said, that's your dad's call. You need to ask him."

"Okay, we will."

The call ends without anyone saying goodbye. I wait, but there is no return call from Eden and Savanna over the next several days. At one time, I told Justin that he and his daughters were a package deal, and now it appears a breakup with him includes the whole family. I also wonder if I have been cut loose from Broward County Greyhound Rescue, too. Although I am reluctant to contact her, I call Debbie Hale-Brown.

After some initial awkwardness, I ask, "Do you have any greyhounds needing a foster home? I'm available."

"Actually, I don't have any in my house either." She tells me that with tracks closing to live dog racing and fewer greyhounds needing rehomed, the rescue group has more adoption applicants than dogs. "When our organization started fifteen years ago, there were around thirty thousand greyhounds registered annually, but last year it was only three thousand."

In the 1930s, the dog tracks in Palm Beach and Miami drew mobsters and movie stars to what was once called the *sport of queens*. Greyhound racing hit its peak fifty years later because dog and horse tracks were the only places outside Las Vegas and Atlantic City where people could legally gamble. But with the rise in Indian casinos, internet betting, and activists fighting against animal racing, dog tracks have lost their appeal and popularity. Since forty-one states have banned greyhound tracks, I can understand how we have reached the point where the demand for these elegant and sweet-natured dogs outpaces availability.

Debbie says, "Sure greyhound puppies will still be for sale, but an untrained puppy who hasn't spent a lot of time with its littermates, hasn't been handled, trained, and socialized isn't the same as a retired athlete. Some rescue groups are looking overseas to places like Spain and the Middle East where there is still a lot of racing. The problem is that it's difficult and costly to get dogs from there back to the United States."

"What are you going to do?"

"I'm looking at other big dog rescue groups I can work with. I'll still stay active with greyhounds, but I really enjoy fostering and finding homes for needy animals. I recommend you do the same thing."

To my relief, the call ends without Justin being mentioned. Maybe Cecilia has contacted her, and Debbie knows he is single again. Now, I'm torn in three different directions. I am glad greyhound racing is in a rapid decline. I am sad that I might not foster more of the dogs I love. And I am mad that Justin is free to hook up with Debbie. How did I end up in such an awful position?

The end of the year slides into the new one without much notice or fanfare for me. As my social life takes a nosedive, my father's calendar is booked solid with the start of the Palm Beach social season.

In one of our now weekly phone calls, he complains, "I'm going to need to buy another tuxedo. I barely have time to get one back from the cleaners before I need it again. The two I own will be worn thin by the time the season's over."

Dennis is surprisingly compassionate when I tell him about breaking up with Justin. "Reminding you of your infertility is a cruel thing to do. I can understand why you ended the relationship despite his later apology. That does bring up a subject I've wanted to discuss with you. Have you ever considered surrogacy as an option for having your own child?"

I pause, surprised my father has even thought about this. "Yes. I've researched it."

"I've heard IVF and the cost of hiring a surrogate can be very expensive, especially if repeated treatments are required in order to achieve a successful pregnancy and birth."

"That's true." Dennis' knowledge of in vitro fertilization is unexpected, and I shake my head with the wonder of it.

"If you're interested in pursuing this, don't let the cost stand in your way. Whatever money you need, let me know and I'll help you out."

It takes a moment until I can speak. "Dad? Are you saying you want to help me have a child of my own someday?"

He clears his throat. "Of course. After all, it would be my grandchild too."

My eyes prick with tears. "Thank you for the offer, but I've invested my divorce settlement for that purpose."

"I'm glad to hear you've planned for a child in the future. Were you thinking that Justin might be a candidate to father your child?"

"I considered him a possibility." I stop myself from telling Dennis that I prefer a man who wants to be a parent rather than a sperm donor. It sounds too much like *his* role in *my* life.

During the first two weeks in January, the only notable occurrences are several bizarre texts from Cecilia.

Cecilia: You didn't think I saw you but I did.

Cecilia: If you don't stop, I'll tell Justin.

Cecilia: You're upsetting the girls. Don't force us to take out a restraining order.

Cecilia: The next time I see you, I'm calling the police.

I don't respond since I have no idea what she is talking about. Maybe she has confused me with someone else, possibly Justin's new girlfriend. She sends the last text the day before I fly to Paris for Fashion Week. Two designers hired me to model their new fall designs. I debate whether I should contact Justin about Cecilia's odd harassment but decide to wait until I'm back home again.

The Max Mara collection is the first runway show on my schedule. It features glamorous and elegant outfits for working women in neutral colors. I wear over-the-knee ecru leather boots paired with a long-jacketed and skirted suit in camel wool and topped with a sumptuous shearling coat. If I lived in a cooler climate, I would purchase the entire outfit for my own closet since it looks that good on me.

The highlight of my week is Karl Lagerfeld's final collection. Not only is the show emotional because of his retirement and recent death, but it takes place in the Grand Palais des Champs-Élysées, a large historical exhibition hall and museum. An an alpine village has been replicated with a runway of artificial snow and backdrops of wooden chalets with smoke curling from chimneys. His fall collection is layers of hounds-tooth suits, pearl and chain jewelry, wintery knits, and ski boots. From the Lagerfeld collection, I place an order with one of the saleswomen for a gorgeous belt worn by another model.

When the show ends, I catch a flight home on Friday at ten-thirty in the morning, Paris time, and arrive in Atlanta at 2:45 in the afternoon. But my body tells me it's almost nine o'clock at night. I have a tight ninety-minute layover to clear customs and catch my flight to Fort Lauderdale. After taking a seat in first class, my phone rings. I pull it from the carry-on bag at my feet. My heart stops when I see the name on the screen.

I hit the button to answer the call but before I can greet him, Justin says, "Do you know where my daughters are?"

CHAPTER 43

A SUDDEN COLDNESS grips my spine. "I have no idea. What's happened?"

"Why haven't you answered your phone all day?" His voice cracks with nerves and tension.

"I've been out of the country. I landed in Atlanta an hour ago and just boarded my flight home. The plane is taking off in a few minutes."

"Where were you?"

"I've been in Paris since Sunday. What's going on?"

Justin emits a sigh heavy with defeat and panic. "I don't know. Cecilia and the girls are gone. I need to find them."

The line goes dead.

At that point, it takes forever until the plane is airborne again. I call Justin upon landing, get his voicemail and leave him a message. "I'm back in town. I'll come to your house as soon as I get my car."

After collecting my checked bag and retrieving my SUV from long-term parking, I contact him again but disconnect when his voicemail engages. I drive as fast as I safely can to his house. When I arrive, two Broward County sheriff cruisers are parked in the street with another unknown vehicle.

I ring the doorbell and, in an eerily similar circumstance to when I brought the twins home from their haircut and Christmas shopping, Justin flings open the door and says, "Where the *hell* have you been?" His posture deflates, and a weary expression of disappointment flattens his features. "Sorry, I thought you might be...Never mind. Come in."

"Oh, my God. You look terrible."

"You would too if your kids were missing."

I ignore his jabbing reminder that the children aren't mine because of the pain evident in his feverish eyes. I am desperate to hug him but don't. Instead, I grab his elbow. "What's going on?"

Before Justin can answer my question, an officer with a phone attached to his ear motions for him to come into the kitchen. The house is crowded. His sister and her husband are there. Several people I do not recognize are talking with one of the deputies in the living room.

I shut the open door. Gretchen and Heath sit at the dining room table, and I approach them. "What happened?"

His sister's face is leached white with anxiety in the stark, full brightness of the chandelier. "Justin got home late last night from a business trip. He called Cecilia, but she didn't answer. He didn't think anything of it because she goes to bed early with the girls on a school night. He waited until this morning to contact her again. When no one answered, he went to her house. They weren't there. It was too early for school, but he thought maybe Cecilia took them to breakfast, or they had gone to a park to walk the dog. He became worried when the girls didn't answer their phone either. He used the *Find My Phone* feature that told him their cell phone was still at Cecilia's house, but he couldn't find it anywhere."

"He didn't talk with the kids while he was gone?"

"By the time he got to his hotel in Jacksonville on Wednesday night, it was late, but he says he spoke to them on his drive up there. Yesterday, he was in meetings all day and tried to call on the drive home, but no one answered. He figured they were doing homework, outside with the dog, or getting ready for bed. That's when he called Cecilia. She sent him a text saying she was busy and would contact him later. Since then, he hasn't been able to reach any of them."

"Were the kids in school today?"

Gretchen leans to the side, looking into the kitchen where Justin and the deputy stand. "That's what they're trying to find out now."

The deputy disconnects the call and shakes his head. Justin turns in a circle, his hands gripping the sides of his skull, his eyes raised to the ceiling.

I sit at the table and point to the people in the living room with the second officer. "Who are they?"

"Neighbors," Heath says. "They saw Cecilia's car leave early yesterday morning but couldn't see who was in it."

Someone's phone beeps with an incoming message. Justin frantically pulls his out of his pants pocket. He touches the screen, reads, and exclaims, "What the *fuck*!"

He holds the phone up so the deputy can see it. Gretchen, Heath, and I wait, frozen in place. Justin and the officer look through the kitchen to the dining room. They focus on me with narrowed eyes. My breath catches in a tangle at the back of my throat when they approach the table.

The deputy speaks first. "You're Annie?"

I nod in reply.

"Mr. Stabler just received an email from his mother-in-law. She writes that she's taken his daughters to a safe place to foil a kidnapping. *By you*."

Chapter 44

I CAN'T SPEAK. My mouth opens and closes, but no sound emerges from my paralyzed voice.

Some of the fierceness has evaporated from Justin's expression, but he watches me with a set jaw. "Annie said she just returned from France today."

The deputy squints, his eyes brimming with suspicion. "Can you prove your whereabouts?"

I pull my passport from my purse. The boarding passes extend out from the pages. I slide both across the table. Afraid this is not enough proof, I unfold a copy of my itinerary, showing my flight last Sunday and my five-day reservation at the Paris hotel.

As Justin and the officer study the documentation, I say in a voice tight with strain, "I can give you phone numbers for the people who hired me and can verify I was there."

Neither says a word. My brain jump-starts, and I pull up the texts on my phone. "Here." A message with a selfie I took two days ago is on the screen with the Eiffel Tower in the background. "I always send a photo like this to my cousin whenever I'm in Paris."

The deputy hands back my passport and phone. "Why would Mrs. Sonnenberg think you would kidnap her granddaughters?"

"I have no idea."

"When was the last time you were in contact with the children?"

"I was with them the Saturday before Christmas and talked with them on Christmas Day."

"Come on, Annie," Justin says with impatience. "You've been waiting for them outside their school."

I blink. "What?"

"Cecilia told me she spotted you a couple times on the street across from the school parking lot. She told the resource officer but when they looked again you were gone. I told her not to worry. You wouldn't do anything to harm Eden and Savanna."

"I swear I've never waited for them outside their school." Now Gretchen and Heath view me with suspicion. I recall the odd text messages from the twins' grandmother. "Is that why Cecilia sent me these texts?"

I scroll through the messages and then hand my phone to the deputy. After reading them, he asks, "Why didn't you answer her?"

"I didn't know what she was talking about. The last one came in when I was packing for my trip. I was going to speak to Justin about it when I came home."

The deputy checks something else on my phone. "The last time you spoke with the kids, what did you talk about?"

I moisten my lips. "They called me to ask about the breakup with their father."

The deputy's gaze bounces between Justin and me. "Tell me about that."

Justin shoves his hands into his pants pockets. "I told the girls Annie would not be here when they opened their presents on Christmas morning because we were no longer seeing each other."

The front door closes, and the second deputy joins us in the dining room. He stands with his hand resting on his gun belt.

The officer with my phone says, "You decided to end your relationship with her."

I immediately connect the dots. If Justin initiated the breakup, that would mean I am the disgruntled ex-girlfriend bent on revenge that might involve kidnapping his daughters.

Before I can defend myself, Justin says, "No. Annie called it quits. It was totally my fault. I apologized, but she didn't want to see me anymore." He licks his lips and casts me a remorseful look. "I was unhappy about it but accepted her decision. The girls were upset though. They like spending time with her."

I swallow hard. "When they called me, they wanted to know if I would still see them."

"What did you tell them?"

"I said it was your decision as their father."

Since I entered the house, Justin has displayed a variety of emotions: anger, hostility, rage, anguish, fear, and disbelief. For the first time, he shifts from one foot to the other. He removes his hands from his pockets and tugs on his shirt. "Yeah, I told them we're a package deal. If you break up with me, you're breaking up with them too."

I drop my head to shield the heartache that must show on my face. Under the table, Gretchen squeezes my leg.

Justin speaks in a hushed and urgent voice. "I'm sorry, Annie. I was hurting and then so were they. I had already changed my mind about shutting you off from them, but then Cecilia claimed you were stalking the girls at school."

My head jerks up. "What can I do to prove I haven't been anywhere near them?"

The first deputy says, "We can subpoena your phone records and check the GPS."

"Do it! You have my permission."

"That's not necessary," Justin interrupts. "If Annie says she hasn't been following my daughters, I believe her. My mother-in-law has been acting squirrely since Christmas, and I've been ignoring the warning signs."

Gretchen speaks for the first time. "Cecilia has been weird since you began dating her daughter ten years ago. Don't forget what happened at our birthday party in October. I know she had a hand in that woman showing up. She hates Annie because the twins love her."

Justin explains to the police that Cecilia had been possessive of her daughter. After Lucy was killed, her controlling nature shifted to his children. "We've had quite a few arguments about that. For a while, everything will be fine then she'll start doing whatever *she* wants again." Suddenly, he closes his eyes and shakes his head. "Earlier this week, Cecilia threw a fit. The girls had switched out pictures of their mother with ones of Annie from fashion magazines they found on the internet."

I recall Cecilia's phone call after she discovered the photographs of Lucy missing from Justin's bedroom. *You may have replaced her in Justin's bed, but you will never replace her in the twins' lives. I'll see to that.* My heart races with an unnamed and unknown fear. Would Cecilia do something to ensure the last meaningful adult woman in the twins' young lives will be her? I look around the room. No one else seems to be thinking this dark and horrific thought but me.

The deputy hands over my phone. "Thank you for your cooperation. If we need more information from you, we'll be in touch." He turns to Justin. "Do you want to have us activate a state-wide AMBER alert? Are your children in imminent danger from their grandmother?"

Yes! I'm screaming inside my head, but the word does not pass my lips.

Justin shakes his head. "She wouldn't hurt the girls. What if we don't issue the alert? What can we do instead?"

"We'll file a missing persons' report and try to locate your children."

"What will happen to Cecilia?"

"With an AMBER alert, she'll be arrested upon apprehension."

Justin bites the inside of his cheek and looks down at the floor.

The deputy continues, "If they're located from a missing persons' report, you can choose to press abduction charges against her or not. It's been at least two days since they've disappeared. Your mother-in-law and children may have left the state by now. In that case, we would call in the FBI for federal jurisdiction."

Gretchen stands and wraps an arm around her brother's waist. "You need to do what's in the girls' best interest."

"I know! I can't think of anything else. Something is going on with Cecilia, more than her usual control and paranoia issues. I'm afraid if she thinks she's in trouble with the law, she'll panic and something bad *will* happen." His voice cracks with a sob. "I can't put Eden and Savanna at risk."

Tears fill his eyes. Gretchen grabs him in a tight embrace, whispering soothing words to him. Heath joins them. After a minute, Justin lifts his head and wipes his eyes with the back of his hand. "Let's give it one more day. I'll keep trying to get in touch with her."

The deputy nods. "We'll put out a BOLO for the car. An alert will be sent if it's spotted."

Everyone heads to the foyer. The officers stop at the front door. Gretchen and Heath bracket Justin like supporting bookends.

One deputy opens the door, and the second deputy faces them. "Let us know as soon as you hear anything."

Do I stay here and offer to help? Comfort Justin? Canvas the neighborhood? Print flyers to post on light poles? Make coffee and sandwiches? Then it hits me.

I grab my purse and approach the people at the door. "How about if I take Fancy home with me until this is over?"

Justin frowns. "The dog isn't here."

I assumed Cecilia had left her behind since he hadn't said the girls *and* Fancy were missing. Hiding and being on the run with a large breed and distinctive dog is not easy. With my focus on the children, I thought Fancy was closed in a room to prevent her from slipping outside with all the people coming in and going out of the house.

"Where is she?"

"With the girls, I guess. She wasn't in Cecilia's house when I checked."

My brain sparks as if infused with a Red Bull stampede. I scramble in my purse for my phone. "Oh, my God! Oh, my God!"

"What?" Justin asks.

"I know where they are!"

CHAPTER 45

JUSTIN'S FINGERS GRASP my arm. "What do you mean?"

I juggle my phone and almost drop it. "I mean, I might be able to figure out *where* they are."

I hit the icon for the tracker on Fancy's collar. Please let the device still be attached. Please let the dog be with the twins. Please let the battery still have juice. Please. Please. Please.

"How can you do that?" the deputy asks.

"I downloaded an app for Fancy's GPS on my phone." While I wait for it to load, I give thanks for buying the device that tracks worldwide and not just locally.

"The dog has GPS?" The deputy looks at me with wide-eyed surprise.

Justin explains that I bought the device in case the greyhound ever got loose. "I forgot about it being on the dog's collar. The app was on my old phone, but I haven't activated it on my new one."

An air of optimistic anticipation fills the room until I say, "The battery is only good for five days. I hope the twins charged it."

Then, my phone's screen lights up with a location and a pulsing dot surrounded by a blue circle. I don't recognize the name of the street, so I zoom out until it becomes clear.

Justin points to a location on the map. "That's the Overseas Highway. They're in the Keys."

Gretchen says, "Didn't Cecilia go to the Key Largo after Thanksgiving?"

"Let me see that." One of the police officers plucks the phone from my hand.

Justin pulls out his cell. "I'll call June, Cecilia's sister, and ask where her timeshare is." He scrolls through his contacts list and disappears into the kitchen.

Heath extracts his phone from a pocket, and says to Gretchen, "I'll call your mom and dad to let them know we may have a lead."

Gretchen looks around. "Where's my phone? I need to check on our kids."

I am left alone by the front door with the deputies. After relaying information about the device's location on the walkie-talkie clipped to his shoulder, the deputy returns my phone to me. "Let's hope the GPS tracker is with them and giving an accurate location."

I sit on the sofa in a dark corner of the living room and watch the screen. The red dot does not move. I click on another screen and review the app's tracking history. An almost southern vertical line is displayed from Coral Springs down past Miami and into the Keys but has not moved more than a few blocks in the last twenty-four hours. Perhaps the little square indicates the girls walking Fancy around wherever they are staying.

Justin confers with the deputies. Heath and Gretchen join him. The murmur of their voices carries into the living room. I yawn but continue to stare at the blinking dot. At some point, I fall asleep because I am awakened by Justin's yelling.

"They found them! They're okay!"

I rub my eyes and push into a sitting position from where I'm slumped against the sofa's poufy arm. He emerges from the kitchen with a big grin dimpling his cheeks.

Gretchen trails him, using her index fingers to wipe away dampness under her eyes. "Were they at June's timeshare?"

"Monroe County sheriffs found her car in the parking lot. It took them a while to identify exactly which unit they were in. It wasn't June's but one in another building. Red-headed twins didn't spark anyone's memory. But the greyhound did."

"Is Cecilia in custody?"

"A deputy is staying with them until I arrive. I guess I'll decide what to do once I get there."

Gretchen hugs him and then pushes him toward the front door. "Go! I'll lock up. Do you have your phone? Wallet? The address?"

He nods. "Thanks for everything. Do you want me to call when I get there or wait until a decent hour?"

"If everything's fine, tell me what happened tomorrow."

Justin kisses her cheek and rushes out the door. Gretchen heaves a ragged sigh. When I pick up my phone from the sofa cushion, the screen comes to life in the dark room. She spins around with a hand on her chest. "Who's there?"

"It's me. Annie." I rise to my feet.

"Oh, my God! Have you been here the whole time?"

"I fell asleep. Everything's okay?"

"Well, at least, the girls have been found. Justin just left to bring them back." She covers her yawn with a hand. "I guess we better lock up and head home ourselves. Thank you so much. Without your help, who knows how long it would have taken to locate them."

"I'm glad it all worked out." I pick up my purse from the foyer table. "Well, good night."

"Wait!" Gretchen grabs my arm. "I'm not going to ask why you broke up with my brother. But I want you to know that I think you're the best thing to happen to him and the girls in a long time. Justin has always had a quick temper and its gotten him into trouble too many times to count. Over the years, he's become an expert at apologizing. You'd think he'd learn. Men!"

"Gretchen, I—"

"I know he apologized for whatever stupid thing he did, and you have every right to not see him anymore, especially when you factor in Cecilia's craziness and lies, but would you maybe give him another chance? Justin and the girls love you."

I'm confident about Eden and Savanna's feelings, but not at all sure about Justin's—despite what Gretchen claims. "Whatever happens after this will depend on how he handles Cecilia and if we can resolve another issue we have. I miss him and the girls, and…" I take a deep breath. "I love all of them too."

She hugs me. "I'm glad to hear that. I really hope everything works out. Come on, let's get out of here."

Gretchen's words swirl in my head on the drive home. It's been a month since I broke up with Justin. If Cecilia had not taken the girls, would he have ever contacted me again? He admitted he was wrong to tell the girls our breakup included them, but did he really believe I was capable of stalking and kidnapping them? Although his sister claims he loves me, he has never said the words. Instead, the ones he uttered to my face tore my heart in two.

Frankie called me a survivor, and I am. But I refuse to live on the crumbs of a relationship. I want the whole loaf. In fact, I deserve the damn bakery.

CHAPTER 46

I SLEEP UNTIL early afternoon. The events of the previous day screwed up my usual body clock reset. Upon waking, I check my phone and find no calls or texts from Justin. I am antsy to hear what happened when he arrived in the Keys and fear what he found. What kind of outlandish story will Cecilia spin about me to justify carrying off her granddaughters without his permission or knowledge? And will Justin believe it?

At four p.m., my doorbell rings, followed by light knocking. When I am a few steps away, a child's voice calls out, "Annie, it's us!"

I rush forward and fling open the door. Eden and Savanna are on the step. I drop to one knee, and they throw themselves into my arms. I release them from my tight hug and look out the open door. "Where's your dad?"

"Here." Justin steps into view with a leashed Fancy at his side. He is scruffy and unkempt in the same rumpled clothes he wore yesterday. His eyes are red-rimmed, and his skin is the color of mushrooms. He looks as though he could fall asleep where he stands, but at the same time, his body movements are jittery and twitchy, making Fancy's leash swing back and forth.

I rise to my feet with my eyes glued to his face. "You look exhausted."

Sounding tired but with a slight smile, he says, "Yesterday you said I looked terrible."

"I know. I was upset. Now I'm happy that you're all home safe and sound."

"The girls insisted on stopping here first." He rubs his face with one hand as if he could wipe away his fatigue.

"You need to sleep." As soon as I utter the words, I know there is no way he will get the rest he needs with two children and a dog to take care of. Perhaps he will call his sister, but instead, I decide to be *presumptuous* like Cecilia said I was. "Why don't you rest here? I'll keep the kids and dog quiet and entertained."

Justin does not speak for several moments. To add weight to my suggestion, Eden says, "That's a good idea, Daddy. You'll just fall asleep on the couch anyway."

It's hard to tell from his hesitation if his sluggish brain is unable to process the idea or if he is trying to think of a good excuse why they should go home. Maybe he's worried he'll wake up and find his children gone and have to search for them again. I hold my breath waiting for his reply.

He blinks and rubs one eye like a sleepy toddler. "You just got back from a long trip yourself."

"I slept until this afternoon and feel fine. I'm worried about you staying awake long enough to drive home." In a preemptive gesture, I take the leash from his hand. "Come in and at least take a nap for a few hours while I give the kids their supper."

In a weary monotone, he mumbles, "A few hours? I could sleep for a week."

Once everyone is inside the house, I hand Fancy's leash to Eden and grasp Justin by the elbow. "Girls, take all the dogs out to the backyard while I put your father in bed. Then we'll see about getting supper ready."

Savanna opens the gate for Juno and Bella to exit the living room, and Eden asks, "Can we do make-your-own pizzas for supper like you did with Daddy?"

"Sure, that's a great idea."

A ghost of a smile curves Justin's mouth as we head to my bedroom. "I hate to miss out, but I'd probably pass out in the middle my pie."

"Were you able to rest at all after you got to Key Largo?"

"I slept in a recliner at the condo for an hour or two." He slips off his shoes as I fold back the duvet to the foot of the bed. Looking down at his rumpled clothing, he says, "Maybe I should take a shower."

"Don't worry about the sheets. You need to sleep first. Get undressed, and I'll wash your clothes."

Justin looks at me with bloodshot eyes. His face is pale, and there's a heavier-than-usual amount of stubble on his cheeks and chin. Despite all this, he is still a beautiful man. He gives me a sleepy-eyed look that falls short of a leer and pulls his shirt over his head. "Are you going to watch me get naked?"

Since we are no longer a couple, I can act dismissive and outraged at his suggestive question. Or I can show him I still care and want him. My gaze drops to his bare chest, and my mouth goes dry. I can't help admiring his rounded butt and muscular thighs when his pants hits the floor. Then Justin steps out of his briefs. Holy Mary, Mother of God.

"Are you thinking of ways to take advantage of me in my weakened state?" he asks.

I force my eyes back to his face. An uncomfortable heat flushes my cheeks and the tops of my ears. "Maybe."

The patio door into the kitchen slams shut, and a child calls out, "Annie, where are you?"

"Coming." I pick up Justin's dirty clothes as he slips under the sheet. Before shutting the bedroom door, I ask, "Is it okay if the kids and I run to the grocery store for pizza fixings? I'm a little low on groceries."

"That's fine with me." He props himself on one elbow and punches the pillow into position. "I want to thank you again for everything."

"I'm glad I could help."

"There's something else I need to tell you, and it has nothing to do with what's happened in the last couple of days."

My beating heart stalls when his brow furrows into deep worry lines. What is he going to say to me now?

He sighs and stares at me. "I was a damned fool and hope that someday you can forgive me."

"I told you that when I accepted your apology."

His head starts to drop to the pillow, and then he stops. "Then, there's one more thing I need to say."

"What's that?"

"I love you."

Blood roars in my ears. "Are you serious?"

"What if I'm not?"

"Then I'll smother you while you sleep."

"And if I am serious?"

My knees quiver. "Then I'll tell you I love you, too."

He lies down and closes his eyes. "I've never been more serious in my life."

CHAPTER 47

I AM DYING to know what happened when Justin arrived at the condo and what Cecilia did with the girls before he showed up. On the way to Publix, in as casual a voice as I can muster, I say, "Tell me about your trip."

Eden says, "Grandma's in the hospital."

I straighten and look at the girls in my rearview mirror. "What happened?"

The answer comes from the right side where Savanna sits. "When we woke up this morning Daddy was there, but Grandma wasn't. He said she got sick, and they took her to the hospital. That's why he came to get us."

Did Justin say their grandmother was taken to the hospital instead of jail to avoid upsetting them? Obviously, they don't know Cecilia took them without telling their father. If they don't know that, then maybe they are also unaware of my role in locating them.

"I hope she feels better soon." I glance in the mirror again to see if my nose has grown longer.

"We visited her on the way home," Eden says.

Savanna's voice softens. "She is having tests today. I hate tests!"

I rub my forehead. Is Cecilia actually in a hospital? Maybe the psychiatric ward? I'm unable to continue the soft interrogation because we arrive at Publix, where I buy more than the ingredients needed for make-your-own pizzas. At home, I sort dirty clothes from my suitcase with the ones Justin took off. The girls retrieve wheeled bags from the car and add theirs to the piles. While one load is in the washer and the pizza dough rises in a warm oven, we take the dogs for a walk with each of us holding a leash.

Back at the house, Juno and Bella seem confused by the small people chattering and running around as well as the excited third greyhound that once lived with them. Usually, a late afternoon walk is followed by their dinner and quiet time on the sofa, but not tonight. Fancy jumps in front of them, spinning, doing *zoomies*, and making let's play noises. Juno and Bella look at me as if to ask what they should do with this canine lunatic who has invaded their usually calm space. Despite their obvious disdain for the youngster's enthusiasm, they wag their tails, which I take as a positive sign, so I don't intervene.

The dogs settle down after being fed. Unlike the night Justin and I prepared make-your-own pizza, we're using jars of sauce instead of my homemade marinara. Also, the toppings are much fewer in number and variety. Despite my curiosity to find out more about Cecilia, I am forced to wait until our pizzas are ready to eat.

I peek in on Justin when I place his clean and folded laundry in the bedroom. He lies on his stomach with his face buried in the pillow. His breathing is deep and steady. I watch his strong back muscles lift and fall for a minute, then shut the door softly behind me. I'm thrilled to see him in my bed again.

The girls and I eat our pizzas at the dining room table while the dogs sprawl on the living room sectional. Eden looks at them lined up in a row on the cushions. "When did Juno and Bella know they were dogs?"

"Um, I think they knew as soon as they were born."

"Fancy thinks she is our sister."

Savanna puts down her pizza. "Grandma says she isn't really and knows it. Is that true?"

"Well, she probably thinks she's a dog when she's with other dogs and a girl when she's with you." The answer seems to satisfy them, so I plunge ahead. "Speaking of your grandmother, what did she tell you about going to the Keys?"

They exchange anxious glances with each other and remain mute.

What are they reluctant to tell me? "I know she thought I was hanging around your school, but it wasn't me."

My statement opens the door for Eden, who is endearing in her earnestness. "We know that! The lady had short hair and a car the same color as yours, but it wasn't you. We told Grandma, but she didn't believe us."

Savanna displays a worried expression. "Are you a staller? Grandma says you are and can go to jail."

I don't want to be contradictive and pit myself against Cecilia with the twins in the middle, but I can't allow misstatements to stand without a defense. "Being a *stalker* means you keep following someone after they tell you to stop. But you're right. The lady at your school wasn't me. Can you tell me why you went to the Keys?"

Both girls draw their narrow shoulders up toward their ears.

Eden says, "We asked, but Grandma kept saying we had to go for our own good."

Savanna's eyes film with tears. "We missed two days of school."

I sit up straight and smile. Time to change the subject. "Well, you're home now and will be back in school on Monday. As smart as you are, I'm sure you'll catch up in no time."

A tear slides down Savanna's cheek. "And we lost our phone."

"No, we didn't." Eden snorts with impatience. "Daddy said it's somewhere at Grandma's house, and he'll find it for us."

"What if he can't? We looked everywhere, but Grandma still made us leave without it."

Cecilia knew Justin could track his daughters with their phone, so she must have hidden it well. "Your dad told me the app on *his* phone shows *yours* is somewhere inside her house. It's probably fallen behind or under something and is hard to see. I'm sure you guys will find it. Who's ready for another pizza?"

We eat, clean up the kitchen, and fold laundry. I check in on Justin again. He makes no sound or movement when I softly call his name and touch his shoulder. Being presumptuous for a second time today, I tell the girls they're spending the night here. While I prepare the guest bedroom, they bathe in the adjoining bathroom. Afterwards, we pop popcorn and watch *Frozen 2*. I insist they get into bed at nine-thirty despite their complaints of not being tired. Halfway through reading a bedtime story on my iPad, I discover both girls in a deep sleep. After kissing them on the forehead, I tiptoe out of the room.

All three dogs are stretched out on the L-shaped living room sofa, snoring and snuffling. Fancy's legs are bicycling in the air. She is more likely dream-chasing Eden and Savanna than a rabbit. Suddenly, I'm tired too. I shower in the guest bath to not wake Justin and dress in a long nightgown. I debate whether to sleep with the dogs on the living room sofa or crawl into my bed with Justin.

With my decision made, I enter the bedroom and slip under the sheet. My internal clock may no longer be set exactly for Paris, but I'm not on Florida time either. I close my eyes and fall into a deep sleep. I wake when the bed dips. Someone sits on the mattress next to me.

"Annie. Wake up."

When I open my eyes, a dishwater-colored light seeps into the room around the edges of the blinds. "What time is it?"

Justin is dressed. "Six."

"How long have you been up?"

"Since four. I took a shower and got dressed. Thank you for washing my clothes. I want to talk with you while the kids are still asleep."

I flip onto my back. "Okay."

"What did the girls tell you?"

"Not much. I know Cecilia's in the hospital, but they have no clue why she took them down to the Keys. They don't seem to know that you had no idea where they were."

"Did you tell them how we found them?"

"No. They think you came to get them because their grandmother got sick. They're more upset with not having their phone and missing school than disappearing for two days."

Justin bends one leg and places his knee on the bed to face me. "Good. I didn't say their grandmother kidnapped them because I didn't want to them scared or worried."

"Tell me about when you got to the condo."

He runs a hand over his bare scalp. "It was three in the morning. I was told a Monroe County deputy would be waiting for me. I thought he would be outside to make sure Cecilia didn't drive off, but they also stationed a woman officer inside too. Thank God, Eden and Savanna slept through everything."

"What happened?" I envision a worst-case scenario where Cecilia threatens suicide or harm to the children.

"The deputy said when they first got there Cecilia claimed she told me where she was going with the kids, but they didn't buy it. They checked on the girls who were asleep and radioed in their location which was relayed to me."

"Did she give the deputies a hard time?"

"Not until shortly before I arrived. Like I said, the woman officer waited inside while her male partner stayed in the patrol car. Cecilia asked if she was under arrest, so she knew she had done wrong by taking the kids without telling me. The deputy told her that I wasn't pressing charges, and they would leave when I got there. She and the woman officer talked for quite a while."

"Did Cecilia tell her why she took the kids?"

"No. She mostly talked about Lucy and the twins then asked if she could get dressed. The officer waited outside the bedroom and when she came out,

Cecilia offered to make coffee. It was a short time later everything went downhill."

I sit up and bunch my pillow against the headboard. "Go on."

"She became agitated and kept running to the window if there was a flash of headlights or the sound of car in the parking lot."

"Was she afraid because you were getting closer to being there?"

"No. She thought it was *you* coming to take the girls away."

CHAPTER 48

I GASP AND clap my hand to my chest.

Justin says, "According to the deputy, Cecilia became more manic and claimed to see you walking past the window. She wouldn't settle down, so the officer notified her partner who called the EMTs. When I pulled into the parking lot and saw the ambulance and police cars with their flashers on, all kinds of horrible thoughts went through my head."

"Oh, Justin." I cover his hand with mine.

"They had her on a gurney when I walked in, but she kept trying to get off. Cecilia usually becomes cold and unemotional when she's upset, but I saw her hit one of the EMTs who strapped her down. I don't know how the girls slept through all that commotion. The condo wasn't that big."

"They said you went to see her on your way home."

"We stopped at the hospital in Homestead." He shakes his head. "At first, she was fine, except she claimed to have no clue why she was there. I sent the girls out of the room and told Cecilia about what happened. She didn't believe me when I described how she acted the previous night with the police and EMTs. Before we left the condo this morning, I talked with her sister, June, who is flying in from Orlando. The doctor wants to keep Cecilia for another day to run tests then June will drive her home when she's released."

"Did you ask why she took the girls without telling you?"

"She couldn't give me a good answer and realizes her reason for going to the Keys doesn't make sense, especially after I told her you were in France. She began to cry, which really bothered Eden and Savanna. When we were leaving, a technician came to take Cecilia for an MRI. Maybe we'll know what's going on after all the testing is done."

There is a moment of loaded silence between us. The only other topic for discussion is our declarations of love for each other last night. A piteous whine sounds from the living room. I raise my eyebrows at Justin.

"I decided to let sleeping dogs lie." Another chorus of wails sings out. "I guess I can't put it off any longer." He leans forward, kisses my forehead, and leaves the room.

While the greyhounds are outside, I get dressed. When I enter the kitchen, the smell of rich coffee fills the air. Justin portions dog food into three metal bowls and places them on elevated platforms. All three greyhounds wait for his signal to eat, then bury their noses in the dishes, chowing down like they haven't been fed for days.

The twins stroll into the kitchen with tousled hair and sleepy eyes. "What's for breakfast?" asks Eden.

Justin points toward the room where they slept. "Go get dressed and we'll head home to eat. Annie deserves some peace and quiet."

In turn, Eden points to the countertop next to the oven. "There's granola in there, and Annie says it's better for us than sugary cereal."

Savanna heads to the refrigerator. "And milk too. We bought it at the store yesterday."

I look at Justin out of the corner of my eye. "When did you last eat a meal?"

"I don't remember. It seems like I've been living on caffeine for days." He glances at his half-full mug by the coffee maker.

"Why don't you and the girls stay and eat breakfast here? I can have it ready in a few minutes."

While the girls dress and pack up, Justin sets the table with dishes, bowls, glasses, and silverware. We all sit down to scrambled eggs with leftover pepperoni and cheese, toast, granola, milk, yogurt, and strawberries. After the kids, their belongings, and the dog are loaded into the car, Justin takes my hand in his at the front door.

He runs his thumb over my knuckles. "I can't tell you how much I appreciate all you've done for us. I know I don't deserve a second chance for what I said, and Cecilia is reason enough for you to wash your hands of our family, but my daughters love you, and so do I. I'm hoping you'll let us try again."

"I would like that."

He glances at the car, where high-pitched chatter filters out the open windows. "It looks like I'm going to have to make arrangements for getting them to school and picked up starting tomorrow."

"Can I help?"

"I'll drop them off in the morning. If you can get them at dismissal, I'll leave your name as an approved pickup."

"What time should I be there?"

"Two is good. When I get off work, I'll check into the school's aftercare program. They've wanted to go, but Cecilia insisted I not spend the money when she could bring them to her house."

"Daddy! Are we gonna leave?" Eden's upper torso leans halfway out the window.

"I better go." He takes a step toward the car and then turns back to me. "I forgot something."

I mentally run through a quick checklist of items brought from his car into the house, but I can't think of anything left behind. "What?"

"This."

He places his hand on my waist and presses his warm mouth to mine, bringing his free hand up to cup my cheek. His kiss is light and lingering, sending a clear message of passion and love.

CHAPTER 49

THE FOLLOWING DAY at noon, I go to Justin's house with the key he gave me to let Fancy out. Rather than leave her there alone, I load her into a dog crate and bring her to my house so she can spend the afternoon with Juno and Bella.

A few minutes before the school pickup time, I secure her in the backseat with a seatbelt harness I have. I hope the girls will be thrilled to see her picking them up today. Fancy pokes her head out the window and inhales all the new scents drifting by on the breeze while I creep forward in the caravan of cars lined up outside the school.

Eden and Savanna spot my car and Fancy when I finally enter the school's circular driveway. They squeal and wave their arms. I stop by the main entrance and present my I.D. while the girls extol the wonderfulness of their dog to the other children waiting for rides.

After arriving at my house, I give them glasses of milk and bowls of Chex Mix while they finish their homework. It takes them longer to find the paperwork and settle at the kitchen counter than to complete it. I suggest we make homemade bubbles. The girls punch holes in plastic lids, then I hot-glue them to craft sticks. After mixing water, dishwashing liquid, and corn syrup, we go out to the backyard with all the dogs. Juno and Bella stroll around while Fancy romps with the twins like she is a third little girl.

The playful greyhound leaps into the air, bumping bubbles with her nose. She shakes her head with obvious distaste when one pops inside her mouth. At one point, Fancy chases a ribbon of shiny globes drifting over the surface of the swimming pool. The girls and I gasp when she falls into the water. The twins coax her toward the steps, and I run inside the house for towels. After we dry her off, I deposit the damp towels in the laundry room. On my return to the backyard, the doorbell rings. I open the door and let Justin inside.

He wraps his hand around my upper arm and kisses my cheek. "Hi. How'd everything go today?"

"Just fine."

"I'm here a little late because I stopped at the school and enrolled Eden and Savanna in the aftercare program. They'll start tomorrow. I gave them your name and phone number as an authorized pickup person along with my sister. There may be some days I can't get there by six. I hope that's okay."

"Of course, it is."

He looks around. "Where is everybody?"

"In the backyard blowing bubbles. Did you know Fancy loves chasing and popping them? The goofball wasn't paying attention and fell into the pool."

"Is she okay?"

"She's fine but wasn't too happy being cold and wet. We just finished drying her off."

"Do we have enough time to talk before they come inside?"

"I think they're good for a few more minutes. Would you like something to drink?"

We sit at the dining room table with bottles of chilled water. Justin takes a long swallow. "I've been thinking about setting boundaries for Cecilia and doing our best to make sure she follows them."

"*Our best?* You want me to help?"

"Of course. We're in this together. I'm hoping the two of us can handle it, but I'm prepared to call in reinforcements, if necessary."

"What kind of reinforcements?"

"My sister, Cecilia's sister, the military, and Homeland Security. I'm preparing a list."

I laugh.

Justin's mouth tightens, and his gaze drops to the tabletop. "I want you to know that I'm going to do a better job of keeping my temper in check. I know I tend blow up before I stop and think about what I'm doing."

"At least, you're very good at apologizing afterward."

He raises his eyes to look into mine. "But by then the damage is done."

Justin may have a hair-trigger temper, but my default position when I am hurt is to go into a hidey-hole to lick my emotional wounds. "I'm not perfect either. You tried to talk to me each time we had a fight, but I overreacted, refused to discuss it, and then shut down. I need to work on that because any successful relationship needs good communication."

"I agree. We'll both tackle our personal issues, and we'll work together on Cecilia."

A door opens at the back of the house, and a girl's voice calls out, "Annie! We're out of bubbles."

Justin pushes back his chair. "Thanks for picking up the kids and taking care of Fancy. I'll get them out of your hair now."

"I have chili in the crockpot. Do you want to stay for supper?"

Both girls enter the dining room trailed by three greyhounds. Eden says, "We're having chili? Can I put cheese on mine?"

"Do I have to eat all the beans, Daddy?" Savanna asks.

He holds his hands up in surrender.

The next day, Justin and I chat via Facetime after the girls have gone to bed. He tells me about their first day in aftercare. "All the kids are required to finish their homework before they're allowed on the playground. Eden and Savanna were so hungry by the time we got home, they didn't care what I served for supper and went to bed without complaint. As far as I'm concerned, that program is worth every penny."

"Have you heard from Cecilia?"

"She was released from the hospital today. The doctors found that a new medication she started taking in December was responsible for her irrational behavior."

I tighten my lips to avoid commenting about her craziness before the recent prescription change.

"Her primary care physician put her on Digoxin because of an irregular heartbeat, but she failed to tell him she was also taking a diuretic. I guess she complained to the gynecologist about being bloated from her hormone therapy, so she was prescribed a water pill. The two in combination caused an electrolyte imbalance that resulted in mania and visual hallucinations. Now she's only supposed to take the medication for her heart. After all, regulating that is more important than being a little puffy."

"Cardiac issues are serious but so are hormonal imbalances."

"I know, but how you feel doesn't matter as much as dying from a heart attack."

Except sometimes you feel like you are dying or want to. "What happens with her now?"

"Tomorrow her sister is taking her to Orlando for a couple of weeks to keep an eye on her. June and I had a nice, long talk. She wants Cecilia to move closer to her and away from me and the girls."

Justin says this with such a placid demeanor that I can't determine whether he's offended or approves of this idea. "Why?"

"She's been worried about Cecilia ever since Lucy's father died. That's when she became overprotective of her only child, the one person left in what she considered her nuclear family. But when Lucy grew older and more independent, she couldn't let her go. They had some intense arguments, and most of them were about me. The more Cecilia tried to hold on, the more

Lucy pulled away." Averting his eyes, Justin sucks his bottom lip into his mouth.

I lean closer to the screen of my iPad, trying to intercept his gaze but say nothing, waiting for him to work through whatever dilemma has silenced him.

After several moments, his eyes meet mine again. "I suspected back then, and I still do, that Lucy deliberately got pregnant to get away from her mother."

I sit back, distancing myself from the screen, unsure what to say in response.

"I wasn't prepared to be a husband and father at that point, but it was the best thing that ever happened to me. My only regret is Lucy won't see what great daughters she has."

"That's a beautiful thing to say, Justin." My heart melts all over the place.

"I mean it."

"I know you do. And that's why I love you."

CHAPTER 50

ADJUSTING TO NOT having Cecilia as our date night babysitter is not easy. The first weekend without her, we spend all day Saturday with the twins. That night, as Justin and I lay naked in his bed, Eden calls out from the darkened family room. I roll off from straddling his hips. Justin hops up, slips into his discarded sweatpants, and opens the bedroom door. He closes it behind him, but Eden's complaint about a nightmare can still be heard.

Justin's voice becomes fainter as he escorts his daughter back to her room. "It's okay. You just had a bad dream. Nothing bad is going to happen to Fancy."

I don't know how long it will be until he returns, so I switch on the nightstand lamp and get dressed. I'm slipping on my second sandal when Justin reappears and halts in the doorway.

"Hey, you're not naked anymore."

I stand and walk over to him. He wraps an arm around my waist, and I rub my cheek against his stubbly one. "I'd love to stay, but it's getting late. I need to let my dogs out."

He sighs. "I miss our childless times together."

The following weekend, Justin and I relax on his family room sofa after dinner. The girls are on a walk with Fancy.

I shift onto one hip and face him. "I'm leaving for New York City next Sunday."

He checks the calendar on his phone. "Are you going to be gone on Valentine's Day?"

"No. I'll be back on the thirteenth."

"Good." He leans back against the squeaky leather and crosses his arms behind his head. "I have plans for that evening. I hired a neighbor lady to watch the girls, so you and I can go out to dinner and spend some time alone. What are you going to do in New York?"

"It's Fashion Week, and I've been hired to walk in three shows."

"I thought you did that last month in France."

"Fashion Week happens twice a year in New York, London, Milan, and Paris. Other major cities also have them, but these four get the most attention."

Justin's eyebrows squish together. "Do styles change that often? I've been wearing the same kind of clothes for years."

"The styles for women change more than those for men and for different climates where there are four definite seasons."

Justin's gaze drops. "You don't have to answer this if you don't want to, but do you make a lot of money modeling for these shows?"

"Not as much as the top ten models in the industry. If designers are strapped for cash, models will sometimes be reimbursed with clothes from the show. Many of us have sold these trade payments online through websites like eBay to pay our bills."

"I guess it's not a bad way to travel and meet new people, even though I'm sure it's hard work."

"It is, and thank you for recognizing that. Anyway, I wanted to give you enough notice, so can find someone to let Fancy out while I'm gone."

"Is your Aunt Linda going to be dogsitting Juno and Bella?"

"Yeah, she is."

Last week, I took a chance and called my father before contacting my aunt, knowing how much he enjoys being with my dogs. He said, "You know I would love to do it, Annemarie, but I have so many invitations for the next six weeks of *The Season* I don't know how I'll get enough sleep, let alone have the time to devote to Juno and Bella. The last thing I want is for them to feel lonely and abandoned."

For a few seconds, I was speechless. This from the man who left me in the care of others throughout my childhood. At least he was finally developing some humanity at this late stage. And as far as his social life was concerned, Dennis has again become that coveted Palm Beach commodity—a good-looking, mature single man.

"That's okay," I said. "I figured you might be booked up, but I wanted to contact you first. The dogs like your company and miss you."

There was a long pause. When Dennis spoke, he sounded a bit emotional. "I miss them too. How are you doing?"

I told him about Justin and I being back together again. I didn't tell him about the twins being kidnapped by their grandmother or the role I played in discovering their whereabouts. Instead, I said Justin apologized for what he said to me in anger. In turn, I admitted I was wrong for refusing to talk to him about what happened. "We both promised to do better in the future."

Dennis' voice was neutral and somewhat parental sounding. "Are you sure about this, Annemarie? He caused you a lot of pain."

Three men have broken my heart at least once, but now I refuse to allow that grief to define me and my future. I said to my father, "That's true. But I've found over the years that pain has made me stronger and heartbreak has made me wiser. I don't want fear to make me lose out on love—and I do love him and he loves me."

"As long as you're happy is all that matters to me," Dennis said.

Now I smile at the man beside me who I love, who makes me very happy, and who needs a dog sitter. "If you don't have a neighbor or relative who can help, there's a service I can recommend. I've used them when Linda wasn't available."

"Text me their information."

I lift my cell phone off the coffee table. "I'll do it now."

He sighs as I locate my contact list. "With Cecilia gone, I'm beginning to realize how much I depended on her. You know, after having kids, buying a house, and holding down a full-time job, I thought I was a mature adult. But without another person around to pick up the slack, it's like I'm forced to grow up and be responsible all over again. What the hell have I been doing for the past nine years?"

I smile and rub my hand over his beautiful, bare head. "Aging, sweetheart."

His phone dings with my text message, and then he turns to me. "Do you own high heels?"

"Of course, I do. Why do you ask?"

"I've never seen you wear them. Would you feel uncomfortable being taller than me?"

"I've gotten used to being taller than most people. Would *you* be bothered?"

Justin snorts. "No. I figured you don't wear heels because you're more comfortable in flat shoes."

"I am. Wearing high heels is not only painful, but have you ever seen the feet of those women who wear them all the time? Talk about misshapen hooves."

A disgusted sound comes from the back of his throat. "I'll take your word for it."

"I don't really think about the similarity in our heights because you're so sexy, and awesome, and self-confident."

"And you look up to me regardless of my inseam."

I place my hand on his thigh and squeeze it. "Your inseam is plenty long for me."

"When I saw some of your past runway photos with those legs that go on forever, all I could think about was having you wear shoes and boots like that when you're with me." His look warms me all over.

"Um, would you want me to wear them only in the house or out in public too?"

His voice drops into a deeper and more gravelly pitch. "Both. Out in public every guy will think I'm a real badass when they see you, my beautiful, tall goddess, on my arm. In private, I have this fantasy of you wearing a pair of killer shoes, with the pointy heels digging into my butt while I—"

When his burgeoning erection bumps against my fingertips, the front door opens. "We're back!"

Justin plops a throw pillow onto his lap.

I stand to greet his daughters. "Hi, girls. How was your walk? Let me help you with Fancy."

Justin leans his head back against the sofa. "Thanks."

I grin at him. "No problem. Just picking up the slack."

CHAPTER 51

IT IS A TYPICAL winter's day when I arrive in New York City. The temperature hovers around freezing, but there is no snow, sleet, or blustery winds. The sun shines brightly when I step out of LaGuardia airport to hail a cab. I am booked to share a two-bedroom Airbnb apartment with three other models, two of whom I know from my agency. We will hardly see each other during the day and may only have contact when we share a queen-sized bed at night.

I've been booked for three shows over three days. In previous years, I had walked in more than one show a day at different venues and would have to dash across the city to get to them on time. A few years ago, the early morning show ran late and affected all the others. It was a nightmare.

My first show is with a new designer and is scheduled for six p.m. on Monday. I arrive early to wait my turn for final fittings, hair and makeup. Smiling, I walk around the bustling backstage in delight. There are dogs in crates and on leashes everywhere. I had been asked by the casting panel about my experience with them because most models they were booking for the show would be paired with a dog. I listed my ownership and fostering of greyhounds. I'm sure that's what got me this job.

I sit on an empty folding chair and burrow through my bag to make sure I have a nude thong, makeup remover, a razor, and deodorant, in case they are not provided by the designer. At least, I don't need to keep feminine hygiene products on hand.

A few minutes later, a striking woman with a beautiful golden retriever points to the chair next to me. "Is this seat taken?"

I shake my head as the dog sniffs my pant leg, which probably carries Juno and Bella's scents. "May I pet him or her?"

"Sure. She loves attention, but you'll have to be the one to stop first. If you wait for Finley to get tired of being petted, you'll be here for hours."

I laugh and stroke my fingers over the dog's square head, then scratch her chest. She raises his nose to the ceiling and closes her eyes. "Is she going to be in the show?"

"I...think so."

The hesitation in the woman's response draws my attention to her face. "Are you walking her on the runway?"

"Me? No. No. I'm not a model. Finley is *my* dog."

"Well, you're both beautiful enough."

The woman leans back in the chair. "Thanks. I'm just doubly nervous right now. I'm afraid Finley might be too much to handle for the model who gets her. The last thing I want is for my dog to ruin Leila's show. She's worked so hard to get her collection ready."

"You said you're doubly nervous. What else is worrying you?"

She runs a hand through her curly, light brown hair. "Several of the clothes are made from my fabric designs. I'm worried people won't like them, and Leila won't get the sales she's expecting or get good reviews."

I know from the initial fittings that the designer, Leila Rue, has some canine-printed fabrics in her show, but none of the outfits I'm assigned is one of them. "I saw a beautiful camel-colored coat with silhouettes of greyhounds on it. Is that one of your designs?"

"Yes. Did you like it?" Her words sound hopeful but tentative.

"I want to order it. I have two greyhounds at home."

The woman's aqua-colored eyes become luminous. "Really?"

"Yes. The coat is a gorgeous design and so is the fabric."

"Oh, uh, that's great," she stammers, and then licks her lips. "Um, I'm wondering, I mean, I guess you know how to handle big dogs if you have two of them. Right?"

I stop petting Finley, and she places one paw on my knee to urge me to continue. Instead, I stand and hold out my hand. "May I?"

The woman hands me the leash. Finley rises to her feet. When I move to stand beside the retriever, she lunges forward. I anticipated her dominance move and jerk the leash sideways. Turning to the right, I walk her in a tight circle, stopping in front of my empty chair. "Sit."

Finley drags me forward a half step. Again, we go no farther than to walk in a tight circle. On the third try, she sits when I tell her. I stroke her head, breathe in and out, wait several seconds, and then once again step forward. "Come."

We advance a couple of feet before Finley hustles to get in front of me. I stop and command her to sit again. We repeat this several times until she walks beside me from one end of the cavernous space to the other, dodging racks of clothes, people, and other dogs. My hold on her leash is loose, and my arm hangs by my side. We return to where her owner waits, staring at us with wide eyes.

"Do you have a treat I can give her?"

"W-what?"

"I don't have any dog treats with me. Do you have some?"

The woman fumbles in her bag and hands me a sandwich bag filled with cheese cubes. "She loves these."

I hold one next to my nose. Finley stares at my face. "Sit."

Her fluffy behind plops onto the floor.

"Good girl!" I feed her a cube. I hold another in my loosely closed fist and bend over with the treat a few inches above the floor. "Down."

Finley sniffs at my fingers. I repeat the command twice more before she slides onto her belly.

"Good girl!" I give her another piece of cheese, pet her silky head, and sit down.

Her owner turns and grips my hand. "Please tell me you're one of the models in Leila's show."

"I am."

"Will you walk with her?"

"Sure, if it's okay with Leila. I haven't been told that a specific dog's been assigned to me."

The woman flings her arms around me. "Oh, my God, thank you so much!"

I smile and hold out my hand. "I'm Annemarie Warden but call me Annie."

Finley's owner smiles back and clasps my palm. "It is so wonderful to meet you, Annie. I'm Rachel, Rachel Karras. Let's go find Leila and see if you and Finley can walk together."

CHAPTER 52

LEILA RUE'S PRODUCTION this year is inspired by her love of dogs and choreographed to resemble a Westminster Dog Show. Astroturf covers the runway lined with low, white picket fencing. Most of the models walk with a leashed dog. A regal black Doberman is paired with a model in a charcoal LBD trimmed in tan braiding around the neckline. A Scottish terrier parades alongside a redhead in a plaid coat dress.

Finley and I strut past the attendees with her shiny, strawberry-blond coat floating away from her body. I'd be surprised if anyone noticed me in the three outfits that I model—a floral print prairie dress, an elegant black, off-the-shoulder tunic top and bell-bottom pants, and a scarlet, smocked blouse with high-waist trousers. In my opinion, Finley is by far the prettier one on the runway.

Other models accompanied by their furry companions wear outfits with more literal canine references. In addition to the greyhound coat, there is a jacket with cameo buttons containing dog faces. In evening wear is a slinky silk gown with an Escher-like print of Dalmatians with the three-D, real-life dog version walking next to it. But the hit of the show is a box-pleated dress covered in black dachshunds with a long-haired wiener dog strutting beside it. Not all the models walk with canines; two with clipboards view the canine lineup like judges, and three hold up giant placards to announce the categories. Like the dog show, they have Sporting, Working, Non-Sporting, and one non-AKC designation—Party Animals.

After the final walk down the runway with all the models, dogs, and the designer, I find Rachel waiting for us backstage. Finley's bushy tail slaps my leg when she spots her, but the retriever remains by my side as we approach.

Rachel hugs me and pats her dog's head. "You guys looked wonderful on the runway. I took a video to show my husband how well-behaved she was. He won't believe it."

I bend down and scratch just above Finley's tail. Once again, she lifts her head and closes her eyes with a look of relaxed ecstasy. "She was a perfect lady, and you are a very talented textile designer. This is one of the few times I hope I'm paid in trade."

"If you want, I'll ask Leila if you can have the greyhound coat."

"Thanks, but you don't have to do that. Since the two of you are new to the industry, you need all the cash you can get. Besides, I have plenty of money from my ex-husband and can buy whatever I want." As soon I say *ex-husband*, Rachel's bright expression dims. I stop petting Finley and straighten. "What's wrong?"

She flutters a hand in front of her face to fan tears that film her striking eyes. "It's just that I might have one of those soon too. I think divorce court is where my marriage is headed."

"I'm sorry to hear that. You're a such a beautiful and talented person, I hate to see you unhappy, but trust me. In time, everything will work out. I learned the hard way that divorce was the best thing that could have happened to my marriage." I extend Finley's leash to her.

A frown pulls at the corners of Rachel's full-lipped mouth. As soon as she has the leash in hand, Finley's head jerks up. For dogs, that tether is often a conduit to their owner's emotional state. In response, the retriever leans against Rachel's legs.

She strokes Finley's golden head. "Can I ask you a question, Annie?"

"Sure."

"What made you realize your marriage was…unfixable?"

What do I tell her? A philandering husband who would never change his ways? A pregnant mistress who was likely the first of many lovers?

Rachel shakes her head, and her caramel-colored curls bounce around her face. "Forget I asked. I understand it's too personal. It's just that I—"

"He wanted a divorce to marry his pregnant mistress before the baby was born."

She flinches like I zapped her with a stun gun. "What the—! You're kidding me."

"Nope. That's what happened."

"What did you do?"

"Since he was on a deadline and I wasn't, I made the cheater pay me big bucks for a quick end to our marriage. Do you know why some divorces are so much more expensive than others?"

"Uh, no?"

I grin. "Because they're worth it!"

To my surprise, I can now joke about being blindsided by Thierry. What has changed? Then it hits me. I've opened my heart to love again.

We laugh, but soon Rachel's expression sobers again. "How long did it take you to get over it?"

I stare into her wide, aquamarine eyes. "I won't lie to you. It's been four long years, and the hurt only recently stopped. Take my advice. Don't lock down your heart against the pain. Yeah, the numbness helps in the short term, but holding onto it keeps out the love that heals you."

Her arms encircle my waist, and Finley presses against both of us.

CHAPTER 53

I WAIT FOR my flight home with other passengers seated in blue vinyl chairs and clustered near charging outlets where they read, text, and talk on their cell phones. Across the aisle from me, a gray-haired man in a rumpled suit and puffy jacket jerks awake after a loud snort, blinks, and scans the gate area. The smell of rich, dark coffee drifts from a Starbucks across the center aisle. The sounds of the coffee grinder and espresso machine are audible above the hum of voices around me.

My phone rings, and Justin's name appears on the screen. I have my earphones in so no one can hear his side of the conversation.

He waves at me. "Hi. Are you headed home?"

"I'm on my way."

"The babysitter confirmed a few minutes ago. Our Valentine's date is on."

"Great. You know, I can't believe how much I missed you on this trip."

"Same here, babe. Talking and texting is no substitute for seeing and touching."

A euphoric feeling fills my chest. I smile and glance at the nearby passengers, like the snorer did. Did any of them note my lovestruck expression? Of course, no one is paying any attention to me, including the businessman who has fallen asleep again.

"Annie, are you still there?" The voice in my ear is laced with amusement.

"I'm here."

"Are you okay?"

"I'm fine, but things will be better…" In an I-want-to-fuck-you voice, I whisper, "When I have you in my arms again."

There is a lag before Justin speaks. "I feel the same way. Damn! You're making me hard. Are you still at the gate or on the plane?"

"I'm waiting to board. We should be leaving soon, I hope. If my flight arrives in Fort Lauderdale on time, it will be after midnight before I'm on the road and headed home."

"Today's going to be a long one for you."

I attempt to stifle a yawn and my eyes water. Since my final booked show was mid-morning, I have been awake since five a.m. There is a hum of muted voices in the background of his call. "Are you in your bedroom watching TV?"

"How'd you know?"

"Since it's after eight on a school night, you're either using the television in there or on your office computer so you don't wake up the kids."

He chuckles. "You've already got my routines figured out. It makes me feel naked."

"Sweetheart, if I wasn't sitting in an airport terminal, you would be."

"You're not helping. At this rate, I won't be able to sleep on my stomach tonight. In fact, how about—"

The jarring announcement that boarding will begin in a few minutes obliterates his words. "Hang on," I say into my phone. While I wait for the loudspeaker to go quiet again, other passengers at the gate disconnect phone chargers, gather food wrappers, and close up their carry-ons. "Okay, what were you saying?"

"It doesn't matter. Get on that plane and come home safe and sound to me."

"I will. I love you."

"I love you more."

The flight is uneventful, but by the time I pick up my luggage, get my car from long-term parking, and enter my house, it is almost two a.m. Leaving my bags unpacked, I shower and fall asleep minutes after crawling into bed.

I'm awakened by the ringing of my doorbell and squint at my phone. Nine-thirty. So much for sleeping late. At the door, a delivery woman holds out to me a huge bouquet of two dozen pink roses in a heavy cut-glass vase tied with a pink velvet ribbon and bow. In the kitchen, I remove the envelope. To my surprise, the flowers are not from Justin.

My name is written on the outside of the envelope in handwriting I recognize but have not seen in a long time. The card reads: *Happy Valentine's Day. I won't make you cringe with a sappy sentiment. You know that's not my style. I just hope your young man knows he's hit the jackpot with you. Your father.*

I hug the card to my chest and sniff the fragrance of the delicate blooms. The word *love* is not in my father's message, but the emotion is evident. *He* sent flowers to me for the first time. *He* wrote the words by hand. *He* personally ordered the flowers at a florist shop. This is the first time I've received anything from him on Valentine's Day.

Then an ugly thought intrudes. Were the flowers a standing order for his wife? At the last minute, did Dennis have to write another card and change the delivery address? Maybe, but I choose to believe otherwise. He could have sent this elegant bouquet to any Palm Beach socialite to curry favor during this busy social season, but my father picked me instead.

I return the card and envelope to the little plastic pick and carry the vase to the dining room table. I send Dennis a thank-you text rather than a phone call, if he is sleeping in from a late-night party. I yawn and return to bed to get a little more rest before my Valentine's Day date with my jackpot-winning young man.

CHAPTER 54

ALTHOUGH JUSTIN AND I have been seeing each other since September, all our dates have been outings to sports bars, movies, picnics on the beach, and casual dining restaurants. This is our first dress-up, fancy restaurant date.

I slither into a golden tube of a dress that flirts with the backs of my thighs. The metallic fabric hugs my body, making it look like thin sheets of gold leaf are pressed onto my skin. Hopefully, Justin will feel proud if other men unwrap me with their eyes. As a result of our conversation about high heels, I push my feet into a pair of Michael Kors snakeskin leather stilettos with double buckle fastenings. These shoes will put me several inches taller than him.

The doorbell rings at six p.m. My breath catches when I find Justin leaning against one of the stucco pillars supporting the porch overhang. He is dressed like a GQ cover model in a pale gray suit that molds itself to his body. Despite all the bulging muscles in his long form, he appears elegant and expensive. My heart thunders in my chest, and it takes every ounce of willpower to keep me from dragging him into my bedroom and forgetting about our dinner reservation.

Justin steps forward and pulls me close enough to feel the heat of his chest, but not so close that we touch. He brings his free hand to the side of my face, cups my cheek, and lifts his warm mouth to mine. His lips tease mine until I open them, and his tongue slips inside. It is wet, and so welcome that I free-fall into a lust I can't hold at bay.

He ends the kiss and steps back. "Lock up, so I can show off the most beautiful woman I know."

"Where is she?" I sling my arm around his neck and crane my head toward his car. "In there?"

Shaking his head, Justin says, "Looks like I need to work harder on you."

"Harder is good."

He smacks my rear end. Once we're headed to the restaurant, I glance down at his leg next to the car's gearshift console. It is covered by sharp-creased trousers, but a picture pops into my mind of his hair-dusted, taut thighs electrifying my sensitive skin as he—

"I'm surprised you haven't asked where we're going?"

"W-What?" I blink as my lurid daydream disappears faster than a prom dress after the dance ends. "Um, is the restaurant very far away?"

"I made a reservation at NYY Steak in the Seminole Casino. Have you ever been there?"

"No, but I've heard good things about it."

The casino is a fifteen-minute drive away from where I live. Justin pulls his car up to the valet stand, hands over the key fob, then comes around to open my door. We enter one of the arched entrances and head down the vibrantly carpeted hallway to the first-floor restaurant.

A hostess in a tailored suit greets us. Justin gives her his name, and she eyes him overly long after checking the built-in screen on her podium. "Welcome to NYY and happy Valentine's Day, Mr. Stabler."

Her second glance at him pleases rather than offends me. I am biased, of course, but in comparison to every man I have seen in the casino so far, Justin is the most striking and sexy. He exudes the masculine self-assurance of an expert who can take care of a woman in and out of the bedroom, and I am the lucky one to have repeated firsthand experience.

"Please follow me." The hostess tucks two leatherbound menus in the crook of her arm.

The décor is elegant, with the addition of the New York Yankee highlights all around. Now, the name of the restaurant makes sense to me. Tables are covered in white linen, surrounded by dark wicker armchairs with black cushions. We walk on red brick floors past a lounge where drinkers sit around a well-lit bar or in comfy club chairs. The distance between me and the hostess lengthens when I slow to peer into a long, glass case where various cuts of meat are artfully arranged. Justin's hand at the small of my waist gently propels me forward.

The hostess stops at a booth in the back. I'm grateful we're not seated near the open front of the restaurant, where the whiff of cigarette smoke from the casino is discernable. After the hostess departs with one last sidelong look at Justin, a dapper man approaches with a carafe of water.

"May I?" He points to the glasses on the table. "This is our filtered water and tastes wonderful. Our guests love it."

Another waiter behind him asks if we would like something from the bar. Justin orders a martini with blue cheese-stuffed olives. I settle on a glass of Cabernet.

When we are alone, I scan the restaurant. "Well, sweetheart, you're certainly following our usual dating tradition."

"What tradition is that?"

"Going to sports bars. Although this one is way classier."

Justin leans close and whispers in my ear. "That's because I always get lucky after taking you to one. I'll never forget our first date at Packy's and what happened afterward."

A young woman approaches the table and introduces herself as Jennifer, our server. She brings with her a basket of raisin bread and mini soft pretzels. Two small ramekins contain house-made chive butter and honey mustard butter. While she lists the dinner specials for tonight, Justin's cocktail and my wine are placed in front of us.

After much discussion and repeated perusals of the menu, Justin orders lobster bisque for two. After being advised of the Caesar salad's generous portion, we agreed to split it. Although I lean toward the whole lobster, Justin convinces me to share with him the long bone ribeye that NYY calls The Tomahawk. Jennifer departs with our orders, and Justin holds up his martini glass for a toast.

I reach for my wine. "You're in trouble now."

He lowers his glass. "Why?"

"I don't think I'm going to be satisfied with date night beer and chicken wings after this."

"I'm know I can always find a way to satisfy you with or without bar food." He smiles and clinks the rim of his glass to mine. "Happy Valentine's Day, my love."

"The same to you, sweetheart. I can't tell you how much I appreciate this romantic date you planned for us." We sip our drinks and, in a few minutes, the soup arrives. When I scoop the last mouthful, I moan. "This is *so* good. The next time we come here, I wonder if I can order it in a mixing bowl."

I'm full after eating the soup, salad, a slice of bread, and a mini pretzel. Since Justin arranged this delightful evening, I want to do the rest of the meal justice. A new waiter brings our side dishes and places them before us. He moves aside, and Jennifer steps forward, bending over the table.

"Bon Appetit!" she exclaims and, with a flourish, sets a white dish between us.

A chunk of seared beef covers half the surface with a long, bare bone extending off the plate's rim by at least three inches. It does resemble a meaty tomahawk.

"Do you need any refills?"

We shake our heads in answer to her question, and stare in wonder at the slab of beautifully charred steak.

"What do you think?" Justin asks when we are alone.

"I think it was a good idea to share this."

"Speaking of sharing…" He turns the plate around, raises his eyebrows, and tilts his head toward the curved hone.

Etched on it in burnt letters are the words: *Will you marry me?*

CHAPTER 55

I STARE AT the blackened words as if unable to decipher them. This is the first time the word *marriage* has been mentioned or, in this case, written in our relationship. I've thought about our next step forward, but we've never discussed a permanent commitment. After all, it's been less than a month since we said I love you. I assumed we would have multiple and prolonged conversations before this, including one with his daughters.

My lack of response wipes the smile from Justin's face. "What's wrong?"

Pointing to the seared question, I say, "I wasn't expecting that."

"I know we haven't talked about marriage, but I love you, and Eden and Savanna love you too. They've been pressuring me to ask you to marry us. I made them promise not to do ask first, even though they want you as their mother and part of our family."

I have dreamed of this moment. Here is my chance with a man I am crazy in love with who has daughters I adore. But Justin did not say the decision to propose is his alone or that he wants me to be his wife more than his children wish me to be their mother. What started out as a romantic date in the Land of Where Dreams Come True has morphed into a precarious situation where a tiny misstep on my part can ruin everything.

"Annie?"

"I don't know what to say."

His smile returns. "Honey, all you have to do is say yes."

I lick my lips. "But we haven't talked about this."

The dimmed lights in the ceiling cast the planes and hollows of his face into shadow. His smile vanishes again. "Maybe I'm skipping a few steps here on the most romantic day of the year, but I can't imagine a life without you in it. Last night when you returned from New York, I wanted you to come home to me and not go to your house. Every time we're apart, it feels like a part of me is missing. When I come home from work, the house feels empty without you in it despite two kids and a large dog. I want you for my wife, and this time it's my decision. It helps to know that Eden and Savanna are on board with it, but I wouldn't ask if it wasn't what I wanted more than anything in the world. I love you so much that being your husband, and having you be my wife is all I can hope for."

His words are sincere. I can see it on his face and hear it in his voice. His green eyes survey me with a tiny glimmer of hope.

Justin shifts on the curved seat of the booth and takes one of my hands in both of his. "I know we have a lot of decisions to make about spending the rest of our lives together. Saying yes to my proposal is not just about a wedding. It's the first step in the process. But I want you to be sure this is what you want too. If you need more time to decide if being a full-time mother to two kids works for you then take all the time you need. A big decision for us is the housing issue. Which one do we live in, yours or mine? Or do we make a fresh start in a new one? A major part of that decision is our finances."

Warnings bells clang inside my brain. Any woman with a bank account containing multiple zeroes worries about how a significant other will react to finding out how well-off she is. Not until this marriage proposal has Justin brought up our assets before.

"It won't just be important as far as real estate is concerned," he continues. "We'll also need to have a good amount in savings when or if we decide to expand our family."

His words are a jolt to my senses. Although Justin knows about my infertility, I have never shared with him my surrogacy plans. "What did you say?"

"Which part?"

"The one about having more children."

He looks down at our joined hands. "I can see what a great mother you would be from how you are with my daughters. Maybe being their stepmother is enough for you, but if not, I think we should adopt or use a surrogate. I researched both processes, and either way there are significant costs involved. We'll need to plan for that. I've got some money saved up, and if we sell one of our houses, we can put any profit towards having another child—if that's what you want." Justin raises his eyes to meet mine. "So, what do you say? Despite the surprise proposal and a hundred important decisions facing us, will you marry a man with two kids who loves you with all his heart?"

"Don't forget you have a dog too."

"How could I forget Fancy? She brought the most beautiful woman in the world into my life."

I can't believe Justin intuited my long-held hope that I would be a mother someday, somehow, some way. I prayed it would happen with a man as eager for a child as me. I smile and bring our clasped hands to my chest. "Yes. I will marry you, my love."

He exhales with a mighty sigh. Pulling me into his arms, he gives me a long, deep kiss that makes me hungry for more. A smattering of applause breaks out in the restaurant. I pull away from him and look around. The clappers are mostly the wait staff, who obviously were in on the surprise proposal tonight. The other diners look around, frowning, or whispering to each other. Then, with some hesitation, several join in the applause.

Justin holds my hand in the air, despite there not being a ring on my fourth finger. "She said yes!"

The sound intensifies as more people clap. At last, we settle in to eat our Tomahawk and side orders. Whether we can't wait to be alone, or the excitement of the proposal has dampened our appetites, or we filled up with soup and salad, we consume only a few bites, request doggie bags, and leave a short time later. We walk to the valet stand with his arm around my waist and mine around his shoulders. We synchronize our steps, moving like two coordinated parts of a single body. In the car, Justin holds my hand on his thigh as if not touching me for the few minutes it will take to reach my house is not an option for him.

Once inside, he places our leftovers in the refrigerator while I let out Juno and Bella. I leave the door cracked open for them to reenter the house as we head to the bedroom, kissing and shedding clothes along the way.

When I sit on the mattress, clad only in my panties, and bend over to unbuckle the straps of my shoes, he growls, "Leave them on."

Sipping on my lower lip, Justin runs his tongue along the seam and gently presses my mouth open as he tips me flat on the bed and follows me down. The kiss is hot and delicious, making my senses spin. My desire for him is so thick and rich that I vibrate with it.

"Tell me what you want," he murmurs.

I am so lost in him that he must repeat what he said. I put both palms on his cheeks and gaze into his beautiful, deep-set eyes. "You. Just you."

"Babe, I'm all yours."

CHAPTER 56

LATER, AS WE lay in the twisted sheets facing each other, Justin stares into my eyes without saying a word. No man has ever looked at me like this before. It is like I'm a cool dip on a hot summer's day. Or a shiny, luxurious car. Or a newborn baby. His gaze conveys a sense of wonder, pride, and delight. The happiness welling up inside me is almost too much to bear.

Justin shifts closer, making more of our skin come in contact. I swing my leg over his hip, and he slips his arm beneath my head. When he speaks, his voice is low. "How did I get so lucky?"

"I'm the lucky one."

"You're perfect for me."

A tear slides from the corner of my eye, and I swipe it away before he notices—except he does.

Justin lifts his head a few inches off the pillow. "What's wrong?"

"It's just…you deserve so much, and I worry that I'm not good enough and nowhere near perfect."

He leans forward, kisses the side of my neck, and then lies back, capturing my gaze again. "Don't devalue what you mean to me. You're my perfect imperfection. I'm happy for the first time in a long time. My daughters are happy. Hell, even the dog is happy, and you did all that. You're the best thing to happen to us, and I love you more than I can say."

"I love you too, Justin. So much."

He pulls me on top of him. Then his mouth seeks mine, and his warm maleness fills my nostrils. I breathe in the scent of his skin, and his mouth tastes like sex. Much later, as our breathing slows, I slide off to lie beside him. After a minute, Justin lifts his arm to check the time.

"Shit! It's eleven-thirty. I told the babysitter I'd be home by midnight." He rubs his eyes with the heels of his hands. "The girls are going to hound me tomorrow when they get up."

"What are you going to tell them?"

"Of course, I'll say I asked you to marry me, and you said yes, but I would prefer we do it together. That way you can share in their twin excitement." He wrinkles his nose. "Which will involve lots of screaming and jumping around."

I laugh. "Then let's do it together. What time do you want me there?"

While he dresses, we kiss and touch, slowing down the process. It is hard to know who this parting is harder on—him or me. We linger at the front door, murmuring endearments, unable to step more than a foot away from each other. I hold onto the jamb as he walks backward to the car, refusing to be the first to break eye contact. I'm forced to grip the doorknob to prevent myself from running after him until his car finally drives toward the street.

Juno and Bella are fast asleep on the living room sofa. I shut and lock the French doors that I left open for them. Thankfully, no intruders found an accessible entrance into my house while Justin and I were lost in each other. I am also grateful that February in South Florida is one of the least buggy times of the year, and my house is clear of night-flying insects. I set the alarm for five so I can be at his house before Eden and Savanna wake up for school.

The following morning, I do my best to look presentable. I use heavy makeup to cover the *too-excited-to-sleep* circles under my eyes. The temperature is in the sixties, so I slip on the greyhound coat the designer insisted I take with me after Finley's owner told her I own and rescue the former racers. A few days later, I ordered the black tunic and pants I wore on the runway and a cream-colored, off-the-shoulder, mid-calf gown to reimburse her for the free coat. On my way to the garage to get into my car, I stop and rush back to my bedroom closet and retrieve my new Leila Rue dress. Holding it against myself, I stand in front of the full-length mirror, cocking my head from side to side and studying the garment.

This would make a lovely wedding dress. Was that in the back of my mind when I purchased it? I return the gown to my closet with more care and reverence, picturing myself in it, standing next to Justin and reciting our vows.

At his house, I use my key to enter. The shower is running on his side of the house, where the main bath is located. The twins' bedroom is quiet. I drape my coat over the arm of a chair in the living room and put the bag I brought in the refrigerator. Toenails click on the tile floor and their greyhound tentatively steps from the girls' bedroom, sniffing the air.

"Good morning, Fancy," I say in a soft voice.

She stops, and then her mouth opens in a canine smile. Coming forward, she leans against my legs and waits for me to scratch her chest or stroke her back. After sufficient petting time for me, if not for her, I straighten when the running water in the shower shuts off. At the same time, Justin's coffee pot timer beeps. I prepare a cup for him, and tap on the closed bedroom door.

"Come in."

His bed is still unmade, and the drapes are drawn, dimming the room. The air is moist with the heat and humidity from his shower and the woodsy scent of the male body wash he uses.

"Good morning. I've brought your coffee."

He emerges from the short hallway to the bathroom with a towel wrapped around his waist. His torso amazes me with all the taut, tan skin and defined slabs of muscle. An errant rivulet of water runs down the hard ridges of his abdomen. He is a work of art, a masculine machine in prime shape that I love looking at it, touching, and tasting.

Justin grins at me and comes forward. "My beautiful fiancée and hot coffee. What a way to start a day!" He kisses me and takes the mug. "Are the girls up yet?"

"Only Fancy."

"Let me get dressed, and I'll be right out."

Fancy waits by the door leading to the pool deck and backyard. I open it, and she races outside, looking for the perfect spot to do her morning business. I scout the kitchen for her dog food and for food I can prepare for the people in the house. A few minutes later, as I reach for cereal bowls from a cupboard shelf, Justin wraps his arms around my waist and kisses my neck. I turn around. He is dressed in jeans and a navy blue T-shirt with a Broward County emblem over his left chest. Scuffed and worn boots are on his feet.

I drape my arms over his shoulders. "How did you sleep last night?"

"Great, except for wishing you were beside me. You?"

"I was too excited for sleep."

"Good to hear." He presses me against the countertop and brackets me in place by placing his hands on the bullnose edge.

I kiss the tip of his nose, one cheek, and his jaw. Then I work my way to his oh-so-kissable lips. When his tongue sweeps inside my mouth, he moans. No, wait. That sound comes from me. I slip my hand inside the collar of his T-shirt. My palm lays flat against the warm skin of his back. The room spins in a dizzying swirl, leaving me in a world where I am only aware of the firm safety of his arms, the warm heat of his mouth, and his earthy male scent.

Sudden high-pitched yells break us apart faster than cheating spouses caught in the act. Eden and Savanna with Fancy between them stand next to the L-shaped countertop extension, smiling and quick-clapping their hands. The girls turn from side to side, making their pink rose-printed nightgowns swish around their legs.

Justin runs a hand across his mouth and states the obvious. "You guys are up."

"Are you gonna do it now, Daddy?" Eden asks.

"Are you?" Savanna adds.

Justin looks at each of his daughters and then raises his eyebrows at me. "Am I going to do what?"

The girls drop their arms to their sides like they are suddenly boneless and useless body parts. With dramatic sighs, they whine, "Dad-dy!"

Justin frowns with feigned cluelessness. "Are you talking about that *thing* you wanted me to ask Annie?"

I join in the charade. "Do you have a question for me about Fancy?"

Hearing her name, the greyhound moves her head back and forth between the twins as if answering no for them.

Eden lays her small hand on the dog's long back. "We want daddy to ask you something else."

"Is it a question about what we did on Valentine's Day?"

Savanna slides her eyes toward her sister and mumbles, "Maybe."

"Well, before we get to that I brought you something from our dinner last night." I step over to the refrigerator and remove a white, foil-lined bag. "I want to give you and Fancy this Valentine's Day present."

As soon as Eden takes the sack, the dog nudges it with her nose. Squeezing the bag in her hands, the little girl's pale red eyebrows squish together. "You brought us a bone? No candy?"

"Just the bone."

"What do you say to Annie?" Justin prompts.

"Thank…you." The two words are muttered with the least amount of sincerity possible.

"Open the bag. Check out the steak bone your daddy and I shared at dinner last night. It's very long and lovely." I realize the double meaning of my words as soon as I say them without Justin's barely suppressed snort.

Eden opens the bag and pulls out the foot-long bone I stripped of meat and washed. Fancy dances around, clearly more excited than her two small owners. I make a sharp, shushing sound. The greyhound plops her bottom on the tile, but her focus remains on the treat. Eden dangles it from three fingers like it's a dead mouse.

"What do you think of your present?" I struggle to maintain a blank expression.

"It's...big," Eden says.

Savanna pipes up. "And brown."

"Check out the writing on it." Justin points to the side facing toward us.

Savanna scoots around Fancy, picks up the dangling end, and lifts the bone until it is level. Together, the sisters flip it until they spot the blackened letters.

Eden sounds out the letters. "Mar...ree..."

Savanna's head jerks up with her eyes wide. "Me! It says marry me! Did Daddy ask you, Annie?"

I nod, my eyes filling with joyful tears.

The usually quiet twin lets out a piercing squeal. She drops her end of the steak bone and rushes to her father and me, wrapping her arms around us. To my surprise and concern, Eden opens her fingers, and the bone drops to the tile with a hollow thud. Fancy rises to her feet, whines, and quivers until Eden says, "Okay."

The greyhound snatches the bone, whirling away to the back hallway.

"Eden?" My question alerts Justin and Savanna. They quiet and stare at the lone person who is not rejoicing. I uncouple myself and approach her. A tear trickles down her cheek. I kneel in front of Eden with my heart in my throat.

Was Justin mistaken? Did only one of his daughters want me as a stepmother?

CHAPTER 57

"EDEN, HONEY. WHAT'S wrong?" I ask in a soft voice. This was not the scenario I envisioned when we informed the girls of our engagement.

She hiccups and sniffs a few times, then swipes her cheek and nose with the back of her hand. "I...I...wanted all of us...to be there...and ask you."

Licking my lips, I clasped her hand in mine. "You wouldn't know it, but there's a *rule* about asking someone to marry you. Especially if they have kids."

I glance over my shoulder at Justin, who rubs his chin with a perplexed expression and shrugs.

"There is?" Eden tilts her head to the side.

I pray this bright child buys what I am about to sell her. "Yes. A man is supposed to ask the woman to marry him, and *if* she says yes, the woman is supposed to ask *his* kids to marry *her*. Your daddy asked me last night using the steak bone." Behind my back, I wave my free hand in a come-here motion. Savanna appears at my side. I take her hand in my free one. "I brought the bone here this morning to ask the two girls I love with all my heart if I can marry them."

The twins look at each other with solemn expressions. Then, without warning, they fling their arms around my neck and scream in my ears, "Yes! Yes!"

In seconds, we are laughing, kissing, and hugging each other. Fancy peers around the doorway with the bone clamped between her teeth. She checks on the excitement and must conclude the girls can handle the situation, which is not worth abandoning her treat. With a flick of her skinny tail, she disappears. Justin kneels on the floor, and his arms wrap around us. I sit and pull Eden onto my lap while Savanna nestles against her father.

We discuss if I will move into their house or if they will move into mine, when Juno and Bella will join Fancy as their new pets, if the girls can wear sparkly pink dresses as flower girls, and a dozen other issues important to them. Most of the answers Justin and I provide them are not definitive, other than the assurance that sparkly, pink dresses are a given.

Then Eden asks, "Can we call you Mommy?"

Neither their father nor I answer. I can understand why she asked the question. They haven't called anyone by that name since they were three years old. I can also imagine Cecilia's volcanic reaction to me, assuming the title was originally held by her daughter.

Justin glances down at his wrist. "Crap! Look at the time. You're going to be late for school."

We scramble to our feet. The girls rush to the bathroom to brush their teeth and wash their faces. I comb their hair while they dress.

Justin calls out from the kitchen, "Cereal is on the counter with your lunches. Hurry up!"

As the kids shovel down Cheerios and milk, I volunteer to drop them off at school so he is on time for work.

Justin kisses me goodbye at the open front door. "We have a lot more to talk about."

"We do, but not everything needs to be decided right away."

"Can you join us for dinner tonight? We have to let Cecilia know about our engagement. I prefer to do it as a united front with the girls."

A cool morning breeze brushes my cheek and whooshes past me into the house. Goosebumps rise on my arms, and I shiver. Am I chilled or simply apprehensive about that phone call? What will his mother-in-law have to say about my status upgrade to Justin's fiancée?

As we prepare dinner that evening, I propose waiting to inform Cecilia until she returns home from Orlando next week. Justin shakes his head. "That won't work now that the kids know. They'll probably let something slip, even if we tell them to keep it quiet for a few more days. All of us doing it together and showing we are united in this is the best way. Trust me."

We are seated at the dining room table with the remains of our dinner when Justin dials Cecilia's cell phone. When she comes on the line, he says, "Hi. I'm here with Annie and the girls."

I call out from the chair next to him. "Hello, Cecilia."

The twins move to stand on his other side. "Hi, Grandma!"

"Am I on speakerphone?" she asks in a querulous tone.

Justin flashes me a be-prepared-for-trouble look. "Yes. We wanted you to be the first to know that I've asked Annie to marry me, and she accepted."

Eden pulls her father's arm with the phone toward her. "Isn't that great, Grandma?"

We wait. There is a hissing silence on the line.

After several seconds, Justin says, "Cecilia?"

"Do the girls know she will never be their real mother? That's she's only...never mind."

I wonder if the woman suddenly remembered she was on speaker phone with her granddaughters listening. Was she about to say I am only the woman sleeping with their father or worse?

Justin rubs his forehead. "For the girls' sake, can't you just—"

"Grandma!" Eden once again jerks the phone down to her level. "We're not babies. We know Mommy is our real mom. Annie's going to be our stepmother."

In a loud voice, Savanna says, "Our friend, Ashley, has two moms because her parents got a divorce, but we don't have any. Now we will."

"Cecilia, we are all very happy about this and hoped you would be too." His voice contains a steely quality that imparts a clear message that our engagement is not up for debate.

"Since I wasn't consulted or informed in advance, I wish you and my granddaughters the best of luck with their new…*stepmother.*"

Justin tells Cecilia goodbye in a polite but terse tone, and the girls shout, "See you soon, Grandma."

I plaster on a tight smile and stay quiet. Justin wraps a warm hand around my neck and pulls me toward him until our temples touch. Although he doesn't say a word, I find comfort in his silent recognition of Cecilia's ability to upset me. His touch is a physical confirmation that he is there to support and comfort me if needed.

Eden appears to sense my mood, too. She comes over to me and pats my arm. "It's okay, Annie. It takes Grandma a long time to get used to new people."

After we clear the table and load the dishwasher, the twins take Justin and me by the hand and move us all into the family room. They direct us to sit on the sofa while they plop down on the large ottoman, facing us. With serious expressions, they cross their arms on their chests, looking like pint-sized detectives about to interrogate suspects with shaky alibis.

"We want to talk about what we're gonna call Annie," Eden announces.

This morning, after she asked if I could be called Mommy, I checked online about the *Name Game*, or what children can call a stepparent. Despite having had one myself, I never realized there is no convenient label for a stepmother. Going with my personal experience, I say, "I'm okay with the girls calling me Annie if they want."

"Well, I'm not." Justin snaps. "It's disrespectful for eight-year-olds to call a parent, even a stepmother, by her first name."

Eden makes a huffing sound, lifts her crossed arms, and slaps them down on her chest again. "You need to listen."

Savanna's gaze wavers between her sister and us. "We're gonna tell grandma that mommy will always be our real mother."

Eden nods. "But Annie is gonna be our stepmother, and we're gonna call her *mom*. That's what we decided."

The two girls stand and march around the ottoman. Fancy rises from her dog bed and follows them toward the back hallway.

Justin asks, "Where are you guys going?"

Eden speaks over her shoulder. "We gonna call Grandma in our bedroom and tell her what we told you."

"What if she doesn't want you to call Annie mom?"

Savanna falters, but Eden holds her chin high. "Our friend, Ashley, said kids can call a stepmother whatever they want. That's the rule."

After the twins are in bed for the night, Justin and I sit in the family room with the TV off. He looks toward their bedroom. "I was impressed with them today."

"They're growing up."

"You know, when they were little and I was the only parent they had, I couldn't wait until they were older. I can't believe I'm sad that they're becoming less dependent on me and are making their own decisions."

I bob my head and give him a slight smile, the one I use when admiring other people's babies and children while struggling not to show my sadness or jealousy.

Justin looks into my eyes. "But I'm lucky that I'll get a second chance to have babies again. And they'll be ours."

My heart expands to twice its size. This is the perfect time to share the plans I've had for the last four years. "There's something I need to tell you."

I talk without interruption, outlining the freezing of my eggs, my investments to cover the costs of in vitro fertilization, and Frankie's offer to be my surrogate. "Even my father offered to help out financially."

When I finish speaking, Justin remains silent for several seconds. Then the corners of his eyes wrinkle, and dimples form on either side of his face. A laugh bursts out of him, deep and rich and beautiful.

"What?" I widen my eyes in confusion.

"Hang on." Justin rises from the sofa, leaves the room, and returns with a file folder. After dropping it onto my lap, he says, "Open it."

On the top is a receipt dated from last month. He had a consultation with a doctor from IVF Florida, a reproductive clinic in the nearby town of Margate. The file includes brochures and testimonials from patients who used a surrogate with high success rates. One piece of paper is a lab report with the results of *his* fertility testing. Tears blur my vision, making it difficult to read.

His index finger taps on the numbers at the bottom. Smirking, Justin says, "Look at that. I'm a baby-making machine."

The next page is a spreadsheet he compiled showing the costs of in vitro and surrogacy, including a breakdown between hiring a surrogate or having a family member volunteer.

I frown. "When did Frankie tell you she and Dale agreed to be a surrogate?"

"She didn't. I talked with my sister about it. Gretchen and Heath are on board too."

My chin quivers, and I cover my mouth with a shaky hand. He closes the file and places it on the ottoman. I crawl onto his lap. He shifts me into a comfortable spot despite my long arms and legs making me as awkward as holding an extension ladder. I rest my head on his shoulder, burying my face in his neck, breathing in the scent of his skin. The peaceful treasure of his nearness and love fills my being.

"Justin?"

"Hmm."

I sit up straight to face him. "I am so happy I chose you. No matter what is thrown at us, I know you'll always be a supportive husband, and you've already proven what a wonderful father you are. I love you and trust you to always love me and our children."

His lips quirk into a smile. "Are you going to say that again when we recite our vows?"

"Do you want me to?"

"Hell, yes. Like you, it's perfect."

The End

Look for the next Love on a Leash book in the series at
www.janetfrankslittle.com

His Golden Girls: A Golden Retriever Love Story

CHAPTER 1

January 31, 2020

The World Health Organization declares a global health emergency as more than 9800 cases of a corona virus and more than 200 deaths are confirmed worldwide.

"I DON'T CARE that you were given a free ticket. There is a serious health crisis out there. Don't you pay attention to the news?" Nick's eyes appear feverish and over-bright as he points an index finger toward the window and the world beyond.

I rub my left eyebrow where the start of a headache throbs. "I may only have a master's in fine arts and not a Juris Doctor degree like you, but I do listen and read about world events. I know the virus is spreading in Asia and Europe, but it's not a public health emergency in the United States yet."

Nick throws his hands in the air. "It will be if large groups continue to congregate. Probably a lot of people at the show today are coming from Asia and Europe."

Finley, my Golden Retriever, enters the kitchen with slow, cautious steps, or canine tiptoeing. She senses the tension between me and my husband. Planting her bulky blond body between us like a boxing referee, she glances at Nick then me. I sigh and rub her silky ears, hating that this sweet creature lives with two angry humans.

"I *have* to go today." I inject conviction into my voice and try not to sound whiny or shrewish. "One of my designs is being featured and so are one of Jasmin's and Alyssa's. Our boss wants us to network for Fab Fabrics and Textiles. I'm not attending just to watch the latest styles walk down the runway. This is my work, my career."

Nick pushes his backside off the countertop. "I don't think you understand the risk you're taking. The coronavirus could be as bad as the swine flu pandemic ten years ago or worse."

I know he's concerned, maybe more for himself and his family, but why can't he support me and my choices for once? "If you had a big commercial closing today, would you cancel it or not attend because a dozen people would have to sit around a conference table signing documents?" I raise my eyebrows, knowing he will say it's like comparing apples and oranges, or because he's Greek—figs and grapes.

Nick closes his eyes and shakes his head. "It's not the same thing, and you know it."

"Why? Because buying and selling real estate is *so* much more important than fashion? Because what you do is business and what I do is just art?"

"Stop twisting my words. The world of commerce won't take a nosedive if consumers can't buy new clothes every year."

This time it's my turn to throw my hands in the air. "The global apparel market is projected to grow in value from 1.5 trillion dollars this year to over two trillion dollars by 2025. If that were to shut down, the world economy would take a definite nosedive."

I keep abreast of factoids for debates like this with Nick and his family. This year's New York Fashion Week show has been an ongoing argument since I told him I planned to attend. I kept checking to see if Governor

Cuomo or Mayor de Blasio would call for a cancellation, but so far everything is on schedule.

Finley leans against my legs as if to remind me that last year both of us played a big part in one designer's show. Leila Rue's models walked the runway with a variety of canines to mimic the Westminster Dog Show. Finley was one of the four-legged ones, as well as clothes using several of my canine fabric designs. I was concerned about my two-year-old Golden Retriever participating in the show, because she often behaved as wildly as a drunken teenager. But we lucked out when Finley was paired with a model named Annie, who was a greyhound owner and knew how to handle large breeds. She took the leash, and within minutes, unruly Finley walked by her side like they had practiced for days. I never had that kind of control with her. Nick and his mother frequently insisted she needed a trainer, or I needed to give her to a rescue group who would find her a new home. After the show, Annie gave me a few quick lessons. I've been using what she taught me and binge-watching *The Dog Whisperer.* Now I'm much more relaxed and confident on our walks, and Finley respects my rules, boundaries, and limitations, per Cesar Millan.

"Why is everything a battleground with you?"

My husband's question snaps me back to our current disagreement. I put one hand on my hip. "You're the one giving orders. *'I forbid you to go'* like I'm your employee or child and not your wife."

His dark eyes close. When they open, he looks somewhat penitent for a man. "Okay, that was the wrong thing to say."

"Yah think, Aristotle?" As soon as the words leave my mouth, I cringe.

"There you go again. I say I'm sorry, and you turn it into a sarcastic comment. That's why I don't apologize more—as you so often remind me."

Nick and I have been like two feral dogs, circling for a fight, lunging, and retreating, snapping with sharp, pointed teeth to gain the advantage. "Fine! I won't be sarcastic when you say *and* mean you're sorry."

"I just did!"

"No, you didn't! You said it was wrong to forbid me from going to the show. You did not apologize for saying it."

"I told you I was sorry."

"No, Nick, you didn't. You said that *I* am sarcastic whenever you say you're sorry, but you didn't say you were sorry for what you said."

He cranes his neck forward and stares at me with a wrinkled brow like I'm speaking gibberish and maybe I am. Sometimes my brain runs off into a Red Bull stampede during an argument with him. But he's an attorney with debate experience. Even though Nick doesn't handle criminal cases, I always feel he views our disagreements like a courtroom cross examination. I'm the witness, and before asking me the first question, he has spent hours laying the groundwork leading up to the moment when the case is blown open in his favor.

In a flat tone, he says, "I'm sorry I said you couldn't go."

From the hallway, a voice pipes in, like the background drone of a vacuum cleaner. "Where don't you want her to go?"

My heart plummets into my ankle boots. Standing in the doorway is Nick's mother, Maria Karras. Her jacketed arms are roped with plastic bag handles. I wonder if the other Saturday shoppers will be disappointed to find the shelves picked clean at the Greek market.

"Ma!" Nick leaps to attention, kisses her cheek, and slips the bags off her as fast as he can. "Why didn't you call me to help you? You shouldn't have carried all this in here."

"Yes. Why didn't you call first, Maria?" I don't know why I ask her this question. Maria does what she wants when she wants.

After relieving his mother of her purchases, Nick helps her with her coat and seats her at the kitchen island. "Do you want something to drink?"

She shrugs one narrow shoulder. "A cup of Greek frappé would be nice. Hot not cold."

I don't tell her there is no such thing as a hot frappé, Greek or not. While in art school, I worked as a barista and often encountered this misconception during the winter months. One customer argued with me for several minutes. Later, the manager said to keep my mouth shut and make him a mocha latte or caramel macchiato because he won't know the difference. Many of Nick's family members drink frappés because the accidental inventor of the drink in 1957 was Dimitrus Vacondios. Yes—like everything else in the world—a Greek, who happened to be a Nescafe sales representative, created the frappé. He was unable to find any hot water at a fair, so he mixed his beloved coffee with cold water in a shaker, and the frappé was born.

"Coming right up, Ma. I'll put the kettle on."

With Nick occupied, Maria turns her inquisitive black eyes on me. "So, where is it Nick doesn't want you to go? Are you going out with the *omofylófiloi* you work with?"

Omo-what? I frown and turn toward Nick.

He looks up from filling the teakettle. "Rachel has a ticket to a fashion show where one of her fabric designs is used. I don't think it's a good idea with this corona thing going around for her to be in a large group of strangers."

Maria nods. "My son is right. You need to listen to him. What happens if you bring this virus home, and he gets sick?"

It's always about her precious golden boy. No concern for me—the half-white, non-Greek woman he married in a civil ceremony without his mother's knowledge or permission. Maria would probably be thrilled if I died from the virus and didn't infect anyone else in her family. No doubt with my obituary notice in the newspaper, she would post our simple wedding photograph so Greek mothers of unmarried daughters all over New York City will know Nick is back on the market. At the end of the article, she'll add a request for donations to a Hellenic charity I know nothing about.

I narrow my eyes. "How do we know *you* haven't brought the virus here today? After all, you were in contact with people at the restaurant all week and now at the grocery store. Maybe you'll be the one to make Nick sick."

Maria rears back in the barstool. "I would never do that to my son! Besides, the people at Taverna Karras and Kiryakos are friends and family. Not strangers from who knows where."

"But you don't know everyone they've been in contact with. It's like AIDS or a venereal disease. You're exposed to everyone your partner...slept with." I don't say the F-word to my mother-in-law. No sense throwing gasoline on that fire.

Maria tips her head birdlike to one side and gives me her usual wintry smile. "You should know all about viruses from those people in the garment district."

It hits me what the word *omofylófiloi* means—homosexuals.

Nick comes around the kitchen island and stands next to his mother. He places his hand on her shoulder. "Until we have more information, we'll live our lives as best we can. I'm still going to the office. You're still running the restaurant. And Rachel can attend work events. I shouldn't have said she can't go unless we stay away from people too. I wasn't being fair to her."

Why doesn't he say that to my face? I always hear these conciliations in secondhand conversations with his mother.

The downstairs doorbell chimes. "Who's that?" Maria asks.

I grab my coat from a barstool. "It's my co-workers."

The tea kettle whistles, and Nick heads to the stove, turning his back to me. "Let me get your frappé, Ma."

For an awkward moment, I wait for Nick to show his mother I am the other beloved woman in his life by kissing me goodbye in front of her. She flashes a self-satisfied smile, as if she knows I'm feeling a bit rejected. I've learned to be cautious when I see that smile.

Finley leans against my leg and I squat down, showering her muzzle with kisses. "I love you, baby girl. You be good while Mommy is gone." I look out the corner of my eye at my mother-in-law. She frowns at my PDA with the dog.

The chime sounds again.

"Your friends are getting impatient," she says. "You better go."

"Yeah. Okay. Bye."

Nick pours hot water into a cup. He doesn't turn around. "Be careful."

I head downstairs, buttoning my coat and pulling on gloves. I step outside and greet the two women. Jasmin is my best friend here in the city. We met in college at the Pratt Institute. Our friendship blossomed at the School of Design program—possibly because we both have white mothers and black fathers. Alyssa is another graphic designer at Fab Fabrics and Textile Designs. She's attractive with straight platinum-blond bangs, natural-toned lipstick, and a tendency to wear only black and white clothing. Today her faux fur coat with a thick, fluffy collar is reminiscent of one worn by Disney's Cruella DeVil.

"Is that a new coat, Alyssa?" I close and lock the door behind me.

"It's my formal winter attire." She drawls in an East Coast prep princess voice. At first, her posh superiority intimidated me until I learned she grew up in Trenton with parents who are public school teachers.

Jasmin slips her arm through mine as we head through the front garden to the sidewalk.

This first week of February has been unseasonably warm with no snow or rainfall. The weak mid-morning sun peeks through the clouds and catches one of Jasmin's silver earrings, making her look like she's touched by an angel.

When we get a few feet in front of Alyssa, she whispers, "I asked her on the way over how many puppies she killed to make that coat."

I bump her shoulder with mine and struggle not to laugh aloud. We wait for Alyssa to catch up with us in her spiked-heeled boots at the corner of Convent Avenue and West 145th Street. In the crosswalk, she maneuvers her way between me and Jasmin.

With calculated nonchalance and a light, airy voice, Alyssa asks, "Is Nick at home today?"

"Yeah, he's there with his mother."

Jasmin's face contorts with a lemony expression of distaste. "What's *she* doing at your place so early on a Saturday?"

My friend knows all about my monster-in-law. Unlike me, hers is perfect. Lula is caring but not overpowering. She is as loving with Jasmin as with her son, Quentin, and their two-year- old daughter, Jade. I don't think Lula has ever had an intrusive inclination in her life, despite being African-America and not Greek. She's just a nice woman.

I shrug. "Maria hits a bunch of shops on Saturday mornings and drops off Greek food for Nick. It's like she's afraid if he doesn't have *soutzoukakia* and good feta every week, he'll forget his heritage."

As we head toward the Broadway-Seventh Avenue subway station, Jasmin asks, "Why do you put up with that?"

"What can I do? When I married Nick, I didn't know about his mother's extreme attachment."

Alyssa simpers, "That's probably why Greek men don't introduce you to their family until after they ask you to marry them. Prior to that, they're planning how to dump you."

Here we go.

On the same night and in the same bar where Nick and I met, Alyssa hooked up with his cousin. When introduced to me, he said: "Hi, my name is Cal or Callisthenes which means beautiful and strong in Greek."

I've since learned that is his standard opening line with women. Cal is the classic bad boy Adonis. Nick told me his cousin breaks up with women after he gets them into bed. I warned Alyssa about him. Either she didn't believe me or thought she'd be different. They lasted for almost twelve weeks, which is like twelve months in Cal-dating years.

After he ghosted her, our working relationship became awkward, and I cornered him at the next family gathering. "Why did you break up with Alyssa? She's smart and pretty."

He lifted a shot glass of ouzo off a nearby table and downed it. "Yeah, she is."

"Then what happened?"

Cal twisted his head until his neck cracked. "She said she loved me."

"Did she say it during sex? You know it doesn't count in the O-zone."

"She said it while we were having dinner in a restaurant."

"What did you do?"

"I paid the bill and took her home."

Since that time, Alyssa badmouths Cal specifically, or Greek men in general, every time I'm around her.

Jasmin stops and pulls Alyssa to a halt in front of the subway stairs. "Rachel and I are sick and tired of hearing you whine. The best way to get over someone like Cal is to get on top of somebody else. Do we need to ask some guy if you can sit on his face?"

Alyssa lifts her chin. "That won't be necessary. I won't bother you with my thoughts and opinions anymore."

"Good." Jasmine links arms with Alyssa and me then leads us to the top step. "Now let's see how good our designs make those skinny bitches on the runway look."

Dear Reader,

I hope you enjoyed reading this book. If you did, I'd appreciate it if you left a review. It really helps me bring more books like this to you that will keep you turning pages instead of sleeping, working, or doing the million other things you need to do.

Don't want to miss anything at Love, Laughter, and Real Life? To find out more about my books, promotions, and competitions (the Golden Retriever in the next book was chosen by a winner in CA), you can keep in touch in the following ways:

Janet Franks Little **Website**: janetfrankslittle.com

Janet Franks Little on **Facebook**: facebook.com/janetfrankslittle

Janet Franks Little on **Instagram**: Instagram.com/janetfrankslittle

Janet Franks Little on **Bookbub**

https://www.bookbub.com/profile/janet-franks-little

To sign up to my **newsletter** go to: Love, Laughter and Real Life https://www.janetfrankslittle.com/about.html or the About Page on my website: janetfrankslittle.com

About the Author

Janet Franks Little is an Ohio native but has lived the last thirty-two years in South Florida. She is a retired Speech Language Pathologist who is now a full-time writer. She began writing at the age of twelve and published her high school's first literary magazine. She is a member of South Florida Fiction Writers, Romance Writers of America, and the Florida Writers Association. Several of her quirky short stories have been published in their magazine, The Florida Writer.

When she's not writing, Janet enjoys rehabbing her second home in Ohio, reading, traveling, and eating good food.

Connect with Janet online:

Website: https://www.janetfrankslittle.com/

Facebook: https://www.facebook.com/janetfrankslittle

Instagram: https://www.instagram.com/janetfrankslittle/

Twitter: https://twitter.com/franks_little

Amazon: https://www.amazon.com/Janet-Franks-Little/e/B00MYERSO6

Goodreads:

https://www.goodreads.com/author/show/8409180.Janet_Franks_Little

Bookbub: https://www.bookbub.com/profile/janet-franks-little

www.ingramcontent.com/pod-product-compliance
Lightning Source LLC
Chambersburg PA
CBHW060851250626
47159CB00008B/2691